MW00774681

Where the River Bends

The History of a Tragedy

by

Elissa Matthews

WARREN COUNTY LIBRARY
NORTHEAST BRANCH

Copyright © 2016 Copake Lake Press
All rights reserved.
ISBN: 0990678601
ISBN-13: 978-0990678601

Cover art by Darren McManus
www.darrenmcmanus.com

Digital editing by Stephen Anderson

DEDICATION

This book is dedicated to the Fischer girls, who showed me what courage looks like. They marched for suffrage, helped cure polio, and taught me that strength comes from sweat.

CHAPTER 1

CELESTE

When the police arrived at Celeste Vandenholm's door that dismal November afternoon, her first thought was Oh God, Peter has found out about me.

But Peter hadn't found out, and later Celeste would wonder why she had even thought that. It would make no sense to think the police would be involved. Perhaps.

The older officer took off his cap and held it against his chest, his fingers brushing pellets of sleet off the stiff brim. "I'm sorry to tell you this, ma'am, your husband has been in an automobile accident." The younger officer solemnly nodded.

Celeste didn't hear a word after that, other than "hospital" and "operating."

The whole day splintered into a kaleidoscope of disconnected fragments from which she tried to snap into action: ringing for Timmins to call a hackney, standing like a stone statue while he opened an umbrella for her, bitter, salty spray catching her in the face as one of the new 1930 Fords sped down Park Avenue.

"New York German Hospital," she instructed the driver, striving to be strong, confident, in control.

"Yes, ma'am," he'd said. "They call it Lenox Hill now," he informed her conversationally. "They done renamed it, must be ten years ago now." He glanced at her in the mirror and fell silent as they drove on, the wheels whirring against the wet pavement.

She had rushed to the hospital, but now the wait was endless. Waiting to be shown to the waiting room. Waiting for Peter to come out of surgery. Waiting to find out what was happening. Waiting for her thoughts to stop whirling so she could pray.

"The first day after any surgery is the most critical," Dr. Stegmann said, when he finally arrived. He wore a clean surgical gown, but a single streak of vivid scarlet crossed his cheek. Oh God, that was Peter's blood. Celeste turned her head, trying not to see what she would never forget. "His wounds were extensive, but we managed to stop all the bleeding, so that's good news." He took her hand and pressed it gently. "But he also has a fractured skull, and three broken bones in his neck. We won't be able to tell how much brain and nerve damage there is, until he wakes up."

It took a moment for the words to make sense. "When he wakes up?" Celeste could barely choke out the words. "When will that be? When will he wake up?"

"We don't know. All we can do is pray it will be soon." He touched her hand. "The nurses will be bringing him up from the operating theater in an hour or two."

Celeste wanted to collapse onto the floor in agony, but had no recourse but to wait and then wait even more.

At long last someone ushered her into what seemed to be an absurdly comfortable hospital room. She stepped blithely through the doorway, and suddenly there he was, shockingly close enough to touch, not even an arm's length away. She jumped backward, startled, and cried out. Bile rose up and for a moment she struggled not to vomit right there. She gouged her nails into the back of her neck, concentrating on the pain until the dizziness passed, then she took a short, but infinitely long step forward and gripped the sheet lying over Peter's arm.

She was barely aware of the nurse moving a chair up to the bed for her, and she sank into it without letting go of Peter. The nurse murmured a few words about calling if anything was needed, then closed the door behind her.

Celeste put her head down on the railing next to Peter's face, listening to his faint breathing. At least he was still breathing, she could cling to that. So many nights she had lain next to him, reaching out for sleep that didn't come, while he dropped into slumber like a rock into a pond, then flopped around onto his back and started to snore. "Roll over, honey, you're snoring," she'd say, shaking him lightly, marveling at how the dim gaslight caught the clean lines of his cheekbones.

How would she live if anything were to happen to her Peter? "Please come back to me," she whispered. "Please."

He didn't wake up the first day. It was an entire day, wasn't it? She couldn't recall. She remembered calling Briarwood Academy and asking Headmaster Hibbeler to put David on a train for New York. She remembered calling home, and asking Nurse Savener to explain to Martina that Father would not be able to play chess with her that night. Martina's addled, confused mental condition would not be able to grasp the situation, but perhaps she was the fortunate one, in that regard, at least. She'd been that way from birth, in spite of all the doctors tried, so who knew what she thought about anything? Hospital staff in white uniforms bustled up and down the hallway in a blur; one of them brought her an cup of terrible coffee with a thin film of oil floating on the surface, and offered her a sandwich. Celeste shook her head. Fear and anger surged through her in alternate waves, ebbing and flowing, like the ocean against the shore. She huddled in the hard chair and waited for Peter to wake up.

Half of his face was mottled and swollen with bruises; the other half was hidden behind bandages that had once been white but were now streaked with blood. He lay motionless, arms at his sides, raised up on pillows, trapped inside a cage of bed railings. The electric lighting cast a peculiar matte look to his skin, as if he were made of a strange, oddly tinted clay.

"Oh God, oh God, why?" she whispered, and bent over once more, clutched the sheets and tried to pray, but it had been a long time since she'd believed that God was an old man with a white beard who stepped in to rescue every puny human in pain.

She rested her face gently next to Peter's. He didn't move. That was the worst part —he simply didn't move. He didn't reach out to stroke her hair, he didn't put his hand under her chin and kiss her, as he always did when she was upset. He was simply gone. This is what Momma had looked like when she died, this eerie, forbidding sense of emptiness, of unknown danger lurking out of sight. Momma and Peter, these were the people who were supposed to keep her safe. Now everything was the wrong way around and she was utterly lost.

"Are you in pain?" she whispered. "Please don't be in pain.   Please just come home. I need you to come home. The children need you to come home." She swallowed down yet another surge of tears.   "I didn't lie to you on purpose. I just always loved you too much to tell you the truth."

CHAPTER 2

MARTINA

He does not come. We wait. We wait. The soldiers are quiet. They stand in rank, motionless, waiting for the battle to begin, but it does not. The general with the big hands, the general of the black army who comes in the evening, he does not come. The gods have taken him away. He must have made them very angry.

CHAPTER 3

DAVID

Father is in a coma.

The train hurtled southward to New York City. The clashing of the pistons wasn't nearly fast enough.

Father is in a coma.

Headmaster Hibbeler had told him only the bare facts. An automobile accident. Severe injuries. David had packed a single bag, and the Headmaster himself had taken him to the station to catch the next train heading for home. November sleet battered the windows, stuck, and slid upward as the train jolted back and forth along the rails, in time to the rhythm of the words banging in David's head.

David pressed his cheek against the cold sting of the window. In the distance, the trees were gray skeletons under bloated clouds, and old corn stalks lay flat and useless in the fields. A wagon full of hay bales beginning to whiten from a coating of accumulated ice trundled by in the opposite direction, the farmer hunched over the reins, collar raised, hat lowered. The horse, too, was head down, its coat shiny and wet.

"I'm the man of the family now," he whispered, trying to make it real, but the words echoed, sounding thin and weak inside him. That's the other thing Headmaster Hibbeler had said when he'd called David into his office and broken the news. Precisely how did one go about becoming the man of the family at seventeen? *Father is the one I would have asked.* He couldn't picture himself in the role, lounging at the head of the table with brandy and a cigar. Father was always been so full of energy, telling a joke, winking at Mother, even making Martina pay attention to him. David sat up straight, he would not cry, not here, not in public like this. The woolen sleeve of his school blazer scratched as he dragged his arm across his eyes.

Father couldn't die, he was a war hero. He'd survived gas and bullets in Flanders. He'd been a Lieutenant in the 27th Infantry, his platoon had stormed a machine gun nest on the Hindenburg Line. He'd survived dysentery, heat stroke and even the influenza that swept through the country after the Kaiser's insanity had come to an end.

Please don't let Father die.

He opened his chemistry book on the polished wood of the table in the first class club car and tried to study. Perhaps Father would be well soon, and David could return to school in time for winter exams. They would miss the annual family outing to the Thanksgiving Day parade, he realized, biting his lip. Father would hate that, he loved parades. He had waved so enthusiastically and cheered so loudly, amidst a shower of tickertape, when Gertrude Ederle had returned from swimming the English Channel. He'd been hoarse for two days and couldn't lift his arm to put on his coat without help.

The whistle screeched as the train slowed, then stopped, at the Rhinecliff station. The car was beginning to fill, as more passengers came on board. David kept his head down and his carryall on the seat next to him.

"Excuse me, is this seat taken?"

David looked up and reluctantly shook his head. He shifted his leather bookbag to the floor under the table.

An older woman stood in the aisle, wrapped in a long coat with thick, dark fur at the wrists and collar and a green beret on her short, gray hair. She tipped her head to one side and smiled, bright blue eyes catching his gaze. Belatedly, it occurred to him to stand, and he struggled to his feet, sending the heavy textbook skidding across the table top. It was nice being suddenly so much taller than his friends, but so awkward!

She motioned him to stay seated. "Don't bother, young man" she said, and tucked herself carefully into the seat opposite. The porter behind her put her large case on the overhead shelf, with her hatbox next to it. She rummaged in her purse and handed him some coins.

David watched, as she pulled her gloves off, one finger at a time. Her knuckles were red and lumpy, swollen with arthritis. She caught him staring, and laughed when he looked away. "Getting old is so tiresome," she said. "But shouldn't you be in school in the middle of the day? Not in trouble are you?" She hiccupped, then laughed again.

"My father's been in an auto accident," he stated. Why did he just blurt that out? Talking to strangers always made him so awkward, he never said the right thing.

"Oh, how dreadful!" She leaned forward, her face softening. "I'm so sorry. Is he badly hurt?"

"Not too badly," David deflected, "but I'm going home to visit for a few days."

The woman nodded her understanding.

Another woman passed them, young and beautiful, stepping daintily on precariously high heels, clinging to the arm of a tall, bent man in a severe gray overcoat. "Oooh," she said, her head turning back and forth between the aisles of spotless tables and plush seats, "This is simply too, too, tricky for words."

David wondered what tricky meant, other than probably something good, from the way she was speaking. Keen? Snazzy? Perhaps he could manage to say it himself, once he was back at school. "Oh, yes, I know Henckles thinks the cut of his new blazer is too tricky for words, but," he would practice the timing of a shrug, "but I say, a school uniform is a school uniform."

"That Vandenholm," the boys would say, "he sure knows what's what."

He looked up to see his seatmate gazing at the other woman's retreating back, one eyebrow arched high.

"Silly twit," she said.

He changed his mind about trying it out at school.

Several businessmen in damp overcoats clattered onboard at Poughkeepsie and congregated at the table across the aisle, scraps of their conversation rising above the thumping of the train.

"Who's got the western accounts?"

"It's here, take it."

"Lewis tallies, looks like eighty-three."

"That's all? That can't be right." The speaker sounded angry.

"Sir, ma'am, would you like anything here?" A waiter stood by them, hands cased in white gloves, holding a silver coffee pot and tray of cups, his black face wrinkled with a smile.

The woman frowned, and nodded. "Thank you, I think I will take a cup."

"For me also, please," David said. He thought about asking for a sandwich but decided he wasn't hungry enough to bother.

"Yes, ma'am. Yes, sir. Coming right up," the waiter said.

"Coffee all around for us," one of the businessmen said. "Man oh man do I ever need a drink. I still can't believe we did so badly. This economy's really squeezing our nuts. Christ." David glanced over. The man thumped his fist on the table, staring at a stack of papers with eyes narrowed to slits.

David glanced across to his seatmate, embarrassed by the man's graphic language.   An eternity passed in awkward silence.

The coffee finally came.

The woman said "Hmmm," and with a mischievous smile and a careful glance around the club car, as if a government agent were about to rise up from under the seat, removed a silver flask from her purse, keeping it hidden under the table. "Cursed Temperance League," she said, "make me carry my own medicine everywhere."

David pretended not to notice as she delicately sipped once and then slyly dosed the cup from the flask. She nudged him with the toe of her shoe and offered the flask to him with a furtive movement.

"Thanks." He didn't like whiskey, he'd tried it once, but he didn't want her to think of him as a righteous stick in the mud.

"It's the real stuff. I know a fellow in the city who brings it down from Canada himself." She hiccupped again, and David realized she was already a little drunk.

He took a large swallow and tried not to gag.

She laughed. "Well, maybe it's not very good. But it's Dutch courage all the same."

David jerked and set the cup down hard on the table.

"Are you all right?"

"Oh, yes, fine. It's, ah, well, my father always says that. Dutch courage." He shut his eyes. He fought the rocking of the train as it tried to lure him to a place where tears were waiting. He wanted to be strong. For Father. And for Mother and Martina as well.

He felt a cool, firm hand on his. "You poor boy."

"I want him to be well, so much." His voice cracked on the last word, and he stared down at his knees.

"Poor boy," she repeated. "Life takes us by the throat and

shakes us around sometimes."

"God dammed coon!"

David jumped at the shout, disoriented. The handful of other passengers in the car craned their heads to see what was happening. The woman pulled back, frowning at the businessmen in the booth across the aisle.

David saw one of the men mopping at his lap with a handkerchief. The waiter stood next to the man's table, holding the coffee pot at an uncomfortable angle. "I'm sorry, sir, I didn't know you was going to move your cup right then, honestly, sir, I didn't know."

The man stopped swiping at his trousers and froze. He slowly looked up and stared hard at the miserable waiter. "Are you saying," he enunciated, "this was my fault?"

The waiter inhaled with a harsh sound, but did not speak.

"Are you saying," the man repeated, loudly enough for the entire car to hear, "this was my fault?" A hush fell over the car as the man's voice rose. "Is it?"

A long silence, then the waiter started to babble. "No Sir, no Sir. It weren't your fault, no Sir. It were my fault. My fault entire. I didn't mean to do it, but it were my fault for sure." He stammered to a halt.

David was so close he could see a dribble of sweat roll down the man's dark face, soaking into the collar of his white uniform shirt, leaving a shadowy mark. Another dribble followed the first. His hands were trembling and ribboned with straining tendons as he gripped the coffee pot.

David shifted in his seat. This wasn't right, tearing into a waiter for an honest accident. David struggled to think of something to do, something to say that would ease the situation, but nothing came to mind. And he would have to stand up and say it to those businessmen, with everyone in the train car watching. Just the thought of it made him shudder.

Outside the stillness of the car, the racketing noise of the train seemed a separate entity. The businessman rose. Everyone in the car was turned their way. Red blotches spread across the man's cheeks and neck. He carefully, deliberately folded the coffee-stained handkerchief and put it back in his pocket. He pulled a pen and small leather notepad out of his breast pocket. "What's your name, boy?" he asked, enunciating each word.

"Sir, it was an accident, Sir." The waiter's voice traveled up and down the scale, out of harmony with itself.

The poor fellow. He shifted nervously and glanced around the car. He caught David's eye, and the blatant terror there made David pull back. He hoped he would never feel that depth of fear. Even his fear of speaking before an audience, why, even his fear for Father seemed mild in comparison. He really wished he could just stand up and tell that lout to pick on someone his own size, so to speak. To go back to the rock he crawled out from under. Everything sounded so childish, even in his own head. Father would have known exactly how to provide the perfect diplomatic interruption. He wished Father were here.

Then the waiter drew a deep breath, audible throughout the carriage, and stood up ostentatiously straight. His shaking stilled, the nervous smile fell from his face. His fear slid from him like a waterfall. He looked directly into the businessman's eyes, and the other man took a small step back.

Good for him, David thought.

His seatmate clicked her tongue. "Unnecessary, making such a scene," she said, facing David, but her voice projecting at least several rows away.

"Excuse me?" David said.

She jerked her chin toward the businessman, who was now looking in their direction. "If he wants to be a complete booby and report that poor colored boy, well that's fine, but he could have been more discreet. He didn't need to make all of us part of his silly drama."

"No, ah, no he didn't." Why on earth was she talking so loudly? Was she so very drunk? People were staring.

She leaned back and spoke even more loudly yet, as if still addressing David but pitching her voice to be clear to everyone nearby. "You know what his problem is?" She paused, and swiveled her head, making sure she had a full audience up and down the length of the club car. "His problem is, his dick's too small."

A sharp retort of shock and laughter shot through the train carriage, mixed with disapproving gasps. David heard the sibilance of "small," the snap of "dick," echo down the rows of passengers, blending in with the laughter, against the steady backdrop of the train wheels rolling along their rails. It wasn't until the waiter strode past him that he realized the obnoxious businessman hadn't gotten the man's name after all. David looked up to see the woman grinning at him. He wanted to stand up and applaud.

CHAPTER 4

CELESTE

The door banged open. "There you are, darling!" A voice shattered her quiet time with Peter. "We came right over the minute we heard!" Helen Voigt, tiny and loud, barged into the room, goggled wide eyed at Peter, then swept Celeste into her arms, smothering her with a face full of expensive perfume and even more expensive Russian sable. Marjorie Sherman flowed, tall and languid, in Helen's wake. She kissed Celeste's cheek then dabbed at the lipstick mark with the corner of her handkerchief.

Calm and strong. She needed to be calm, to be strong, to be in control. She didn't want to face anyone right now, she wanted to be alone with Peter, but apparently it was too late for that. "How did you know where I was?" she asked.

"When you didn't come to the lunch, we called round. It was such an important fundraiser we knew you wouldn't have missed it on a whim." Helen said. "Your Timmins didn't want to tell us, but clearly he and his wife had both been crying." She shrugged, indicating the rest was obvious. Of course they would tell her. Helen always found a way to be the dominant presence in any room.

Celeste couldn't even remember what charity the fundraiser had been for. Helen danced from one cause to another without clear direction, sucking friends along in her wake. Medical fees for unmarried women having babies out of wedlock. Legal fees to support a wrongful death civil suit for some servant or factory worker. Rent and food for disabled soldiers. It all made Celeste's head spin.

"We came by to see if we could do anything for you," Marjorie said. "We thought you could use some undemanding company."

Oh God, undemanding company, Celeste thought. If only she knew how hard it was to hide from them, to keep her mask in place, to keep her mannerisms polished and perfect. "Thank you ever so much," she said, touching Marjorie's shoulder lightly. She appreciated their gesture, she truly did. She tried to remember if she'd let her accent slip at all.

"It's odd," Peter had once said after an argument about a long forgotten triviality, "when you're angry you sound more American than when you're happy." Celeste didn't remember now what she'd said to steer him away from that thought, it was always ridiculously easy to put him off a topic, but she had taken it as a warning to keep her guard up. When she was upset, or simply tired, a younger, earlier person took over her body, a person who hadn't yet arrived in New York City, hadn't become French, hadn't learned what it took to be rich. Certainly she was in turmoil now. She would have to ease back into her accent in front of the nurses, when Marjorie and Helen weren't around. Perhaps a witty comment about hospitals in Paris? The closest she'd ever been to Paris was the foreign language shelf of the public library.

Helen shifted a chair away from the wall and sat down. "Can we help you with the notifications? Is there anyone we can call? Do you have family back in France who will be coming to help you out?" she asked.

"*Non*," Celeste answered brusquely. "Dealing with family I haven't seen in so long would be too much right now," she added. "It's a long journey from Paris, after all, and winter crossings are never pleasant."

"We're here for you," Marjorie said.

"The same thing happened when my mother died," Helen said, launching into the story with her usual arm-waving theatrics. "This cousin no one has seen in years just shows up out of the blue at the funeral. I'd never met her, but it turns out everyone else simply hates her, and I can understand why. She came and annoyed us all with chatter about herself, her son, herself, her two daughters, herself, and finally my father got fed up, left the room and came back with the cousin's coat. 'Florence,' he says, 'here's your coat. I'm so sorry you have to leave now.' He stuffs her into it and escorts her straight to the door."

Marjorie choked on a laugh. "How awful," she said. "But how perfect!"

Helen laughed at her own story as well. "It was awful, but it was funny, you must admit. Of course, Cousin Florence didn't speak to any of us on the way out, and I haven't seen her since."

Celeste pretended to laugh along with Marjorie and Helen. She wished she had the nerve to show her own visitors straight to the door. She wanted to be alone with Peter, but that would leave her alone with only her own lies for company. That would be worse.

As it happened, Dr. Stegmann made the decision for her. When he arrived at the doorway with two students following behind, there simply wasn't enough room for all of them. Dr. Stegmann turned to Celeste. "I don't have much to tell you, but we can move to my office to talk, if you'd be more comfortable." He looked pointedly at Helen and Marjorie.

Helen didn't look like she was planning to leave, and placed a proprietary hand on Celeste's arm, but Marjorie caught Celeste's eye and reached for both of their coats. "Celeste, dear, we'll come back tomorrow to visit again, please call if there's anything we can do in the meantime."

"I don't have much more information than I did yesterday," Dr. Stegmann said after they had disappeared down the hall. "I'm sorry. He is not responding to stimulus yet. We've run a full set of neurological x-rays and while there is some bleeding inside his brain, it's not enough to account for his condition." He rubbed his fingers across his forehead. "I wish I could tell you when he will wake up, but I don't know. The truth is, we don't really know how the brain actually works. I certainly hope he will regain consciousness or we will have to start giving him food and fluids manually."

One of the students made a noise, and Dr. Stegmann shot a sharp look at him.

"Manually? What does that mean?" she asked.

"Through a small tube we insert down his throat, directly into his stomach."

Celeste felt her own throat close up, gagging in response. She tried to think about anything other than nurses standing over Peter, ramming a hose into his mouth. The room flickered into a mosaic of purple and green swirls, tilted sideways, then turned black.

A spike of ammonia fumes pierced her. Pain stabbed behind her nose, behind her eyes, as the smelling salts did their job. Her neck arched back and her eyelids shot open of their own accord. Light flared. Pieces came together: the rumble of the doctor's voice, the feel of a nurse slapping her wrists, the wide eyed faces of the two students.

"There you are, there you are, you're back with us," Dr. Stegmann soothed. "I'm sending you home now, and I'll give you a prescription to help you sleep, you probably didn't spend a very comfortable night here." He smiled calmingly at her. "Nurse Fritsch will take you home, you shouldn't be alone right now."

Celeste stared. Peter not wake up? Impossible! She

knew what she had to do. She rose from the floor, Dr. Stegmann's arm supporting her, leaned close to Peter, and cushioned her lips in the hair on the side of his head that wasn't covered in bandages. "I love you," she whispered. "I didn't marry you for your money, truly I didn't, no matter what your father said." She took a breath, smelling the mix of Peter, smelling salts and medicinal astringents. Her decision was made. "When you wake up I will tell you everything. But you have to wake up."

CHAPTER 5

MARTINA

Still he does not come. The general with the big hands does not come, and the soldiers wait. I wait. The mother one cries in the morning. The david one comes and goes away and goes away. All the crying. All the leaving. All the noises are wrong.

CHAPTER 6

DAVID

New York City in the middle of a school day was a beehive of activity. David sneezed as he moved from the dim interior of Grand Central Terminal, into the midday sunlight. He always sneezed like this when hitting the outdoors; long ago the doctor said it sometimes ran in families. But Father didn't sneeze like this – maybe his father did?

Autos and wagons, horses and hansom cabs all streamed up and down the avenues as the taxi delivered David home. He mounted the stoop of the tall brownstone at Park and 78th and rang the bell. "Hello, Mrs. Timmins," he said when the housekeeper opened the door. Her red rimmed, swollen eyelids made it clear she had been crying, but her gray hair was pinned into a neat bun from which not one wisp escaped. She patted the pins. She'd had this habit as long as David could remember, smoothing her hair into place whenever she was upset, as if personal tidiness would put everything into order in the world.

She stepped away and pulled a handkerchief from her pocket to dab her nose. "Och, Master David. Terrible, terrible thing, this," her Irish brogue heavy. She tucked the handkerchief into her sleeve, then pulled it out again, wiped her eyes, and put it back, the tears still flowing.

David nodded. "Yes, terrible." He felt awkward, not

knowing what to say. He'd never seen Mrs. Timmins so distraught.

It was strange to see the familiar sheen of the marble foyer and the bowls of fresh flowers Mother changed every day, to hear the ticking of the grandfather clock and inhale the lingering scent of Father's cigar smoke from the night before. It was all so familiar, and David had trouble remembering why he had thought it would be different. The violence of Father's accident should have been mirrored in the surroundings here, but inside these walls a typical winter afternoon passed by.

Before David could ask where Mother was, a door banged open at the other end of the hall, and with a great thudding of feet his sister shot into the room. Martina barreled up to him, auburn hair flopping in short curls, her delicate face blank.

"Circles!" she shouted.

David wrapped his arms around her and lifted her off the ground, spinning her around with a happy shout. She didn't laugh, but when he set her back down, she leaned her forehead against his chest. He hugged her tight, bouncing her up and down on her toes. She always liked rhythmic movements. At fifteen, she was tall for her age, she'd been growing almost as fast as he had, and leggy besides. She fumbled in her pocket for the small pink comb she carried everywhere and started to rub it methodically back and forth across her cheekbone. David was surprised at how beautiful she was becoming; she was starting to look just like Mother.

Nurse Savener arrived with a squeak of rubber-soled shoes, panting from the chase, smoothing down the pleats of her uniform and scowling. "The minute she heard your voice she came running straight out." She said this as though David had deliberately engineered Martina's escape. "I do not understand why you insist on whirling her around in that unseemly manner. She is not a sack of potatoes."

"Hello, Nurse Savener," David said. "How have you

been?" He always tried to ignore her disagreeable temper because she was so protective of Martina.

"I could be better, Master David, and that's the truth." She shook her head. "He was a good man, your father."

David stiffened. She spoke as if he was dead.

Martina stopped rubbing the comb along her cheek, pushed her face an inch from David's, and stared at him without blinking, her sapphire eyes startlingly bright. "All the blue," she said. Her voice was husky, and her tone intense. This was important, David knew.

"Very blue, Martina honey." He lifted her hand, the one holding the pink comb, and rubbed his own face with it. For a minute he saw a glimmer, a spark, behind those blank, drifting eyes. If only he could cure her with hugs and love.

"All the blue," she repeated, calmly, satisfied now. She pulled her hand out of his and resumed rubbing, up and down, up and down. She turned, and walked back down the hall. "Boxes," she said as she left, apparently to the wall. "The line is bent."

"She already misses your father something fierce," Nurse Savener said. "Poor little mite, she knows something's wrong."

"Bothers us all, it do," Mrs. Timmins said.

"Father will be home with us very soon, I'm sure," David declared.

Timmins and Nurse Savener stared at him. "Of course he will," the nurse said gently, the way she spoke to Martina.

David was startled by this soft response. "Is he so very badly hurt then?" he asked in surprise. "Is he going to die?" He swallowed, hard, against the painful tightness in his throat.

"His condition is severe indeed," Nurse Savener said. "But Lenox Hill is a good hospital, with good doctors." She sniffed. "Only the best for the Vandenholms," she muttered.

"Louise!" Mrs. Timmins exclaimed.

David was surprised. Savener liked Father, didn't she?

And how very upset indeed Mrs. Timmins must be to speak like that to another staff member, right in front of him.

She patted her hair. "One never knows what the new day will bring," She had a way of stating the obvious as though she'd just thought of it. This was a skill David practiced often for his elocution class, but never quite pulled off in the housekeeper's natural manner.

"Does Martina understand what's happened?" David asked, peering down the hall after his sister.

"Perhaps yes, perhaps no," Nurse Savener said. "She sat in front of their chess board for hours waiting for him, I couldn't budge her. Tonight you can play with her, maybe that will help calm her, she has been quite tense all day."

David tried to smile at her. "I still say you should learn how to play, Nurse."

"I do know how to play, young man, I was playing chess before you were born. But your sister, she's out of my touch. If someone is going to lose to her every night, I'd prefer it were you."

"I'm not sure she can beat me yet," David said, "but Father always let her play the white pieces, and he always let her win. I shall too, now." He started to say, "Now that I'm the man of the house," but it sounded so pretentious he stopped himself. It was only a temporary promotion anyway. The words didn't fit, and he wanted Father to come home before they did.

"She's improved quite significantly since you were last home, she's gone back to reading those chess books of hers. You may not win even if you tried." Savener smiled triumphantly. A thump came through the wall and she spun around. "I'd better find out what fell," she said, and headed rapidly back down the hallway as well, one shoe squeaking as she went.

David sighed. There was no pleasing the woman.

"Would you be wanting a cup of hot cocoa or a mite to eat, Master David?" Mrs. Timmins asked.

"No thank you, I had coffee on the train." He thought back to that woman's marvelous rescue effort, and wondered how anyone could behave like those businessmen had. He would never treat any of the family staff so poorly, colored or not. Why, they were practically family, after all. Well, from now on he would make an extra effort to be courteous, even to Nurse Savener.

"I'll take your bag up and tell your mother you've got home safe, shall I? She returned from the hospital a few hours ago and went up to rest, but she asked to be woken when you arrived."

"Thank you, Mrs. Timmins," he said. He should, he thought, be industrious and follow the maid upstairs to his room, but the door of his father's study, standing slightly ajar, beckoned to him.

The afternoon sunlight highlighted the reds and browns of the rug and curtains, picking out glints of gold among the clutter everywhere. Swimming trophies Father had won, including the ones from his own time at the Briarwood Academy, lined the fireplace mantel. A signed photograph of Gertrude Ederle from the celebration after the ticker tape parade held pride of place in the center. Chess books sat neatly on the shelves, the only tidy thing in the room, books he and Father had studied together, along with classic reading never touched and dog-eared novels that had been shoved into untidy rows. He pulled down a volume of chess openings, saw Father's notes on the margin of every page, and slid it back into place. How could this man, who had always been laughing, always been ready to play a game or throw a party for his huge crowd of friends, how could he be in a coma? David sat behind the walnut desk with its scarred leather blotter and inhaled the scent of cigars and brandy, pretending Father would be home from work soon and they would be able to talk. Before the need to cry overwhelmed him, he jumped up from behind the desk and moved away, leaving the door, the room and the memories as he had found them.

Upstairs, a voice halted him before he reached his room. "*Bonjour*, David, you have arrived safely, this is good." Mother glided in on a cloud of French accent and rich perfume. Every time he came home it struck him, as if his senses had grown dull at school and only now were waking up again. As she approached him she slowed, then stopped with her arms out. He advanced and she opened her arms fully, enveloping him in her warmth. A plume of smoke from the end of her ebony cigarette holder drifted over David's shoulder.

Father always said Mother was an artist's ideal of contrasts: thick hair the color of cocoa with streaks of dark and light, high cheekbones from her French parentage, hazel eyes so smoky they were nearly gray, and pale skin that burned so easily she never exposed it to the sun, even at Newport Beach in the summer. Father had pointed out to him once as they walked down Fifth Avenue on a spring Saturday, how a space always appeared around Mother as if people were afraid to stray too close to her radiance. How their eyes angled sideways to take in her beauty without staring. "I loved my mother very much," he had said to David. "She had a sterling character and I wish she were still alive, but she was damned plain." How long ago that seemed now, as if Father was on the other side of a narrow but immeasurably deep rift in time.

From inside the cocoon of Mother's arms David breathed in her scent and tried to relax, but even as he did she stiffened her spine and step away from him. She held her cigarette at an awkward angle and wiped her eyes with a lacy handkerchief, then pinched the curl in front of her ear. "All will be well, *mon cher*," she said, patting David's shoulder distractedly. "We will get through this, you will see." She took a deep breath, blinked a few times, drew on the end of her cigarette holder, and moved her lips in a rigid smile. "Come, rest. You must be hungry and tired after such an interminable train journey." She pronounced the word een-ter-mee-na-bleh, and David smiled in spite of himself. "You go to your room now and I shall bring to you a morsel of something on a tray." She would send up enough food to feed three people, he knew, including scrambled eggs with cheese, and croissants from the French bakery on the corner.

"Father had much surgery, there was much bleeding, but it is stopped now, and that is good, *non*? Soon, yes, we will return to the hospital." She seemed uncertain what to say next. She appeared to forget she'd already asked him about food, and brought up the topic again. "You are always hungry after that long train ride. Are you hungry now? Do you want something to eat? I will get you something to eat." She left before he had a chance to reply to any of her waterfall of questions.

He had barely thrown his bag on the bed and washed his face when she returned, followed by the butler carrying a loaded tray. "Thank you, Timmins," David said. Like his wife, he had been crying; the skin around his eyes was inflamed, his swollen eyelids hid all but the tips of his eyelashes. His thinning gray-blond hair straggled in uneven lines behind his ears, shoved back without care.

"Would you like to eat in the sitting room or would you rather have time alone right now?" Mother asked. Her toe traced a tight arc in the weave of the rug.

David tried to guess which one she would prefer. He always tried to read the subtle hints in her posture, her tone of voice. "I'd like the company, please," he said, and relaxed when she relaxed.

Together they walked to the warm sitting room looking

out over Park Avenue. Timmins followed them with the tray, and set out the coffee service. "*Merci*, Timmins," Mother said, "I'll pour."

"Very good, Ma'am," he replied. "Will there be anything else?"

"*Non, merci*, that will be all."

With a nod of his head, the servant disappeared.

Mother was always a concerto of tight movements, a violin played pizzicato, but today she was edgier than usual. She fussed with the ritual, handling the sugar tongs with great precision, adjusting and readjusting the amount of milk in each cup. She grasped the handle of the coffee pot carefully and poured slowly, tremendously focused on the simple task, as though without immense concentration the pot would rise to the ceiling and the coffee run to the floor. She leaned forward to better gauge the flow, then set the pot down on the tray and shuffled her feet across the weave of the rug, making a soft sound.

David too began to fidget as Mother's nervous activity started to grate on him. She clearly had something to say, and was having trouble saying it. What should the man of the family do? He picked up a few crackers and put them on a plate. He took a napkin, shook it out onto his lap, and rubbed his finger over the silk stitching of the monogram in the corner.

"They say he might not wake up." Her voice burst out in the quiet room.

David jerked so hard the napkin fluttered to the floor. "But," he blurted, "but he can't!" He couldn't form a more coherent sentence.

Mother lowered her voice to practically a whisper. "The doctors say the injury to his," she coughed, "his skull, his brain, is too severe." She spoke rapidly, without inflection. "I shall have to arrange for friends to know, of course, even though they can't visit. He wouldn't like people to see him like that."

"What do you mean, he might not wake up? Aren't the doctors going to do anything?"

"When the swelling went down, they took a second set of x-rays, and there was greater injury than they first thought. They say they've done what they can."

David shut his eyes, shook his head and rejected her words. His stomach churned and he felt close to throwing up. If Father were going to die, David would be able to feel it, to sense it. "Father will wake up, I know he will," he insisted.

"But what if he doesn't?" The turmoil of her emotions showed in the twitching of her eyelid, the tremor of her shoulders. David felt the air hum with her pain, echoing his own. She turned to him and trembling overtook her, as if invisible hands were shaking her by the shoulders. "Oh David, what will we do?" she whispered. She stared at him with huge eyes. "What will we do without him?" She picked up a pillow and hugged it to her stomach. A single, racking sob escaped her.

David sat frozen on the edge of the couch. Her one, lone sob ripped down his spine. What did one do with a crying woman? What did one do with a crying mother? His muscles burned with the conflict between staying still and lunging forward to, to do what? She sat on the end of the sofa, kneading the pillow. Her hands looked so pale, so small, with their thin, short fingers and delicate, rosy nails. Steam from the abandoned coffee twirled upward, and he wanted to take a cup, move the spoons, anything to occupy his own useless hands. Should he put his arms around her, pat her back, and say everything would be fine? It's what he would have done for Martina. His face burned with the shame of his impotence. The intimacy of the desperation and the need in those hands overwhelmed him. He felt small and helpless, and more than anything he wanted his mother to hold him, to comfort him, to make him feel safe. The air between them felt like a cement wall.

He shut his eyes. A fire engine screamed in the distance then faded away. A hot tide rose up in him; he longed to grab his tiny cup and hurl it against the window, grind the sugar into the carpet, anything to break this immobility. There was nothing he could do about Mother's pain. He had never thought failure could be so simple. "The only thing necessary for the triumph of evil is for good men to do nothing." That quote had been on a history exam in the far past, and it came back now with ferocious meaning.

Mother took in another huge ragged breath, the harsh sounds contrasting with the murmuring of the city street below, then shifted on the seat. "*Non*, it is enough of this nonsense," she said sharply. "Father will be fine, and we will be fine. We will proceed as normal, and *enfin*, all will be normal." She looked like a statue carved out of ivory. In the reflection in the window David saw her touch her eyes. "Our coffee, it is cold," she said, her voice crisp and stern, and almost, but not quite, steady. "I shall ring for more, *oui*?"

"No, no," he said, "this is fine, it's still fine." He knew by her minute motion she had wanted him to say this, offer this everyday courtesy as proof the world still followed the rules.

She turned toward him. "*Eh bien*. We will go to the hospital soon. Nurse Savener will come with us to help with Martina." She looked through the window out toward the street and spoke to herself. "I should not take her, the hospital is no place for a child, but she has been so upset, so *déséquilibré.*" She turned her gaze back to David. "Yes, that is what we shall do." She placed her cup and saucer carefully on the tray and curled herself into the cushions, head tilted as if she were settling down for an afternoon with a good book. Her hands rested calmly, one in her lap, one on the couch. Silently they accused him of the things he could not do.

David had never been inside a hospital before. The only exposure he'd ever had to serious disease was in novels, and he didn't think H. Rider Haggard's descriptions of jungle fever and skin rot had taught him what he needed to know now. He followed Mother, with Martina and Nurse Savener following behind, through the high arches of Lenox Hill Hospital, to a large nursing area heavy with the quiet rushing of people hurrying about on errands of life and death. An old man sat alone in one corner, shoulders shaking as he sobbed. David tried to ignore the cramping in his stomach. To the left as they went toward the elevator, David saw a small chapel with rows of chairs covered in dark red, and a podium at the front flanked by huge sprays of bright flowers. They looked garish and out of place in the somber room. David turned his head away; he wanted to tear them down so no one would have to see how cheerful they were.

He lay so still, looking waxen inside the cocoon of bleached white sheets. Behind David, Martina squeaked like an injured bird, and it suddenly made him viciously angry with Father. Whatever doubt he had before that Father was not really hurt, that this was a nightmare he would wake up from, disappeared in the agony of Martina's little sound. He wanted to push Mother out of the way, grab Father by the edges of the white gown and shake him until his eyes opened, until his lips parted and he was with them once again. "How dare you," David wanted to shout at him, "Look at us, a woman, a boy and a sick girl. We need you! This is so selfish, taking yourself away from us in a silly driving mistake. I hate you!" But he kept silent, turned away and stumbled to the window, to stare blindly out across the quiet courtyard.

Behind him Martina spoke. "Hurt," she said. David spun

around. She stepped up next to Mother, and was running her hands slowly up and down the corner of the bed railing near Father's feet.

Nurse Savener stood next to her. "Yes, dear, your father is hurt." A tear ran down the woman's face, and David remembered that she too had known Father almost fifteen years; she had come when Martina was an infant.

"Not sleeping," Martina said, grasping Father's foot with both hands and twisting back and forth. Nurse Savener pulled her hands away. How did Martina know Father wasn't sleeping? But then, David never fully understood what Martina knew about anything.

"No, he's not," Nurse Savener said to Martina. "God and the good doctors are taking care of him now."

"He's not sleeping, God is looking after him," Martina said, so clearly and lucidly that all three turned to stare at her. At this most primitive of levels, at the fundamental core of life and death, the real world and her imaginary world had merged. Death, and loss, the great going away, is the same in all lands, David thought. What poem was that from? Tears rolled unchecked down Martina's cheeks; she rocked to her own inner lullaby, her pink comb once again clutched to her face.

How was he ever going to be the man of this family? How could he possibly take on this impossible task? The anger inside him bubbled like hot, black tar. He couldn't do it. Father wouldn't want him to leave school, but more imperative, he would never be able to face Mother again if he failed.

CHAPTER 8

CELESTE

Celeste had never been to the office of Sherman and Browerman, Peter's financial advisors, but she knew it would look like this -- subdued and wealthy. Designed to impress the new client with the power of those in charge of this financial stronghold, and to reassure the current client his money was safe, no matter what was happening in the rest of the country. In the outer office, large seats and antique side tables clustered in a corner, offering a comfortable wait. Crystal bowls of grapes and chocolates waited patiently, offering mute decadence. The air smelled of old books, old leather and old money. Sounds faded quickly; thick carpet in swirls of brown, gold and bronze stretched from one wall to another, softening footfalls after the ringing of the marble hallway. The clatter of many typewriters, and assistants on errands dissipated into the luxury of plush surfaces.

It had been three months since Peter's accident, three months of seeing him lying in that hospital bed day after day, and in that time she had managed the complexity of their household finances quite competently, if she did say so herself. Yet merely stepping through the doorway of these broker's offices transformed her into an amateur of no importance. She jolted to awareness of every eye that might be watching her. Brokers were the gatekeepers of the power holders, and this was their territory. Peter was a man to be noticed in this world, but Celeste was merely a wife. She took a breath and prepared to step up and stand up for herself. A mere wife she might be, but this was a question of survival.

A pudgy, young man sat behind a large desk in front of two doors. He was writing in a ledger, his head bowed down, one finger holding his place among a copious stack of notes. He stopped, slid a marker into the notes, stood up and smiled professionally at Celeste. "You must be Mrs. Vandenholm," he said. "Mr. Browerman is expecting you, please come this way." He rubbed the cramps from his fingers with a furtive motion as he led her through one of the doors behind the desk, into a corner office with a spectacular view of Madison Avenue. Windows in the buildings across the street glittered in the sun.

Behind a massive, heavy desk sat a large man with broad shoulders, a large, bony face and perfect stillness of bearing. He looked more like a duke than a broker, with his fine posture and his charcoal suit with subtle pinstripes. A chunky, gold signet ring with a dark stone flashed on his finger, and the pen he used seemed as fragile as a toy in his large hand. Celeste froze two steps inside the doorway.

It had been a mistake to come; this man would spot her lies and her ignorance in a minute. She should have stayed home and pleaded illness. She should have arranged to do this by post. She should have at least worn a veil.

Mr. Browerman stood when she entered and as he did so his head crossed through the path of a sunbeam. The light shone for a second on his bald scalp, then rippled across his face, causing him to wince in the glare. This tiny, visible weakness restored some of Celeste's balance. She strode to his desk, reached for his outstretched hand and shook it firmly. If he was as good with money as his confident appearance suggested, he would handle her affairs well, which was the most important thing. Peter had chosen wisely, as he did with all things when his emotions weren't entangled.

"I'm so sorry to meet you under these circumstances." His square face showed sincere concern and, she thought, a calm willingness to wait for her to cry, if that's what she needed to do.

She sat where he indicated, in a tall-backed Flemish antique chair, with curved wooden arms and blue velvet upholstery. He remained standing. "Might I get you a drink? A cup of coffee or tea? Perhaps fruit juice?"

Celeste knew what he meant by fruit juice, and she paused for a minute over the possibility. "A glass of wine would be delightful, but perhaps not, *oui?* I have much learning to do if I am to take over the reins of my financial future." She tasted her words to make sure her accent was solidly in place. She smiled at him, hoping her confidence was evident, but her smile brought no response.

"That's an admirable attitude, Mrs. Vandenholm," the broker said matter-of-factly, without making it sound at all like a compliment. "Let's get started then, shall we?" He opened a manila folder and handed her a sheaf of papers. "I'm here to help you with this, in any way I can." He turned his hands palm upward on the desk, trying to look unthreatening, she supposed, but the wary detachment in his eyes was impossible to miss.

"Thank you." She nodded. "While I would like to review my finances in detail in the future, for the moment I only need more funds available for daily expenses."

"I'm afraid it's not quite so simple," he said. "I won't mince words. Your finances are in a weak position, and we're going to have to work quite hard to rescue anything."

Celeste frowned. "What do you mean, our finances are weak? Our finances are fine."

"To be honest, Mrs. Vandenholm, your portfolio suffered severely with the downturn in the economy. And since your husband lost his job, there has been almost no revenue to offset expenses."

As a girl, Celeste once saw a cottonmouth snake catch a vole that had wandered down to the stream to drink. At one moment the snake was lying quietly by the water's edge, sunning itself in the warm shallows. It seemed unaware of the vole, which was busily washing behind its ears with its tiny paws. The next minute the snake had the vole in its mouth, fangs buried in the dying creature's neck. In between the two moments no movement had occurred. Just two photographs, one next to the other. Life and Death. Before and After.

Bad news had always come to her with the speed of a striking cottonmouth. When the police came to tell her Peter had failed to negotiate a turn, when the doctors told her Martina would never be normal, when her mother had stopped stirring the pot of stew on the stove and sat down on the floor, she knew in those moments how the vole had felt. She knew what it was like to be stricken by a fate both violent and unforeseen; and all the more violent precisely because it was unforeseen.

When had Peter lost his job?

When she had called his office to tell them about the accident, that he wouldn't be coming back to work, what had they said? Had they already known he was lying to her? Had they in fact said something that should have given her a clue, but she had been oblivious to it?

She raised her chin. If nothing else, she knew the role she was assigned to play. Her heart beat hard and her palms slicked with nervous sweat.

"Tell me," she said, her voice calm, her survival skills clamped hard in place. Under the water, she thought, the swan's feet may be thrashing for all they're worth, but above the surface she glides like a queen.

Browerman nodded slowly, as if a sudden move might

startle her into hysterics. Perhaps it would. He shifted a few papers without looking at them.

"Tell me how bad it is." She didn't know if his hesitation was chivalry or sympathy.

"Extremely bad," he said at last. "To start with, due to the fall of the stock market, many companies went out of business, and your husband had his insurance policies with one of them."

Beyond the wide glass panes, the traffic moved up Madison Avenue. In the stream of automobiles, a horse pulling a delivery wagon went past, an increasingly rare sight these days. "Life insurance?" she asked.

"Oh no," Mr. Browerman said. "I sincerely hope Mr. Vandenholm will recover and return to us quite soon." He shook his head. "I was referring to automobile accident coverage." He said the word automobile oddly, as if he didn't say it often. She thought perhaps he had never driven one, never owned one. "Since the automobile was so badly damaged, the Buick Company your husband purchased it from will not agree to repossess it."

"Repossess it?"

"Take it back. Buy it back."

Celeste shook her head, once, puzzled. She knew what repossess meant, for heaven's sake, it was the other concept her mind was stumbling over. "You mean, the car company still wants its money, but there's no insurance company to pay for the damage? Is that what this means?"

"Yes, precisely. I have talked to the company manager, and he will not move from this position. Their company will require full repayment of the purchase loan."

"That's ridiculous. I won't pay it," she declared. She felt her neck and shoulders tightening, and the back of her head was beginning to throb.

Mr. Browerman sighed and shook his head. "Then they

will come after you with a payment order. I would like to be able to say the courts would treat you kindly, as you are a woman on your own with two young children, but that isn't likely to be the case in the current economy. There have been too many cases like yours to make any more exceptions." He coughed, spitting delicately into a large, pale blue handkerchief. "In these hard times, no judge will allow you to keep your assets but not pay your creditors."

"My husband paid the insurance company for coverage. Even if they went out of business, where did that money go?"

Mr. Browerman shrugged, turning his pink palms upward. "A business can fail for many reasons. Almost certainly, the funds your husband and others provided were invested in stocks that collapsed last year. 1929 was hard on all of us." He looked down and rubbed the surface of his desk with large fingers. "And of course, if the accident were in fact deliberate, that would mitigate against any claim you might have on the bankruptcy proceedings."

Celeste had been staring at a dark splotch on the wall near the window, but now she caught his eye and stared at him, hard. "It was not deliberate, it was an accident!" How could he even suggest such a thing? Peter was vibrant and optimistic; Peter had everything to live for. "I'll thank you not to mention that again." The thought was not to be considered, even for a moment. She crossed her arms over her chest. "How much of a drain is this going to be on my other resources?"

The broker exhaled, in one long, soft sigh. "You don't have any other resources," he said.

The statement, stark and fatal, struck her like the cottonmouth, shifting its grip on an already dying prey. The bad news traveled through her system, her arms and legs felt powerless to move, as if she weighed a thousand pounds.

"I don't have specific instructions, of course, but Mr. Vandenholm and I did discuss some generalities. The townhouse has been mortgaged twice, and the loans are both nearly a year behind in payments. You own several large blocks of stock of negligible worth. Over the last year, your husband sold all of the stock that had any remaining value. When the Bank of New Amsterdam failed, he needed to liquidate what he could."

"But he told me we hardly suffered at all when the bank crashed. I remember that night. We celebrated our close call with champagne."

Mr. Browerman's smile was a study in gentle, fatherly patience. "Men often like to protect their wives from bad news. I would do it myself, if I had a wife." His attitude was certainly meant to be gentle, reassuring, and understanding, but his pity was clear. He rubbed his bald head.

"He bought that brand new roadster."

The kind smile didn't waver. "Men don't always do the right thing, the sensible thing, even in hard times."

His tone, paternal yet patronizing, riled her. "I think you mean," she snapped, "that Peter bought expensive toys he couldn't afford, just to impress his friends." Peter's beautiful, laughing face flashed in front of her. She shouldn't be angry with this stranger for stating the truth. She loved Peter very much, but yes, he was foolish in some ways. It struck her that she had not heard the words "I love you," in more than three months. Before, she and Peter had said it every night for nearly twenty years. She ached with the senseless, tragic waste of it all. She ground her nails into her palms, fighting to find control, to refocus on the problem at hand. Calm and strong, she repeated in her head, calm and strong, but her thoughts whirled like a river in a flood. Beyond the steep edge of control lay a long, sharp and frightening drop into that swirling oblivion. She clamped her mind onto how much Martina and David needed her, holding the floodwaters back with an almost physical effort.

"This is plumb crazy! I have practically lost my husband, I am alone with my children, there are two mortgages to pay, and on top of it all, the car company wants money as well. It ain't fair!" Even as she said them, she knew the futility of the words. She heard their impotence in the very loss of control, of accent. Fair was a creature you couldn't fight. Fair was something the other people, the people with power, the haves, decided for you. Plenty of fools, and plenty of bright people who should have known better, tried to fight it, but they lost, of course, because there was no way to win a rigged fight. The eternal cry of the doomed, failed, miserable have-nots who were too weak to win and too stubborn to lie down and give up, their motto was "it's not fair!" And who the hell gave a damn, except the other doomed, failed and miserable have-nots?

Mr. Browerman made a sound that indicated agreement perhaps, or possibly only acknowledgement.

"I have two children to take care of," Celeste said, "David has another year of school, and then university. I can't allow this to happen to us." What did they expect her to do? How did they expect her to earn a living?

"Have you no family you can turn to? The Vandenholm's are an old and well established family. I know that Peter and his father fell out some time ago, but surely, under the circumstances? " Mr. Browerman let the sentence hang.

She tried to force the anger back, but failed. Peter's father had the money to help them; she was damned sure that miserable old bastard had protected his finances just fine, thank you very much. But she knew he would never give her or her children a cent of that money, and she would starve before she went on bended knee to see him. He had forced Peter to choose between them, and Peter had chosen her. Peter's face rose before her again, his blue eyes capturing her, the faint scar on his chin calling to her fingers. She broke the skin on her palms trying to redirect her pain, but it was no use. The anger, the hurt, the betrayal of Peter's simple failure to follow the curves in the road gagged her. "No, there is no one." She struggled to draw each breath; she heard the air rasping in and out of her lungs in shorter and shorter gasps. She put her hands over her face as shudders ran through her, shaking her against the arms of the chair.

Large hands pulled her up and out of the chair. A warm arm guided her down the hall to a lavish ladies room, and then left her alone.

Alone, oh God, alone. She needed to be alone. She did not want to weep quietly, she wanted to wail, to shout, to scream loudly enough for Peter to hear her and come back. But she was trapped, locked in this private hell, a whirlpool of fear and anger.

As she stood in the bathroom stall, the cottonmouth swallowed her, whole, with wrenching violence. Huge, loud, ugly sobs moved through her, building deep inside and bursting out in a violent torrent. She sank to the floor, leaned her face against the cold tile wall and wailed. She felt the rough edge of an uneven tile scraping her cheek as she shuddered, crying, and she thought she should pull away, but she couldn't move, she could only cry.

Images of Peter stampeded her: Peter laughing, Peter sleeping, eating, smoking. He might be immature, silly, childish and overly concerned with his appearance and his standing with his friends, but he was gentle and loving, and he had chosen her. They had been a wonderfully happy family, in spite of their secrets. Yes, Peter had kept this news from her, but she had kept so much from him, as well. She could see Peter joyously swimming with David, and seriously, carefully teaching Martina to play chess. She could see Peter pushing his shining golden hair out of his face as he rose above her as they made love, propping himself on one elbow as he stroked her face.

Celeste's chest hurt from sobbing, her throat ached. Her eyeliner ran into her eyes and stung them, bringing more tears. She didn't want to cry anymore, she wanted to scream, she wanted to throw something fragile, throw it hard with all her might and listen to it shatter into thousands of glittering shards. She pounded the wall until, at last, the anger ran out of her, down to the dregs, and she huddled on the floor, damp and drained. She wondered if she would ever have the strength to stand up and go on.

She took a deep breath, held it, and then slowly released it. She took another breath. She didn't know what she was going to do, but she would come up with a plan. She had to. Once upon a time she had been able to run from her problems, but she had David and Martina to think about now.

CHAPTER 9

MARTINA

The general with the big hands is not here. The fast general david one used to come before and do battle, but he went to the school place. The gods have taken them all away. All away. All away.

The soldiers are quiet again, again, again, standing motionless in rank. The gods are angry.

Where are the circles? I am all alone.

CHAPTER 10

DAVID

"*En garde*. Fencers are you ready?" asked the student directing the bout. All around David, the Briarwood school gym resounded with the clash of metal against metal, of other students shouting, of white shoes lunging and sliding across the surface of the fighting strips on the floor.

"Ready, Sir." David touched his epee to the front of his mask in salute, bounced once tightly on the balls of his feet and crouched into a ready stance. Behind his mask he grimaced at James Troast, his opponent.

"Ready," James said.

"Fence," Evan called.

David shot forward into attack. Lunge. Parry. Riposte!

"Halt!" Evan called. "Point. The attack was good. That was fast, David. You're usually so polite!"

David laughed more loudly than the comment deserved. He pressed the point of the blade against the floor to bend the tip a little more. He'd taken one of the new, whippier blades out of the cabinet today; it moved awkwardly through the air, not quite right. Maybe the balance was off. "Ready."

"Aren't you the eager beaver," James said. "All right. Ready."

"Fence."

The expanse of white chest before him appeared huge,

the scoring area large enough to plant crops on. Time and space were distorted since he'd returned to school. He had been glad to leave the tension of home behind, but school had been no better. Every hallway seemed to surge with boys whispering the vicious lie that Father's accident had been no accident at all. David thrust his epee forward then drew back and shifted his aim downward before James recovered from parrying the first thrust.

"Halt!"

David's arm vibrated with the effort to stop his forward motion.

"Point to David. You're moving in double time today, for certain."

"Am I?" David asked.

Evan and James stared at him.

"I'm ready," David said.

"Sheesh. I'm ready."

"Fence," Evan said.

Advance. Lunge. Thrust. The whole world had collapsed to include only David and his target. David grinned.

James skipped backward.

"Halt. James, you're off the strip. Slower, David, you're starting to slash."

Lunge, parry, riposte.

"Halt! Point!"

He saw James and Evan exchange another quick glance. Was he acting strangely? He didn't feel different, but yes, tight and wild and happy. Or not happy, he wasn't sure of his feelings at all anymore. "Ready," he said, before Evan could ask.

A shimmer of electricity sizzled under the skin on the back of David's hands, rippling up his forearms and through his shoulders. He could not name it, but the buzz of it flowed upward across his chest, across his cheeks. Not excitement, not anger, but yet it was both. What could he call it? The right name for it, the sense of it, hovered just beyond the reach of his thoughts. He was surging with strength, and he wanted to drop the courtesies of the fencing rules and strike out in whatever direction his body chose.

"Ready, let's go."

"Okay, all right. Ready."

David leapt forward into a flying attack, his feet leaving the floor, his arm and blade extended as a single unit.

The point of the weapon landed squarely in the middle of the other boy's chest. The blade arced sharply under the pressure then suddenly snapped in half. The crack of the shattering metal ricocheted through the gymnasium like a gunshot.

David stared at the foot of metal blade still attached to the handle. "I could have killed you," he said, horrified, but at the same time jubilant.

James touched a finger to the jagged point of the weapon. "I've never seen a blade do that up close before," James said, wide-eyed.

"You okay?" David helped James to his feet.

"Yes. Maybe. I think so." He rubbed his chest, looking dazed. "It's the ones that don't bend that hurt you."

David secretly hoped there would be a large, huge bruise for everyone to see.

Boys hurried over, pushing in at each other to touch the lethal weapon, murmuring their shock. "You would have been *skewered* if that hadn't snapped," one boy said. "You would have been absolutely *punctuated*."

The burst of laughter that followed was rich with the release of tension. "Punctuated," another repeated, "that's a good one."

Master Fellows, the fencing master, rushed up, pinching the corner of his perfectly waxed mustache. "Is everyone all right? What has happened?"

"I'm okay, Sir," James said.

David held up the damaged epee. "Blade snapped, Sir."

"Oh my," Master Fellows said, pinching his moustache. "Oh my goodness. What a close call. Are you sure you're not hurt, Troast?" One of Master Fellows' feet tapped the wooden floor, making rapid clicking sounds.

"No, Sir." James patted his white jacket for emphasis. "I'm fine, Sir."

Master Fellows clasped his hands together as if they would stop twitching if they had each other for company. "Well that's a relief. All right, everyone put away your gear and take your showers. This period is over."

James fingered the rough edge of the metal. "Nearly killed me, it did. I'd like to keep the blade, Sir. If that would be okay?"

"Unacceptable slang, that word. Okay indeed." Feet tapped, fingers went back to mustache pinching. "You need to speak properly at all times. All times. But yes, you may keep the blade." James led, as they all hurried off to the locker room, broken epee under his arm. David walked behind, flexing the muscles in his arms and legs, engaged in his own thoughts. He tried to catch a glimpse of his reflection in the window as he passed. Could everyone see how glorious he felt?

David slammed his physics book shut; he did not want waste his evening thinking about calculating the angles of rowboats crossing streams. Curfew and lights out would not come for another two hours, he did not want to study any longer, he wanted to retrieve the exhilaration he'd felt that afternoon. He opened his Coleridge assignment, but the very start of the mariner's endless, allegorical ramblings made him angry. He was trapped in this airless room. "Enough, I'm done," he announced, standing up from his desk. "Come on,

Chad, let's get out of here, I cannot sit still for another minute."

David's roommate, Chad Schuyler, lay on his back on the lower bunk, his feet pressed up against the springs of the upper bunk. He was holding an anthology of American literature over his head, his lips moving as he read semi-silently, with occasional dramatic pauses. Clearly Chad thought Coleridge was fine.

"I don't know why we bother with this garbage," David said. "What difference does it make how well I do on some test or other? What difference does it make if you go to Yale like your grandfather and great-grandfather, or stay home and have a good time? Life comes to nothing in the end anyway."

Chad rubbed a hand in his hair and peered around the edge of the book at David. "You're at it again."

"But it's true." David paced back and forth, weaving a path through the clothes strewn on the floor. "What good does it do us to accomplish anything, when in the end we're still dead? Isn't the whole point of life to explore now? To actually feel alive right now?"

"You're not going to start this same argument with me. Go find someone else." Chad rolled over and turned his back to David. "Besides, you're a fine one to talk, Mister my-whole-family-went-to-Dartmouth. Mister I'm-class-president-and-I'm-going-to-be-a-great-success-one-day."

Yes, Father would have wanted him to study, work hard, and move on to Dartmouth after graduating with high marks. Father had always been thrilled with his success at school. But wouldn't Father also have wanted him to honor this victory? The courage to travel a different path? He didn't know which one was more important, he only knew which one felt better.

In the short pause in the conversation, voices from the hall were clear.

"Did you see that broken blade Troast has? Vandenholm

snapped it right off against him."

"Not on purpose?"

"No, but you should have seen the look on his face. Like a wild man, he was. Pretty scary."

"Vandenholm's been a touch, well, odd since his father took the big dive."

"I hear they're completely out of money."

The fury that had been flirting with David roared out in full strength, surging through him as it had that afternoon. To hell with petty courtesies and rigorous manners. He burst out of the room into the lounge where a handful of boys were sprawled on chairs, chattering idly among books strewn haphazardly. He knew exactly which one had made that foul comment about Father taking a dive, it was Michaelson, the little worm. He grabbed the boy by the shirt and shook him, hard. "That's not true," he shouted. "My father was in an accident, he did not try to kill himself." He was peripherally aware the boy in his grasp lived in the same dormitory, shared many of the same classes, and could be counted as a friend. He pulled back his fist, about to let fly, when his roommate caught hold and yanked his arm down.

"Calm down, David," Chad said. "He didn't know."

"He shouldn't be spreading lies if he doesn't know the truth," David snarled. He shook Chad off and drew his arm back once more. The smaller boy threw an arm up to cover his face.

Chad grabbed David's fist again. "No, he shouldn't," Chad said, "but he's about to apologize, aren't you, Mikey?" Chad glowered at the other boy.

"I'm sorry, old man," the boy said, peering out from under his elbow. "I thought," he looked at the faces eyeing him, "I'm sorry, I didn't mean it."

David drove his fist forward and just to the right of Michaelson's head, slamming his knuckles into a lamp and sending it flying. It landed with a crash, and glass shards flew outward across the floor. The boy cringed in David's grip.

David started to laugh and the sound of it, harsh and raw, scraped up and down his throat until he was breathless.

More hands reached out to pull them apart and David released his hold. He sucked on his knuckles, regaining his breath, the wild laughter gone and tears threatening to arrive. "My father didn't try to kill himself, it was a car accident," he mumbled.

"I know," Chad reassured him. "Ignore them, they're morons." He pointed at one of the younger boys. "Get a broom and sweep up the glass. We'll see about getting a new lamp in the morning." He pushed David back into their room.

"By the way," Chad added, "when I said you should find another chump to pick a fight with, I didn't mean it quite so literally."

David grunted in reply. The victorious sensation was gone. David swung himself up the bed ladder onto his own bunk and collapsed onto his stomach, his head cradled in his arms. His hand hurt. His head hurt. "Did you see the look on Vandenholm's face," one of the boys had said. "Like a wild animal." He had felt so powerful, and so right, why couldn't they see it? He hated this jumble of emotion and consciousness, and yet he loved it. He hated not being in control of himself, but he loved the flying, soaring splendor of losing control. He was a Roman candle, piercing the night sky with glorious flame. He fell asleep the happiest he'd been for months.

Thoughts of his triumph were still with him the next morning in American History.

"Vandenholm."

"Hmmh?"

"Mister Vandenholm!"

David's focus snapped back to the hushed classroom and an impatient Master scowling at the front. He scrambled to his feet. "Yes, Sir?"

"Your presence is required in the Headmaster's office. You may be excused." The history master crumpled the message slip and dropped it into the trash basket, then pointedly swiveled back to the blackboard to resume his lesson.

David gathered his books and left the room, his heart pounding. In five years at Briarwood Academy, he had never been summoned to the Headmaster's office before. When they told him the news about Father last fall, Headmaster Hibbeler had come himself to collect David from class. A summons like this usually accompanied the discovery that one of the boys had been caught cheating on an exam, or stealing. This had to be about the fight in the lounge last night. But maybe not. "Please don't let anything be wrong with Mother or Martina. Please don't let Father be dead."

The hallway was infinitely long; David heard each individual footstep echo along walls hung with faces of senior students who had died in the Civil War, then the faces of those who died in the Great War, a mere year older than he when their pictures were taken. They looked stonily down on him from their places of honor, those rows of pale oval outlines and wide eyes, judging him. The occasional dark face mixed in, Briarwood was quite proud of its history of educating former slaves and their children, even now still accepting a colored student every five or six years. The closer he got to the headmaster's office the more his hands shook, and the stronger the protest in his stomach grew. He paused for a minute. It would be even worse humiliation if he threw up now.

Headmaster Hibbeler waited behind his massive oak desk, his brown hair streaked with white, short and carefully trimmed. Heavy robes falling perfectly in place, blue eyes, sharp and stern, watching from behind the silver rims of bifocals. He waved David to a chair. "I understand there was a disturbing altercation in the dormitory last night."

"Yes, Sir." David shut his eyes and gripped the arms of the chair. A tremendous ringing started in his ears. He concentrated on the smell of lemon oil from the big polished desk and tried to resist the dizziness.

"I understand that damage was done to school property, and another student was endangered."

"Yes, Sir." David stared at the toe of his shoe.

A long silence followed, and David finally looked up into the old man's face, sad and waiting. "Would you like to tell me what happened?"

The gentle tone poured straight through David. Huge tears formed and dribbled down his cheeks before he could check them. He wiped them away with a balled fist, head bent down to hide the movement.

"I don't know, Sir," he mumbled. "I couldn't seem to stop myself. I just ..." He stopped, clearing his throat. "I'm sorry, Sir, it won't happen again." He wanted to say it had been that worm Michaelson's fault, for spreading vicious gossip about Father. He wanted to explain he was only doing what a good son should do -- defending the reputation of a man who was not there to defend himself, but the words froze in his throat.

"You've been angry since your father's accident. All the Masters have mentioned how much trouble you've been having with your studies."

David had been having difficulty concentrating, but he didn't think anyone else had noticed. He thought he'd been hiding his lack of enthusiasm for school quite well. He tried to make eye contact with the Headmaster, skittered his gaze over the man's shoulder and out of the window instead. "I know my grades have slipped, but they'll come back up, I promise."

"It is understandable that you have a great deal of

resentment and worry. It isn't fair, you think, that you should have to concentrate on an activity as remote as studying." Master Hibbeler leaned forward over the surface of the huge desk, speaking sadly and softly. "You're right, it isn't fair. You miss your father, and you are frightened for his sake, but that is the human plight. The greatest of philosophers have railed at the Almighty for performing His works without explanation. However, knowing that others have been where you are now does not help, I know."

David nodded. It was strangely comforting: the formal words, the gentle tone.

"It will not go away, this fear, this sense of being overwhelmed by life. Nor will the questions surrounding your father's accident."

David looked up and found the headmaster watching him intently. He nodded, and the headmaster nodded back. David realized that whatever rumors he himself had heard, of course the headmaster would have heard as well. David was glad at least one person understood what he was enduring.

"The gossip will fade, although not as quickly as you would like. Your fear and anger will become easier to live with as well, although they will never go away. A tragedy like this will become part of you. It is your job to make sure it is a source of compassion, not an excuse for moral laxity. You have sunk to brawling and fighting because it feels exciting, it is rousing, isn't it?"

David nodded, surprised. How did this man know exactly how he felt?

"Rage and violence are always exciting, we are human animals, human yes, but animal at the core. Do not confuse an action that *feels* good for an action that *is* good. It will take character to move beyond this time of trouble, but I have faith that you have that character. Remember, 'we acquire the strength we have overcome.'"

"Yes, Sir. Emerson, Sir." David held his eyes open wide, trying not to cry again, and focused his attention on the leaves waving at the edge of the office window. It was ivy, still glossy and green even in winter. A few stray brown oak leaves, curled and crisp, were trapped against the wall next to the ivy. As the leaves trembled in the wind, David found the thought of Father's coma slipping away. He tried to retrieve his exhilaration of yesterday and think of it as wrong, as lacking in compassion. He wanted to be a man with a good character, more noble than he had been yesterday. He wanted to be redeemed.

Master Hibbeler was still watching him. "I know you are in turmoil, and the Masters will give you some leeway in your studies until your concentration returns to you. But I must draw the line at brawling in the hallways like a barroom thug. Giving in to your self-pity is a pernicious habit to acquire, even for a short period." The headmaster's long fingers rested together, steepled among the impedimenta of his work.

David looked away from the leaves, aware that a response was expected. "Yes, Sir," he said.

"Your father was a fine man."

"Yes, Sir," David answered. He gripped his hands together.

"Class of '02, I believe."

"Yes, Sir."

"I didn't know him, I'm afraid, he was several years behind me. Your grandfather was class of 1874, was he not?"

"I believe so, Sir." David hadn't a clue. He'd never met the man.

"You come from a good family, you have a proud tradition to live up to. Work to find that strength inside yourself."

"Yes, Sir."

"Look within yourself, and become a man that your father

would have been proud of."

"Yes, Sir."

"I hope this has helped," Master Hibbeler said.

David nodded and rose. Oddly enough, it had.

CHAPTER 11

CELESTE

Celeste sagged against the cold glass of the jewelry counter and tried to count the number of times she had heard the words "I'm sorry" in the last few months.

"I'm sorry madam, I cannot give you any more for that necklace."

"But it's worth six times what you're offering!"

"I'm sorry madam, not in today's market."

Chin up and shoulders square she marched out of the store, pretending a courage and a confidence she did not have, determined to find the right buyer for each necklace, each ring, each painting. She would not give up a single one of these treasures without a fight. She felt like a child chasing a balloon, arms outstretched, running to catch hold of her dreams as they wafted tantalizingly out of reach. She had been just as powerless to stop Peter from floating away into whatever lost world he now inhabited. She should have gone with him that day, she should have been in the car, holding his hand. He had wanted to drive around aimlessly; she had wanted to finish the novel she had been reading. She would never read Sinclair Lewis again. It seemed like only a moment since Peter had been gone, yet an eternity at the same time. She found herself struggling to remember the sound of his voice; at frequent intervals during the course of a day she would stop what she was doing and concentrate on bringing it back to mind. She pressed her fist to her chest to stop the knot of pain from engulfing her.

Her feet tapped the cement sidewalks in time with the endless looping of her thoughts. From one dealer to the next, from the foreign traders in Chinatown with their quick, shrill language and their nose-tingling spices, to the pawn brokers in Washington Heights with their pitying looks and their smug offers; up and down the length of Manhattan, she stubbornly held on for each pathetic dollar more. She walked all the way to Harlem, where black faces jumped out at her in waves. She tried not to stare. She had never seen such well-dressed Negroes as a child. She had never seen anyone well-dressed at home. She would make damn sure she got every cent possible, in order to buy one more moment of medical care for Peter, one more test that might restore him to her as husband, lover, father. She refused to acknowledge what the doctors told her. She would not, could not, give up hope.

But in the end, she settled for what she could get. Once solid stocks sold for pennies. Tables and chairs practically walked away. Artwork and jewelry tumbled for a tenth of their value into the hands of dispassionate merchants, each profiting from her downfall. Every night she scrutinized her checking account, totaled and retotaled her pages of sums. Every night they told the same story, only a sentence here, a phrase there, different than the night before, but the ending always the same.

The old survival skills came back without any effort, like sturdy, leather boots that had shaped themselves to her feet and still slipped on easily, although they'd been in the back of the closet for years. She bought end cuts of meat in the butcher shop, day old bread in the bakery. She haggled over the size of eggs, she turned her head and refused to see the oranges, bananas, and tomatoes, all out of season and out of reach.

There were more steps she would have to take, and they were hard steps. She would go to Helen first. If she convinced Helen, that would help sway Marjorie. After all, Helen did pride herself on being a philanthropist and the queen of charitable giving.

"I'm sorry, darling," Helen said, lounging casually on a divan quite inferior to the one Celeste had just sold. "You know I would, but Lewis would never hear of it. Of course I'll ask him, but I don't hold out much hope."

"It's not for me, I hope you know," Celeste laughed gaily. "Make sure Lewis understands that. I have plenty to live on, and to keep Martina and David, but with all the medical bills, it's simply not enough to keep David at Briarwood, and that is so important to Peter." Through eyes crinkled with laughter, she analyzed every nuance of Helen's expression. How much more could she push? Would it help to be more pitiful? Less?

"Of course I know that," Helen leaned forward and put her hand on Celeste's. Her eyes were wide with a sincerity that Celeste did not believe for an instant. "Of course I know it's for David, but Lewis is practically primeval about appropriate finances, even about loans to his own family."

The Voights gave so generously to charity, why couldn't they help her now that she was in such need? She knew the answer, of course. They were front and center when there was a lawsuit with newspaper coverage, but here in private, with no credit attached, they would leave her out cold on her own. "If you only would talk to him, I know he would come around."

"I'll talk to him, of course, but he doesn't pay much attention to me when it comes to money matters." Helen wrinkled her nose winsomely and shrugged one shoulder.

Celeste knew what she should do. She should smile cutely back and laugh, ah, the dear men, what would we do without them? She knew she should do that, but with help so tantalizingly close to her reach, she opened her mouth and the wrong words came tumbling out. "If you could talk to him, I know he would do anything for you."

Even before she heard the tense overtones of her voice, the near-demand of her plea, she saw in Helen's eyes that the battle was lost. If it hadn't been before, it certainly was now.

"Of course I'll do my best," Helen said tightly, and immediately glanced at her watch, seeking escape from the awkward conversation. "Oh dear, look at the time, I must be getting ready. Lewis has an absolutely tiresome business dinner tonight at Sardi's." She stood, smoothing her dress over her knees. "Tilly will see you out. Perhaps if you're free some time or other next week, we could have lunch."

"Yes, that would be lovely," Celeste said. She walked away, and did not look back. She had never been handed over to the maid in a friend's house before. Perhaps she still hadn't, she thought.

Celeste summoned the staff. They knew what she was going to say, of course. They had seen the townhouse being stripped to the walls, the closets emptied, the meals reduced. They nodded as she spoke, tears in their eyes. Celeste gripped her hands together behind her back and tried to meet their eyes. "I will give you as much pay as I can," she said, "and of course provide the best possible references for all of you." It was as if she, herself, was being torn into shreds, not just her circumstances, not just her family. "I wish there was another way."

The murmurs of "Yes ma'am, I'm sorry ma'am, we understand, ma'am," all broke over her in a gentle tide. She stared at their shoes fidgeting nervously on the bare floor. Timmins' were large and black, Mrs. Timmins' brown and Nurse Savener's dark blue. Three pair of shoes, three different colors, lined up in front of her like a display in a shoe store. She concentrated on this image. "This is temporary, and I will get our finances sorted out soon, very soon. Everything is in such a muddle since Peter's accident, he was a good man but had no head for paperwork, I'm finding out." She tried to provide a reassuring chuckle, but it scratched harshly in her throat. Mrs. Timmins choked back a sniff, and Celeste made the mistake of looking up to meet her eyes. Sorrow lay heavily there, with sympathy, and the deep knowledge that this was the last time they would meet.

Late that night, in the darkness of her room, staring out the window at the lights traveling up and down Park Avenue, she entertained the slim chance that going directly to Peter's friends and business associates would be of use. For only a minute or two, alone in the darkness, without the hard corners of reality intruding, she embroidered a scene in which money poured forth, easily and happily, keeping David in school, keeping Nurse Savener for Martina, keeping the Timmins's here and the brownstone for herself. Best of all, there was money to get Peter the best care. Money to bring Peter back to her. She tried hard to ignore the images in her head of her husband, once so strong and vibrant, now withering, supine, dissipating by the spoonful each day. Celeste huddled in the blankets and tried to pretend she was still a young girl, hoping a magical, delightful, astonishing future lay ahead of her. She floated through a dream in Peter's arms, wrapped in warmth and silk, shining as brightly as her diamonds. She'd been so happy then, she tried to hold fast to the scattering wisps of her fantasy and force it to come back.

The dream scattered when she woke. The new day arrived without bringing any magic wand to wave poverty into retreat. The numbers continued to tell their stark tale, and Celeste repeatedly breathed deep and searched the mirror for a sign of the strength she knew had once been there, sighing in defeat.

The dreadful, mournful spring dragged on. David came home from school for the summer break, looking as dashing and alive as Peter once had. He moved around the empty apartment in shock, shifting his shoulders forward and back in a way that caught Celeste's attention. That's exactly the way Poppa moved when he was restless. She studied him. She had never seen anything of either of her parents in David before, and this vivid snapshot of the past caught at her throat. Maybe he had her own stubborn streak, but physically he had always been all Peter. Day by day, drop by drop, Peter was trickling away from them. With a tiny movement she clutched the cloth of her skirt.

David's face went completely blank when she broke the news of how bad their finances were. He stammered for words. "Go back to Briarwood as a charity student? I can't do that, I'm the class president. I'm," he paused. He stared at her as if she would be able to speak for him. She could, she thought. "I'm not a charity student," he finished. He looked so confused, Celeste felt her tears well up yet again. Was there no end to the crying?

Celeste thought he'd been about to say that he was too important to go back on a scholarship. And too proud. She would have to put a stop to this nonsense. She forced the tears back into the black depths they'd come from, and locked them down there. "If you don't go back to Briarwood, you will have to go to public school, and your father would never agree to that. Public schools can be excellent, but you come from a Briarwood family, and don't you forget it."

He leaped to his feet, his fists clenched and his tone fierce. "Never. I will never go back to Briarwood as a pauper. I have a reputation to uphold, Father would have understood that."

"A good education is what your father would have wanted for you."

"I am a Vandenholm. Maybe you don't understand because you're only one by marriage, but it is important to me. You were nothing but an orphan when Father married you!"

Celeste halted, the rebuke she'd been about to deliver for his loud voice forgotten. If only he knew, the thought boiled. He thought he could wound her by calling her an orphan. He didn't know how to hurt her, he was like a puppy snapping at a shadow on the wall. He had tried to, though, and the pettiness of his intent bothered her. On the other hand, she understood his frustration, they were trapped. She knew that better than he did, that all the avenues of escape were sealed off. Except one, but she would not go there. Well, except two, the thought came unbidden. "No," she vowed. "I will not go there either."

She spoke to David at last. "Insult me as much as you want, but there is no money. You go back to Briarwood on a scholarship, or you don't go back at all. I'm sorry, I've done the best I can, but no money means no money."

He was silent for so long, she began to wonder if he'd heard her. Then he shifted his weight and took one step away from her, his shoulders square and bony and young. "Very well, Mother, we will do our best." But she saw the rebellion in his eyes, and the effort he was making to conceal it. "Will we be able to go to Newport this summer?"

"No, *mon cher*," Celeste told him gently. "It is out of the question. In fact, you will have to look after Martina, while I look for work. We will find an affordable apartment with a park nearby."

"Without Nurse Savener? That's not possible!"

"You always do quite well with her. She will be fine, and so will you." She smiled at him. David would feel better if she set a good example for him. "*Alors*, we will proceed admirably, *mon cher*, you will see. It is only temporary, only until your father wakes up and returns to us." She wanted to hold her arms open, cuddling away his hurt as she had when he was a baby. She put one arm around him and pressed her cheek into his shoulder -- he had grown taller than her -- and after a minute, she felt him lean in and turn his face to her hair.

Sotheby's auctioned all of the remaining furniture, books and household items, then handed her a pitiful return, which she took with a grateful hand. Even a tiny windfall was more useful than a large number of ornate, oversized tables and chairs. Celeste found a damp apartment at the southern end of Manhattan, in a squat brick building, in a row of squat, brick buildings, all huddled next to each other like mushrooms. One dreary, rainy day in June, they loaded their meager pile of boxes, carrying the last of their clothing and trinkets, into a rented wagon and rode downtown.

David took a few steps into the apartment, sniffed once and hunched wordlessly over the box he was carrying. Martina ricocheted among the boxes stacked in the cluttered space, patting each one. Occasionally she singled one out for special attention, shoving it into a new place. "They are hungry. There are no circles," she said, forehead furrowed, hands fluttering. "They need to be fixed."

Celeste pretended not to see David and Martina's distress. There was not a thing she could do about it, this was their new reality. Where once Celeste had swept through a broad marble foyer and formal rooms with a glowing view of the city lights, now she commanded a hook by the door and a tiny space with a couch, which she made up at night for David. She and Martina slept in the one miniscule bedroom. Where once she had decorated and redecorated with joyous abandon, here the walls had been slapped with paint in a shade of beige that Celeste suspected the landlord had chosen solely for its ability to hide dirt and stains. The attempt was only partially successful, and was overlaid by the dull grime of inattention, coal soot, and the exhaust residue from the ever-growing population of motor vehicles clogging the streets. The ceilings were low and the windows narrow, looking out onto the brick-walled side of the next building in the row.

Celeste moved through the days without allowing herself to think. She went from one task to the next, not permitting herself to react to her surroundings.

After weeks of applying for every job advertised in the newspaper that she was even marginally suited for, Celeste found a receptionist position at Clawson's Electrical Supply. "You're the prettiest girl who's applied," Martin Clawson chuckled. "You can call me Marty. I know it's not strictly proper, but everyone else does." He grinned sweetly at her. He was younger than she had expected, no more than thirty, with round, puffy cheeks and a round, puffy body. A great deal of light brown hair stood out all around his face, in soft curls that any girl would be proud of. She liked him at once, even though his hand rested lightly on her right buttock as she passed him to take the seat he indicated.

She swung around and glared at him. He jumped back almost a foot, his eyes wide and startled in his pudgy face. "Are you married, Mr. Clawson?" hoping there was a wife she could use to keep him in line. She needed this job.

"Oh, no, no," he waved a hand and attempted to chuckle, while continuing to back away. "Too much the fun-loving bachelor. No, it's just me, Tibby, Taffy and Motro."

"Cats?"

"Gerbils. Oh, they make terrific pets, I don't know what I'd do if anything happened to one of them. And they're adorable, you should have seen what Taffy did the other day—"

Somewhere between the end of the anecdote about Taffy and her bit of string, and the beginning of the one about Motro and the raisins, which she heard the next morning when she reported to work, she finally escaped with the job, an

advance on her paycheck, and the confidence that this man
would never put his hands on her again.

Celeste did nothing to brighten up the apartment. It was
dark, dreary and uninviting, but she couldn't seem to stoke
enough energy even to put up curtains. Her final reserves of
power had been spent in salvaging a few remaining scraps out
of the ashes Peter had left behind. Each day, she struggled to
survive the unvarying routine of weak coffee made with too
much water, cold showers in a bathroom shared by all three
flats on the floor, and the grind of menial office work.

She found three jigsaw puzzles in the trash and fished
them out when no one was looking. She could make up any
missing pieces out of cardboard. It was the kind of game that
Martina was so good at, and it calmed her. Celeste licked the
tip of her finger and tried to flatten one bent corner.

She boiled beans and scraps of meat for supper, chopping
in whatever wilted and sprouted greens she had found in the
cheapest grocer's bargain bin. She then did her best to choke
down the result, without making a face, trying to set a good
example for David. Over bowls of the cheap stew, she sat up
straight, held her knife and fork like a countess, and tried to
engage him in discussions about history, philosophy, or what
life would be like when these hard times were over, when
Father was better, as he surely would be soon. "You'll go back
to Briarwood, of course, and then on to university. Have you
decided where you want to go?"

"I, ah, no." David stammered. "I haven't thought about it
much recently." He finished his food with gulps and stood up.
"May I be excused? The tailor on the corner said he might
have a few errands for me if I came in right after he closed up
the shop tonight."

Celeste sighed and nodded her permission.

On Sundays, she took Martina to the tiny triangle of park
across the street from their apartment. Other mothers chatted

or read as their children played, and on weekends, the occasional father joined them, forming poor but tidy families seeking the free entertainment of the summer in the city.

"Is that your sister?" the man sitting next to her asked. She had noticed him when he first sat down, because he looked a bit like Peter. Like Peter used to, she amended. He wore an expensive suit, fine Italian shoes, and a heavy gold signet ring. He had beautiful hair, so blond it was nearly white, and sharp, high cheekbones. His hands were strong and precise. He barely rustled his newspaper as he turned the pages. A heavy tang of lime aftershave clung to him. "She is exquisite."

Celeste smiled. Martina was indeed beautiful, spinning around, her arms stretched out as if reaching for the world. "I thank you, *Monsieur*, she's my daughter."

He swiveled theatrically back to her, eyebrows raised. He was acting, Celeste knew, but she applauded how smoothly it was done. "She can't be your daughter, you're much too young to have a daughter that age."

Celeste gave the obligatory responsive chuckle, and said, "I have a son who's even older." She smiled at his clumsy attempts to flirt with her, and tried not to wrinkle her nose. He had on altogether too much aftershave. He wasn't like Peter at all.

Peter, on the other hand, was slipping farther away from her with each passing minute. At long last came the day when Lenox Hill Hospital would no longer accept excuses and promises, instead of payment. "I'm so sorry, Mrs. Vandenholm," the nurse on duty told her, "Mr. Vandenholm was moved to the public ward this morning."

Celeste put her hand over her mouth, giving herself time to regain her composure. "Where is that?" she whispered.

The large room at the bottom of the stairs in the back of the building was not filthy, not crowded, not the hell she had been imagining. But it was poorly lit, with only a short row of small windows high in the wall. It was cold, and there were only two nurses present, who proceeded briskly and efficiently among the many beds filled with moaning, suffering patients. Celeste patted Peter's hand, as motionless against the slightly shabby, slightly gray sheets as it had been against the pristine white ones. These indifferent-looking nurses wouldn't work as hard to give Peter the care he deserved; they wouldn't work as hard to feed him, to keep him alive. He would die if he stayed here much longer.

She had no choice. If she was going to be able to save Peter, she would have to find the strength to do what she had promised herself she would never sink to. "I'm not a charity student," David had cried out, and she wanted to scream that she wasn't either. "I can do this one thing," she said. "Just this one thing."

If she knew anything about him, old man Vandenholm still kept his precise business hours. She debated whether to confront him at home or in his office. At his office he could not turn her away without causing a scene, and that image-conscious old buzzard would never cause a scene, oh no. In the end, she decided in favor of the privacy offered by the secluded surroundings at his home. She took a taxi, an extravagance to be sure, but the day was a hot one and she did not want to arrive sweaty and disheveled.

The imposing front of the Vandenholm mansion did not face Fifth Avenue in that vulgar modern way, but nestled on a quiet cross street, guarded by high granite steps and dense, intricate wrought iron railings, each spear tip gilded and polished. At the top of the steps, a heavy, dark oak door with raised panels waited for her. According to family legend, Peter had told her, the door had been hewn from timbers salvaged from the first trading ship in the budding Vandenholm fleet, the ships which had ferried a fortune between the Dutch colonies in the New World and eager buyers in Amsterdam.

"Don't think about it," Celeste whispered. "Don't think about what you've done, don't think about what you're going to do, there is no other choice." It's not as if she hadn't become immune to the burning shame of begging. She could—and would—do anything necessary to keep Peter, David and Martina alive. She lifted the heavy brass knocker, a curved cornucopia of fruit and grains, and let it drop once.

The door opened immediately. An elderly butler, with cheekbones like hatchet blades and gleaming silver hair, inclined his head a scant few inches when he saw her.

"Please tell Mr. Vandenholm that Mrs. Vandenholm is here to see him on a matter of urgency."

"Madam," he said, showing no surprise at learning who she was. Of course he already knew, that was his job. His posture displayed a blend of the respect due her as Peter's wife, and the repudiation of that marriage, heaped on her by father-in-law. He bowed again, but left her standing in the hall, not offering to take her coat.

She had been in this house twice before; once when Peter had brought her to meet his father, and again when they had come to announce their engagement. Peter's mother had died only a few years before they married, but the house almost immediately taken on the feeling of one never breached by woman or child. That feeling ran even deeper now. Black and white marble floor tiles were polished until Celeste could see her muddy shoes reflected in the black squares. Dark portraits, no doubt by famous Dutch artists, marched along the walls and up the stairwell in precision. The senior Vandenholm may sneer at Henry Frick's modern mansion just a few blocks away, built with flashy new money, but Frick's art collection sang with color and life. In contrast, this place had become a morgue.

The butler returned promptly and this time he did take her coat before leading her down the hall to the last door, and ushering her into the old man's study.

Her father-in-law's desk was not huge, nor was it ostentatious, but it was an antique, *probably brought over to New Amsterdam with the original colonists*, Celeste sneered. The Vandenholms never let go of a thing, except their sons. The man behind the desk appraised her, his face a stolid mask, his bald scalp as smooth and taut as the finish on the desk. She sat, without being invited, refusing to stand before him like a supplicant.   One eyebrow arced in amusement at her effrontery; his gaze humorless, blue ice. She was glad that he didn't look much like his son.

"I take it you're here for money," the older man stated. "It was merely a question of time."

I will treat this as a strictly financial negotiation, Celeste told herself. *Nothing good will come of losing my temper.* "Yes," she said, "I'm here for money. Peter has been moved to a public ward, and the care there is not good enough. It's terrible. He needs to be moved back to private care."

"Why is this my concern?"

Celeste was shocked. "Because he's your son!" she exclaimed.

"He was my son. Then he chose you. I told him what you are and he didn't believe me. So he stopped being my son."

Be calm, be calm, Celeste repeated. She took sips of breath. "I married him because I loved him, not for his money. Now he's sick and he needs you, or he will die." She shut her eyes at her own words.

"He's already dead to me."

She was ready to leap across the desk and slap the smug bastard, but his tone, not his biting words, aroused her suspicions. He had agreed to see her; he had let her lead the conversation, without launching into a twenty year old tirade against her unsuitability to marry his son. "What do you want?" she asked slowly.

"What I always wanted. I want my son back. I had annulment papers drawn up twenty years ago, sign them now and I will take over Peter's care." The man might as well have been ordering coffee from a waitress.

Celeste stood. "I'm not that desperate yet." She would never give Peter up like that. Annulment meant they had never been married, that her children were bastards, that they had no father. The world would have to come to end before she would sign her family away into oblivion.

"If you truly loved him, your decision would be about what he needs, not about what you want," the old man called after her as she stalked out.

She tried not to hear them, but the words stabbed at her heart. It was true, she thought, but it was not true enough.

At the door she paused only long enough to snatch her coat from the butler, and yanked the door open by herself, not leaving him enough time to say whatever he clearly looked like he intended to say. She staggered through the summer heat to the dark apartment where her children waited, trying to shake off the old man's final words, trying to focus on the mundane chores she needed to do. There were so many things she should do.

She should find good city care for Martina.

She should find a way to help David get past his pride.

She should add color to the apartment.

She should find a better job.

She should.

She should.

But she couldn't.

CHAPTER 12

MARTINA

The gods have turned night into day. The general with the big hands does not come. The mother comes in the evening, not in the day. The fast general has come home from the school place again, and he comes during the day. The mother cries because the gods are angry, she is afraid of the gods. The army hurts. The fast general, the david one, does not like the daylight. "It is not fair," he says. "It is not right."

The boxes are in a line and that is good.

The mother has brought a new general to command the white army, and mightily do the armies battle. He is a poor general, and every night the black army defeats his army without a death. He has angry eyes. He would like to be a god, but he is not.

The new general smells like paint.

CHAPTER 13

DAVID

David glanced up from his book to make sure Martina wasn't breaking whatever she was banging now. "Come away from the window, it doesn't open anymore," he said. Since the beginning of summer break, he had been stuck babysitting for Martina, and even the act of waking up each morning was like pulling on a cloak of lead. Life had changed so much he barely recognized himself.

Martina continued to yank the window up, banging the top edge against the nail that kept it from opening more than a slim inch, then slamming it down.

"Don't bother kiddo. I'm tired of jumping over the fence to pick up all the things you throw out there." The courtyard was completely enclosed by a tall iron railing, with no access except the locked basement door, whose key was held by the nasty and suspicious apartment manager. He usually sat, sullen and drunk, in a damp corner of the furnace room like a pale, hairy spider.

"It's you again, God damn brat." The manager would heave himself out of his chair and glare at David with bleary eyes. The rancid, yeasty stink of homemade whiskey wafted around him. "Retard sister of yours still pitching shit down? That's who lives in this crap-hole, retards and losers and snooty bitches like that God damn mother of yours." Then he'd fumble in his pants for the key, sometimes finding it, other times giving up and sinking back into his chair with a grunt and a snarl. It was less complicated to scale the railing for the jettisoned pillows, books and clothing than to ask for access. Easier still to hammer a nail into the window frame so the window would only slide up a few inches.

"Come on, Martina, leave that alone and stop banging. Let's draw a picture, how does that sound?" He pulled Martina's arm and led her to the folding table where he folded her into a chair and handed her a pencil and a piece of paper. Then he settled once more into the depths of Ivanhoe's adventures.

Mother was thumping in the bedroom, probably trying to put the heel back on her shoe yet again. "Don't forget, if Richard asks, Father got sick eighteen months ago, not last fall," she called out.

The move from Park Avenue to East 12th Street seemed to have eliminated the rule that ladies and gentlemen did not shout from one room to another. In fact, Mother often initiated conversations from whichever room she was in now, although there were only two. David tried hard to maintain the standard Father had set for him, but it was becoming easier and easier to indulge in laxity, as Headmaster Hibbeler would have referred to it.

"Did you hear me, David?" Mother shouted.

"Yes, ma'am," David called back.

"Then answer when you're spoken to. Your manners have become *absolument* shocking of late."

David scowled at the wall. He wasn't the only one whose behavior had deteriorated since they'd left Park Avenue behind.

"Don't forget, eighteen months."

"Yes, ma'am." As if a longer time lapse would make stepping out with another man more acceptable. As if that would make abandoning Father the right thing to do. Of course it would, he sneered. Even worse, she was stepping out with this Richard Biscayne. Maybe he was blond like Father, but he wasn't Father. He wasn't smart, he wasn't funny, and he wasn't distinguished, dignified or noble in any way. He had clammy hands, flashy clothes, and his chummy manner made David uncomfortable in a way he could not describe to Mother, or even to himself.

The doorbell rang and Mother swirled out of the bedroom and into the living room, trailing a hint of perfume. Even without jewelry she sparkled. She'd draped a silver scarf around her neck. One end floated in the vee of her neckline, the other fluttered along her back and she had tucked a blue silk flower in her hair. David wanted to tell her she looked beautiful, but he was too angry. She opened the door and stepped forward to kiss Richard on the cheek, and David looked away, itching to deliver a cutting and brilliantly sarcastic riposte but unable to think of one. He crossed his arms over his chest, decided he must look as belligerent as he felt, so he dropped his hands and slid them into his pockets, striving for a casual man-about-town pose.

Richard held out his hand. "Good evening, young David, I certainly hope you've been practicing your chess game, because I have." He chuckled richly, leaving David wondering if he had practiced that tone in front of a mirror. "You might have won last time, but I've been studying, you won't take me so handily next time we joust."

"Sure thing, I can't wait till our next match." David tried not to sneeze as the cloud of aftershave engulfed him, and returned the limp handshake firmly. He didn't even want to touch the man. It was terrible, what Mother was doing. It was embarrassing for a woman her age, a mother, to be prancing out on the town with a man she barely knew, carrying on like a flapper. And she was still a wife! Father wasn't dead, and here she was, lining up a replacement. It would serve her right if Father got better tomorrow and caught her running around with this peasant who reeked like he'd fallen into a vat of lime juice.

"And there's the lovely Martina." She sat at the card table, with one hand lining up scraps of paper with minute precision, and the other rubbing her cheek with her pink comb. "I hope you're feeling well today, sweetheart." He tried to catch her eye, but settled for a quick kiss on top of her auburn curls, before Martina scrunched away with a shriek, then he and Mother swooped out the door, calling cheerful farewells and leaving David alone with his sister.

He was a servant, that's what he was, a servant for practically the whole city. He spent all day with Martina, and went to visit Father any time that Martina was in a manageable mood, no matter how hard it was to see him so broken and wasted. At first David had tried to talk to him, tried to pretend that the father he'd once had was still in there, tried to act as if they were both sitting comfortably at home in the study, surrounded by books and cigar smoke. But he was too self-conscious when he heard his own voice in the long ward, rambling out loud to no one. And if that wasn't enough, the other patients in the ward felt this was their cue to wake up and demand that he attend to them next.

Well, he wasn't going be a servant any longer. He would tell Mother the first chance he got, as soon as he assembled the right words. "Mother," he would say, "I will not stay home and play nursemaid any longer. The time has come for me to find a job and become the man of this family."

"But of course, *mon cher*," Mother would say. "That's the perfect idea, you are so clever."

Or she would say, "Of course, that's ideal. Mr. Ruder from Father's firm called ages ago, while you were still at school. He'd like you to work for him, to take Father's old position."

Yes, he would settle down neatly at the furniture company, and hire a pretty girl as his secretary. He would come to work each morning and she would smile shyly at him, then she would bring coffee into his office and stand a few inches too close as he took the first sip. A blonde, or maybe a petite, perky redhead.

"David, I'm hungry," Martina yelled. "Hungry, David, hungry."

David opened his eyes, then shut them, trying to recapture the wisps of the fleeing fantasy. "Go away!"

"Hungry, David. Hungry!"

"Oh all right." David abandoned the petite redhead with a sigh, knowing that Martina would not stop yelling until she got her way. He loved her, and he loved Mother, but there were times, entire days, when he wanted nothing more than the courage to pack a bag and take the first train headed anywhere else. If he was old enough to drop out of school and be responsible for the care of a mental patient, he was old enough to fend for himself out in the world, out in a place where nobody knew him.

"Peanut butter," Martina shouted. "Candy."

"Oh, all right already." David headed for the kitchen corner to deal out the leftovers from the icebox. "Potatoes tonight, not peanut butter," he warned. He wondered what restaurant Mother was in, and whether she had ordered steak or lobster. He didn't like steak as much as lobster, but it was less obvious for her to hide in her purse.

He thumped the plates down on the table and shuffled Martina into a chair. God, he'd turned into Cinderella, waiting for his stepmother to return from the ball. It was obscene, there was no other word for it. He wished he had the courage, and the money, to get on a train and get out, before he turned into a permanent mushroom. Go to a new city, where he could live life as a man. Not a nanny, not a boy, but a real man. Oh for heaven's sake, now he sounded like Pinocchio.

And if Mother lost her job because she had to stay home with Martina, well so be it. She could always marry Richard and who cared if she was already married? The man was a toad— how did Mother tolerate his moist hands? His sour breath? Did they kiss? Oh God, David gagged at the thought.

When Mother had told him he would be taking care of Martina during the day, David had imagined playing a game or two of chess, perhaps going to the park, then settling down later in the afternoon with a book. He would have a chance to read the mysteries he had stacked up. He would lie back, relax and enjoy being out of school, in spite of the reason for it. He would have a chance to be alone. He had never been alone before, he had always been in the company of others: his family, school friends, one social group or another. Sure there had been some scattered moments when he'd been on his own, but to have the whole house to himself, well, the whole flat at least, that was different. He was quite looking forward to it.

The first morning Celeste went to work she kissed David goodbye with a flurry of words. "Now don't forget that Martina eats at 9, 12 and 3 o'clock, I've put her meals in the icebox, she's impossible to handle when she gets too hungry. You know where her clothes are if she has an accident, and Mrs. Gheitrys upstairs will dress her for you. Don't forget to make sure she wears a hat if you take her to the park, she likes the park and it should be warm enough."

"Mother," he said, "I know what to do, everything will be fine." A tight knot of nervousness lodged in the pit of his stomach, but he was sure he could handle anything that came his way. Martina was his sister, after all.

Celeste stopped talking and laid a hand gently on his arm. "So grownup, if only your father could see how quickly you're turning into a man." She shut her eyes as the pain traveled across her face. With a short breath, she reached out and yanked David against her, pressing her cheek to his. "Oh God," she gasped, "Oh God, please give me just a little more strength to hold on." As abruptly as she had grabbed him, she pushed him away and strode down the hallway to the stairs with a fading clatter of high heels.

David struggled to control his jumping thoughts. It frightened him, this brittle, erratic, woman his mother was turning into. Next to him, Martina babbled, "Mum, mum, mum, warm, warm, war-um, war-um, mum, mum, mum." David wrapped his arms around her and pulled her away from the blank face of the shut door. Her hair smelled clean and sweet.

"Don't cry, Martina, it'll all be fine. Mother will come home later. She'll be back." It wasn't fair, Mother should be here taking care of her children, not the other way around. He should be in Newport with his friends, playing tennis, playing golf, skimming a boat across the harbor with Chad and Teddy, waiting for the girls to come back from shopping.

"Mum mum mother mother mother," Martina wailed.

"Come on, Martina, let's sing a song." He held her tightly in his arms and rocked back and forth with her for what felt like an hour, until Martina at long last reached for her comb, and with a few final hiccups, settled down into quiescence.

They sat quietly, without moving. David wriggled his foot back and forth, trying to fight off the pins and needles starting to invade. Was he going to spend the whole summer like this? What would happen when the school year started? He pushed Martina to her feet and stood up.

"Let's play a game." He led her to the elaborately inlaid side table, left over from Park Avenue, which served as their dining room set, and pulled out a jigsaw puzzle, a colorful scene of two golden haystacks, an impossibly blue sky and a herd of chestnut horses. He dumped the pieces onto the table and a drizzle of dust and grit floated down. Martina sat with her hands in her lap, quite still. "Isn't this nice, a new puzzle?" David coaxed. "Look how the pieces fit together. You have to put them where they belong." He picked up two joined pieces clinging crookedly to each other. " See this? You have to put all the pieces together, like this."

Martina fidgeted in her chair, her eyes darting from his fingers, to his face, to the pile of pieces. She wiggled her fingers at the edge of the table and rocked side to side in her seat. She had often sat just like this, while Father taught her the rules of chess and the different moves and strategies. David ached for Father to be with them now, and he fumbled to teach Martina with the same patience and skill.

"See here," he pointed to a piece, "see how this looks like a little man? And how this part looks like a little mouth? See how the man's head fits into the mouth?" He snapped the two pieces together. "*Voila*," he said.

"*Voila*," Martina repeated, in Mother's voice, her fingers still desperately clutching each other, waiting. "*Voila, voila, voila.*"

"See, all the pieces fit together. You have to put all the pieces where they belong." He picked up another piece with a distinctive line angling across it, rummaging through the pile for its mate. "See the knob here, how it looks like a monster's head? He held it up for her to examine. "It fits here, with this piece."

Martina grew still. Clearly an idea was trickling through the mis-wired pipelines of her brain, to take on meaning of a sort, of a certain Martina shape. She touched the seam of the two puzzle pieces ever so delicately with the tip of one finger. "Put the monsters where they belong," she said.

"Yes, Martina," David said, encouraged that a few of his words had successfully traversed the difficult pathways. "Put the monster shapes where they belong."

She reached out and grabbed two more pieces, and jammed them against each other.

"No, no." David stopped her. "They don't fit. See how the colors are different and the shapes don't line up? You have to put the pieces exactly where they belong."

Martina went quiet again, staring without blinking as David sorted through the puzzle pieces for straight edges. Then she reached out, deliberately selected a single piece from the pile, then another piece, and tentatively fit them together.

"That's right." David clapped once. "That's right. You did it, Martina. Good girl!"

Martina reached for a third piece and tried to fit it in with the other two in her hands, but the first pairing fell apart, one of the pieces landing back on the table with a soft clunk.

"Oh no," Martina shrieked. "Oh no oh no oh no oh no no no no no." She reached out and snatched at the piece, knocking others to the floor in her panic. "Monsters monsters oh no no no." She tried to scoop up more pieces, as others scattered around her feet.

"It's ok, Martina, it's alright," David soothed, startled by her outburst. It was completely unpredictable what his sister would take a sudden reaction to. "It's ok, don't be afraid." He took her flailing hands between his and held them still until they stopped fluttering. "It's ok, we can fix it. It will be fine, you'll see. Watch me." He pried the bent cardboard from her fingers, and laid the pieces down. "If you keep the pieces on the table, they fit together much more easily." He slid two, then three, of the pieces toward each other, building her a base to work from. "See how they go together? They stay on the table."

Martina sat rigid in her chair. Then she gave a sharp cry and bent forward, as if in pain. She seized a piece from the table and slammed it into place against another piece. She grabbed another and another and crushed them against each other. David was about to stop her when he realized with surprise that she had completed a short section of the picture's edge. Her hands flew, her eyes flickered, and her head froze in a peculiar, strained position, thrust forward over her task. David started to worry she would collapse because she was holding her breath for so long, but she continued assembling the puzzle at the same rapid pace. David scooped up pieces from the floor and flipped them right side up for her, as she knit them rapidly into the body of the picture. When the last piece dropped into place, Martina sighed and her posture unlocked. "Where they belong, where they belong." She traced the outer perimeter of the puzzle with her index finger. "Box," she said.

"Yes," David said. "A rectangle, like a box."

"Box," Martina declared, and patted the puzzle with the flat of her hand. She turned her face up to David, studying him with her amazing sapphire gaze, and smiled as beautifully as an angel in a church painting. He put his arm around her shoulder and she leaned stiffly against him. Perhaps, he thought, even without Father, things might be alright. Not good, but manageable.

"Monsters," she said, "All safe."

"Right-o," he said. "Make the monsters safe."

"No no no no!" Martina lunged across the table, grabbed his arm and shook it. Her elbow slid against the puzzle, which fell to the floor and fractured back into its individual pieces.

"Of course, we need to be safe. Not the monsters." David reassured her. Damn. Just when he thought he'd finally done something right, it all came apart.

"Safe! Safe! No monsters!" Martina leaped up and barreled headlong into a chair, toppled it over and stepped on the puzzle container which had fallen off the table as well.

David glared at the mess scattered across the floor, the crushed container, and Martina trembling in the middle of it all. The apartment was suddenly too claustrophobic to breathe in. The knot he had tied around his anger burst apart.

"God damn it!" he shouted, shocking himself. "Damn it, damn it, damn it! And damn you too, you stupid, horrible lump!" He stepped forward and grabbed her shoulders to shake her. "You pick those pieces up right now!" David yelled.

"No!" Martina yelled back. "No no no monsters!" Beads of sweat welled up on her forehead and trickled down her face.

"They're not monsters, you sick retard. They're puzzle pieces, and you're going to pick them up, do you hear me?" He shook her again.

"Circles, circles!" Martina shrieked. She put her hands over her head, hunched her back and sank, curling in on herself, transforming into an inert bundle held up only by David's hands. He let her slide to the floor where she rolled into a ball. "Circles," she moaned. "Circles."

He wanted to kick her. The sight of her lying there whimpering, weak and pathetic, made him burn with the desire to hurt her. She was the reason he was trapped in this box, day after day after day. "Box!" he shouted at her. "A box with no escape!" He pulled back his foot. He wanted to feel the impact through his shoe and into his bones, but he held onto enough sanity to restrain himself. He crashed his foot into the leg of a chair instead. It flew forward, hit the table and fell over, taking the table and the rest of the puzzle pieces with it. A long gash showed in the wood where his shoe had connected, a white wound in what might have been Martina. A single stray puzzle piece, dislodged from precarious balance on the other chair, fell to the floor with a flutter.

David stared, aghast at how tempted he had been to hurt his delicate little sister. His anger completely evaporated, leaving only cold sweat drying on his skin and a bitter taste in his mouth. He took Martina in his arms, holding her as close as he could, rocking back and forth. "I'm so sorry, I'm sorry I frightened you. I'll never do it again." He embraced her, warmed her, murmuring reassurances, until she relaxed against him and her panting slowed down to a regular, even pace. He took her into the bedroom and settled her down for a nap.

He cleaned up the mess then dropped face down on the couch, limp. How astounding, that such a huge, black wave of anger could build up and burst over, then simply ebb away. He was infinitely thankful that he hadn't actually hurt Martina, in fact he'd only shaken her, only scared her a bit. She would get over it. In fact, all that turmoil, and nothing had actually occurred.

In the quiet following the storm, an insidious, poisonous thought snuck in and the feral freedom of his uncontrolled outburst tingled inside him. This was different than the night in the dorm at school. He could have kicked Martina and no one would have known. Even when he'd punched the wall, he knew he would be called to account by the headmaster. He'd never acted unruly before and gotten away with it, or even hoped to do so. This time there were no witnesses, no one to reveal his secret. "Do not confuse an action that feels good with an action that is good," Headmaster Hibbeler had said. But what was wrong with feeling good, if he wasn't going to get caught? Sure, his parents, teachers and the chaplain at school might say virtue was its own reward, but they didn't understand this new, vigorous energy. Perhaps this new life had advantages after all.

He spread out his arms and spun in a circle like a four year old. He shouted as loud as he could. "I'm free, damn you all!" He wondered if Mrs. Gheitrys upstairs would come to find out why he was yelling. He doubted she cared enough.

These wicked new thoughts lifted David off the ground. He knew exactly what to do with this liberation, and he didn't care who thought it was wrong. He shuffled through Mother's things until he found her meager pile of nickels and stole four of them. Yes, he thought, let me start out my new life by stealing. He laughed out loud. He had been emancipated today, freed from the constraints of proper behavior that had followed him from his old life. Well, the old life had died, or at the very least, it was sleeping in the deep, deep recesses of an unending coma. The clinging miasma of Mother, of teachers, of everyone knowing and seeing his every move was gone.

He snatched Martina's coat and hat from their hook by the door.

"Come on, kiddo, let's go to the park. There are no monsters in the park." He whistled as he propelled her out the door.

When they reached the noise and bustle of the city street, Martina squeaked with excitement. A few blocks north of their tenement, a busy park lay wedged in the angle of Union Square and 14th Street, under the rattle of the Canarsie El. Tables and benches invited pedestrians to sit and enjoy the view of passing horses and motorcars on the wide street, but, in fact, the shaking and screeching of trains overhead obliterated any pleasure this park once held. Pairs of men now sat at the tables, gambling. They were playing chess for money, and David had the perfect weapon.

He put a nickel down on the side of the chessboard and gave Martina a push into an empty seat across from an old black man with thick, white hair, and the most knotted, gnarled hands David had ever seen. Each knuckle humped up like a small, brown egg, and every now and then the man would rub the fingers of one hand over the bumps of the other. The skin over the knuckles darkened where it thickened in the creases and folds. Perhaps he shouldn't let her play with a black man, but it was the only open seat, and he was eager to start. He stood behind Martina's chair with his hands on her shoulders.

Martina's opponent held out his two closed fists, and David tapped the back of the left one. He would have to teach

Martina the opening ritual for selecting black or white. The man opened his hand to display a white pawn. Good—Martina would have the opening move, and the army she was used to. With swift and fierce concentration, Martina launched a pawn into battle. Her shoulder muscles bunched into hard knots under his hands.

The black man smiled at David, his crooked teeth glinting in a bony, stubbled face, then focused as intently over the board as Martina. The stained cuffs of his shirt flopped over the board on each move, ragged tears coming close to catching on the king each time. More poor people crowded into this part of town than David had ever met or associated with before. Of course, since the fall of the stock market, there were more poor people everywhere. He may be poor now, but he was not one of these crumpled men, these used up candle stumps, and he hoped none of his friends happened to wander by to see him sitting here like this, as if he were one of them.

David massaged Martina's shoulders while she calmly destroyed her opponent's army. She had him on the run now. Deep furrows ridged the man's forehead, turning dark in the folds like the skin over his knuckles. His brown hands hovered tentatively over the remaining pieces.

"That your sister?" a man next to him asked. David nodded. He looked around to find they had amassed a sizeable audience. He wondered if it was because she was pretty, or simply because she was young, female and white. "She has the look of you," the man said, "And she's beating old William, and that's not easy. She's good."

"She is. Thank you."

The black man pushed his king over and rose. "Dat one good game," he said to Martina, puzzled when she didn't respond. The man leaned down and peered into Martina's face, then stood with a resigned shake of his head. He put out a hand and stroked her hair, very lightly, but Martina jerked away. David was about to warn him not to repeat that, but the man turned and walked away, rubbing his knuckles as he went.

David grinned. Gambling was thrilling!

Another black man laid down a coin and took the place opposite, as Martina began to reset the pieces on the board in front of her.

Within a dozen moves, Martina had her second opponent on the ropes. David thought he recognized the pattern of the strategy from one of Father's books. He sizzled with excitement. The audience around them grew, whispering and nodding, as Martina displayed her skill. In the good times, it was awfully easy to be proud of his sister. She was so beautiful, her movements so graceful, her game so incisive. Martina neatly moved her rook into position, threatening the opposing bishop. The man's bishop was pinned; if he moved it, a line of attack would open up to his own rook. He moved his knight instead, and stared, as Martina left both rook and bishop in place to move her own knight in for an angled assault. "Check," she called. The man moved his bishop then, hoping to draw Martina's rook out of position with an easy target, but she ignored it and moved her own bishop up to complete the box closing in the man's king.

"Checkmate," Martina said, and breathed a deep sigh, as if she'd run a long distance, and had finally arrived at safety.

David stepped forward and put his arm around Martina's shoulders. "Good work, kiddo," he said. He stood tall next to her.

"She plays real good, for a dummy," the man said as he rose, shoving forward the pair of nickels with a short jab.

David flinched as the words struck him. He caught a few derogatory looks from the bystanders. Were they all thinking the worst of him? Were they all despising him for taking advantage of Martina in this way? Okay, yes, he knew this was wrong. He couldn't wheel Martina around the parks of New

York like a chess-playing circus freak for a nickel a show.
Father would be livid if he knew; Mother would be too. Even
Master Hibbeler would be.

He tried to recapture the sense of invulnerability he'd had
earlier, but it eluded him. On the other hand, it didn't matter
how he felt about it, it didn't matter what others thought of it,
and it didn't matter that he'd lost his moment of fleeting
elation. This was a good idea, or rather, it was a necessary idea,
and he would do what he had to do. They needed the money.
He needed the money if he was going to earn enough for
tuition by the start of the school year. He only had a few
months left.

He pushed forward a nickel while another old man settled
into the seat opposite Martina.

CHAPTER 14

CELESTE

Celeste poked a curl into the lopsided twist of hair lying at the nape of her neck. She pinned it in place and crooked her head to the side in a futile attempt to see the back more clearly in the mirror. The mirror overwhelmed the wall space it occupied, looming too large and too formal for the shoddy apartment, much like the other stray bits of her life she couldn't seem to let go of. She remembered buying it with Peter, when money had been nothing more than paper to play with. She'd even been able to send huge sums home to the family, although not enough to attract Peter's notice. The mirror had cost too much, but they didn't care, they had fallen in love with the handsome couple staring back at them, one so blond, one so auburn. Of course, in hindsight, everything had cost too much. She bit her lip in her effort not to cry. "Oh, Peter, I wish I could tell you I love you more than a useless mirror. So much more!"

She pressed her forehead against the cool glass. Her body felt as if sandbags had been strapped to her shoulders and hips. The effort to move, to smile, to keep Martin Clawson and his gerbils amused, to keep Richard Biscayne enchanted, to keep David and Martina fed and sheltered; it all bore down on her with renewed force. At night she fell into bed and lay flat on her back, sapped and flaccid. Sleep would descend like the dowsing of a candle, swift and irrevocable, until the morning alarm recalled her to foggy awareness of another day. Even at the best of times the pain never left, she could only ignore the weariness and think of what Martina and David needed; burdens might be all this life held, but she couldn't afford to let any of these burdens drop.

Celeste sat up straight and turned back to the mirror, concentrating on her makeup. She didn't enjoy angling for a new husband, even if the time wasn't right yet. She wanted Peter back, but one didn't always get what one wanted in life. Peter used to say *"sol lucet omnibus"* which he told her meant, the sun keeps shining no matter what happens. In other words, get over it. She fiercely focused on her face. Makeup was armor. Years ago, she had turned makeup into a science, a study of art and technique, from Cleopatra to Helena Rubinstein, and she needed that intellectual diversion now, both to distract and to prepare herself. She once shared with Peter that whores in ancient Rome wore lipstick to signal their willingness to perform fellatio, and after that, all she needed to do was check her lips in her purse mirror and his erection roused, no matter where they were.

She would not, absolutely could not, think about Peter right now. *"Sol lucet omnibus."*

When she was young and ignorant, she used to think that clothing kept you warm and makeup was to highlight your best features. Now she knew they had the same function—to project the image you wanted people to believe of you. Two or three years ago she had gone with Helen and Marjorie to a rehearsal of "Abie's Irish Rose" at the Fulton Theater as part of a charity benefit. She had already seen the play and was looking forward to seeing it again; she didn't care what the critics said, she found it enjoyably silly. But the magic wasn't there. The songs were the same, the lights were the same, the lines hadn't changed, but the actors weren't in costume. They were simply ordinary people, walking about on an ordinary wooden floor. She imagined them out back between scenes, smoking cigarettes and arguing about where to have dinner after the show. She knew them now as plain workers, not as the characters they played on the stage. She had always known, of course, that actors and roles were not the same, but she had never seen through the illusion quite so clearly before that afternoon.

"Get over it," she said to herself as she made a final adjustment to her hemline. "With your shield, or on it." Peter often said that as well, but of course he'd said it in Latin, so she'd teased him by pretending not to know what it meant.

"Mother." David accosted her as soon as she left the haven of the bedroom, "I need to talk to you."

"Please David, *mon cher*, not tonight. I had such the terrible time at work, and now I must to sparkle for Richard. Whatever it is, it can wait, *non?*"

David muttered under his breath.

"That's rude behavior, David. If you have something to say that cannot wait, then say it. If not, *reste silente.*"

He scowled at her. "I said," he enunciated, "I'm going to get out of this rattrap. Soon."

Celeste tried not to sigh. David was a good son, he was so patient with Martina, but he always seemed to pick the most inconvenient times to become a dramatic teenager. She was invariably surprised by these outbursts, and invariably in the wrong mood for them. Peter used to say it was because David was so much like her, she couldn't be objective. She thought David was more like Peter: innocent, optimistic, perhaps weak, but so good-hearted no one would ever take advantage of him. She wished Peter were here now. She wished she could stop thinking about him.

"David," she tried to infuse sincerity and love into her tone. "I know you need to talk, and I can tell this is important to you, so I think we should discuss it later, when we have more time." There. That sounded fine.

"You're just saying that because you think this is something I'll forget. You think it will blow over."

Actually, she had thought that, but his clenched fists and forward-leaning stance underlined his serious intent. "No, no, I'm sure it's important, and I know it won't go away. But Richard will be here any minute, and I want to give you more time than a few minutes."

As if on cue, Richard's evenly spaced three knocks sounded on the door.

"Richard, Richard, Richard!" David exploded, not quite shouting, but certainly speaking loudly enough to be heard on the other side of the thin panels. "All you think about these days is Richard. Father might as well never have existed."

Celeste did heave a sigh this time, and made no attempt to hide it. "David, we will discuss this later. *Maintenant*, you will behave like a gentleman, because we have a guest." She slipped into the hallway before he could respond.

Richard, with a bouquet of red roses and white carnations in one hand, kissed her on the cheek. "Sounds like there's a problem?" He held out the flowers.

She took the flowers, and found that he was peering at her with such caring, so gentle, almost haloed by the dim bulb hanging down from the hallway ceiling, that she felt completely subsumed. She buried her face in the bouquet, absorbing the comfort and scent, until she had regained her composure. "I'm sorry about that," she said at last. "David, he is in one of his moods tonight."

"We can stay home, if you need to be with him." His soft, brown eyes shone with sympathy. "Would a man's point of view help at all?"

"No, no, it is nothing more than a bad mood. Perhaps too much being home with Martina."

"Because I hope you know I'm here to help in any way you need." He took Celeste's hand in his, moved the flowers to the side. Her eyes fluttered shut as he kissed her, so lightly, a feather-weight on her lips. She tried to enjoy kissing him, in spite of the specter of Peter halting her, comatose in his narrow charity bed. All she could smell was Richard's aftershave.

She pulled away at last, attempting to breathe a little more heavily and smile a little more naturally. "Thank you for your help, but David, he wants to grow up too fast, I think. I will talk with him tonight when we return, and let him to clear the air, *oui*?"

"Oh, my darling," Richard held her close. "It must be so difficult for you, so difficult to be a parent on your own, especially in these hard times." He cupped the side of her face gently with one warm hand, and the smooth skin of his palm slid against her lips. "You're doing a superb job."

"Thank you," Celeste whispered. "You are so kind."

"I mean it," Richard said. "Your strength and your courage are only two of the things I love about you."

Celeste peered up at him in the feeble light, trying to gauge the appropriate level of commitment needed in response, but she saw from the change in his face that she'd waited too long. She must be more tired than she'd thought.

"I do love you, I hope you know that," he said, and placed a finger over her lips as she started to reply. "No, don't say anything, I know it's too soon for you, and you have other things on your mind tonight, but I wanted you to know."

Celeste pressed his hand. "Thank you, for being so understanding," she said. "Thank you." She stepped closer into his embrace, trying to empty her mind and think only of pleasure, of the sun sparkling on blue ocean water. The look on Peter's face when he held David for the first time.

Richard pulled away from her suddenly. "I have an idea.

You need to be alone with David, you two need to have some privacy. Why don't I stay with Martina and you take him to the concert?"

"Oh, I couldn't!" Celeste said. She stepped back from him and patted her hair, pulling herself back from the furrows of complacency she'd been sinking into. "Martina can be difficult, if you're not used to her, and if she's not used to you." She had carefully limited Richard's exposure to Martina, keeping their interactions to the occasional chess game, and only when Martina was in the best temper.

"Please don't worry," Richard said. "I won't love you any less after I spend an evening with her. He slid an arm around her. "Everything will be fine, and I won't take no for an answer."

Celeste stared at him. Had he always been so perceptive, or was she being particularly easy to read tonight? As for his offer, tempting as it was, it was out of the question. One of Martina's tantrums, and Richard would be gone forever. "Oh, that's not it," she lied, "but you don't know what she can get up to."

"Is it me, then? Don't you trust me?"

Celeste heard Richard attempting to keep the chill out of his voice, but he wasn't succeeding. In trying to avoid scaring him off, she was managing only to insult him even more in this clumsy fashion. "Of course I do, but I don't want you to put yourself out like that. You were looking forward to this concert so much."

"Then it's settled, I'll stand guard here while you and David mend your fences." He smiled, the tension released from his shoulders, and his tone was gentle and reassuring. "It will be fine, you'll see."

"I'm sure it will. Thank you for doing this." She did trust him, of course. She kissed him once more, and said a silent prayer to the fates that Martina would behave herself. She drew a deep breath. She had made her decision; it was out of her hands now.

"Don't worry, go and enjoy the concert." Richard rubbed the furrow between her brows with his finger. He reached around her and opened the apartment door, leading her through. "David, you and your mother are going to the concert tonight. Better hurry and change into theater clothes."

"Really?" David looked at them in surprise.

Celeste nodded. David's expression turned flat. Celeste wanted to smack him—in an instant he had turned back into a surly teenager. Richard's offer had been a perfect and sincere gift, and here he was turning his nose up at it. She squinted at him, and tilted her head the smallest degree in Richard's direction.

"Thank you, Mr. Biscayne," David said. "This is extremely generous of you."

"Don't give it another thought." Richard swept his arm in a curve, indicating the door. "Have a good time, that will be all the thanks I need."

Ten minutes later Celeste and David were alone in the hallway, and David turned on her. "Mother, is this the right thing to do?"

"Of course, I'm sure it will be fine. Martina is having one of her good nights, I think it will all be fine."

"That isn't what I meant. I don't think they should be alone." He paused. "Are you sure they—," he paused again.

"It will be fine," Celeste declared. "Richard will take good care of her."

"What would the neighbors say?" David persisted.

Celeste sighed, "I know it wouldn't look right." Her glance swept up and down the narrow hallway, the closed doors. "It's not as if Martina has a reputation to protect so she can make a good marriage."

David looked as if he wanted to say more, but he simply

nodded once and then bit his lip.

They stepped out of the building and turned up Twelfth Street. Celeste took David's arm, determined to have a good time and not think about Richard, overwhelmed by one of Martina's screaming fits. "You've grown in this last year." She tipped her head back to see him at his full height, then glanced down at the cuff of his dress pants. "You're all leg, those trousers should be let down again. I wish I had the money to buy you new ones."

"It's fine, Mother, we don't go out often enough for me to worry about it."

"But I worry about it."

David laughed and squeezed her hand.

They walked on in silence for a few minutes before David spoke. "I want to leave, Mother. I want to head out on my own, stop taking care of Martina and start earning my keep."

Celeste stopped short on the sidewalk. "No, no, you can't!"

"I have to. I've made up my mind."

"You're much too young! You're my baby." She tried to control the panic in her voice. Was this what he'd meant when he said he had to get out? She couldn't let him go.

"Oh, Mother, I'm not a baby. I'm old enough to find real work and start contributing to the family finances." His cheeks reddened. She knew she had insulted him, but she couldn't seem to stop the flow of words.

"That's nonsense! You do earn your keep. If you didn't take care of Martina, I would have to find a nurse and pay her a salary."

"I could earn more than you would pay a nursemaid. And I don't want to be a nursemaid any longer."

How petulant he sounded. She wondered how she sounded to him. Did she sound terrified? Anything could happen to him, what would she do if something terrible happened to him as well? She had lost Peter, she simply couldn't lose David too. She groped for the right words. "I can't stop you from leaving." Her breath came in tight, short, bursts. She rubbed her chest with her fingers and tried to relax. Around her the storefronts were closed and grated, squarely fenced in. Safe. "It is truly, truly a bad idea." She resisted the urge to point out, yet again, that he was too young. He didn't feel young, she knew. She tried to be patient, because she could remember when she was his age, when she too knew with certainty how ready she was to leave, and the only path for her was out and away. In fact, she was barely older than this when she'd left home and come to New York. But she'd been older in so many ways other than years. "I don't want anything to happen to you, and Martina needs you so. I know you think I'm saying that because of the money, but it's not true." She stopped and knuckled David's chin down to make him meet her eyes. It always surprised her that he was taller than she. "It's not true." She smoothed a lock of hair from his forehead. "I love you," she whispered. "I would be lost if anything happened to you."

The youthful start of his Adam's apple slid up and down his neck as he swallowed. The emotions in his face were so easy to read—longing, guilt, love, indecision. He wanted to leave but knew he shouldn't. Wagons and motorcars rolled past them, splattering through the mud in the street. She wouldn't be able to hold him forever, but maybe, maybe she could hold him long enough to let him grow up just the littlest bit more.

Celeste replaced her arm in his and they resumed their progress to City Center where the New York Philharmonic played a selection of pieces Celeste did not hear a note of. She wanted to find exactly the right words to make David feel better about staying, but she couldn't think of a thing, so she simply stayed silent.

He was quiet as they walked home from the concert hall,

leaving the beauty, lights and elegance all behind them. Even as a little boy he had been this way—shouting out a tantrum, then withdrawn and penitent. Celeste speculated that having said what he wanted to say, he was now reassessing the consequences. The bright lights of midtown Manhattan grew dimmer in the distance as they strolled quietly through the night.

Their tenement loomed darkly before them, its few feeble lights a bitter contrast to the glittering world they'd left behind. Its narrow stairwell swallowed them back into its ugliness. The baby in 2C was crying itself to sleep, and the couple in 1B was arguing. Meanwhile, a Victrola down the hall was turned on too late, and up too loud. Their footsteps echoed against bare tile floor, the odor of boiled onions and mildew permeated the air. A few spots on the floor caught Celeste's eye, they looked like paint. A few more spots higher up the stairs, then a smeared handprint on the tile wall, palm coming toward her, finger pointing back up the stairs. A handprint, just at shoulder height to her. In the weak, yellow glow from the single light bulb dangling from a bare wire, the mark looked dark brown.

Why would someone be smearing paint in the stairwell?

When David asked, "Is that blood?" in a hushed voice, she shook her head. It couldn't be blood. Blood would mean Martina was hurt. Blood on the stairs would mean Martina was badly hurt and Richard had carried her out to the street—to a doctor, to a hospital. It couldn't be blood, it had to be paint.

Her feet sped up; she raced to the apartment, where the splatters on the floor and the smears on the wall outside became thicker and wilder. Another handprint on the wood above the doorknob pointed grotesquely inward to the waiting apartment.

The door was open a few inches, the apartment terrifyingly quiet. Nothing was out of place except an overturned chair and the streaks of scarlet on the floor.

"Richard?" Fear scraped at her, filled her voice, sounding sharp and high in the empty room. "Richard?" It was clear there would be no answer. "Oh God," she said. "Oh God, Oh God." She tried to figure out where to go, what to do next. A hospital? Which hospital? Which one was closest? She couldn't remember. Her teeth were banging together but she couldn't stop them.

David stood next to her, and across the short distance separating them, she saw her shuddering pass to him. Anger welled up inside her, pushing out from behind her skin. She didn't want to put her arm around him, didn't want to bear his fear as well as her own. He wanted to go out into the world and be a man, to ride off into the west on a steed of independence, then so be it. Let him start now. "Go see if Richard left a note," she snapped. Anything to move his fragility out of reach of her sympathy.

Her chest heaved and the room began to swirl around her. "Stop it," she told herself. "This is no time to panic. There is nothing you can do until you hear from Richard. As soon as everything is all right with Martina, he will return straight here." She tried to breathe evenly, tried to force her arms and legs to move normally, but her mind wrenched itself back to the splatters of blood in the hall, and a vivid image of Martina, pale and bloodless, hanging in Richard's arms as he raced through the streets with her, looking for aid. "She can't be dead, I won't let her," she screamed silently. She scraped her fingernails into the skin of her arms to lock the wailing inside, not let it into the open air.

She had to do something. She had to move. "I'm going to clean this mess," she called to David, and marched into the hallway to get a bucket from the cleaning closet. She wanted to bang her head against the wall. She shouldn't have left them alone; Richard didn't understand how mindless Martina could be. He didn't understand how quickly she could fling herself into harm.

"Mother! Mother!" David shrieked. Celeste dropped the bucket and raced to him, squeezing the sponge in half in her fist.

Martina lay in the corner of the kitchen, curled up on the floor. Celeste fell to her knees and scooped her into a desperate embrace, her mind a swirl of black and gray forming no pattern, no meaning.

Time came to a halt.

Celeste knelt and held her daughter. Martina's mouth gaped dumbly open, lips thin and pale, skin almost blue against vivid streaks of blood. Her eyes were shut, her lashes lying long and shadowed on her cheeks. Her back alone was tense, pulling her legs all the way up to curl under her chin.

Through the fog of her thoughts, Celeste realized that Martina was warm, she was breathing, and Celeste buried a sob in her hair, releasing the frightening idea that had clutched at her when she first saw Martina lying so still and small.

"Oh Lord," she cried, and couldn't form the plea for this night to be undone. Had that monster attacked her baby? Had Martina had one of her fits and he had tried to restrain her? Hit her? Had he started it? Had he raped her?

Martina's eyes blinked open, and she stared blankly at her mother.

Celeste would be damned forever. A great weight pressed down on her, seeping into her bones and rolling out through her muscles like an oily stain. She lacked the strength to stand, so she bowed her head and kept her face in Martina's hair. "I'm sorry darling, I'm so sorry." If only there was a penance she could perform, a payment she could make to mend the shattered places, to repair this jagged tear in their life.

Anything.

She had been so blind, so stupid. Her fantasy came raining down around her in crystalline shards. She had tried to hold the family together on her own, without Peter, without help from friends, refusing to bend to the demands of family. She thought she'd found the perfect solution to her problems, she thought she'd found a man to take care of them. Here in her arms lay the damaged harvest of that delusion. Even David had tried to warn her, even he had sensed something was wrong with Richard, and she hadn't listened.

"Oh Lord," she prayed, "Please tell me what to do to make this right. Tell me what I can give you to make this all right."

The answer came to her before she was aware she had a decision to make. She was defeated. Done. There was only one place left to go. The thought leapt into her mind fully formed, all the pieces coming together at once. She stopped rocking and levered herself up from the floor, cradling Martina carefully in her arms. She breathed slowly, feeling the pounding beat of her pulse slow, settle, and resume its normal pace through her veins. She knew what she had to do. They would start packing tonight and leave first thing in the morning.

David hovered over her, wringing his hands.

"Get some towels, please," she told him. "A wet one and a dry one." How calm her voice sounded! She had only calm left. She would clean Martina's wounds, take her to the hospital if necessary. She knew what to do.

David's panicked voice swept over her. "What? What is that?" He was gagging. The tip of Richard's finger lay by the edge of the rug, lying white and pale in a garish pool of crimson blood and scattered chess pieces. "That's why there's so much blood, Mother. See, look, it's not Martina's."

Celeste looked at it and started to laugh, loud, so loud, the sound scissoring out of her like serrated knives. It filled her with pride that Martina had fought back. She was the strongest of them all.

"Mother?" David's voice pleaded for her to say

something, anything, to make this nightmare less horrendous, but there was nothing at all she could say. Tomorrow she would sign the annulment papers and relinquish Peter to the care of his father, then she would take her children where they would be safe. She would take them home.

CHAPTER 15

MARTINA

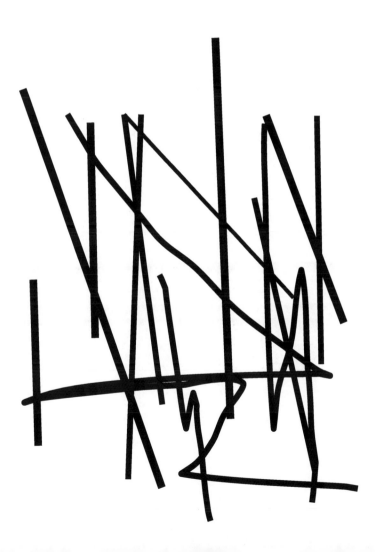

CHAPTER 16

DAVID

Mother sat wrapped in a deathly stillness. David glanced at her out of the corner of his eye, not wanting her to catch him staring. She appeared calm; but it was a disturbing calm, like the sudden silence after lightning has hit, but before the thunder rolls in. David found himself hunching his shoulders up around his ears when he was near her, his neck stiff and his jaw aching. "This is my mother," he tried to tell himself, but in fact Mother had disappeared the instant they found Martina, leaving behind this empty space that only looked like her.

She progressed from one task to the next with deadened, trancelike movements. She no longer moved smoothly and gracefully, but jerkily, one step at a time, as if working her body had become an enormous chore. Her eyes were flat and dull, like stagnant pond water. Like Martina's.

When he went to check on Martina, he found her on the bed, still curled into a ball, barely breathing. David kept imagining the fight that must have taken place. How could that monster have done such a thing? He gripped the edge of a table and shook it. How could they have left her with that man? He had known. He couldn't fool himself otherwise. He had wanted to get out, he had wanted to get away, and he had left her alone with that fiend. Why hadn't any of the neighbors come? Martina's screaming must have been loud enough for the whole building to hear. Why hadn't he been here? He kissed her gently on the cheek. "I'm sorry." He stroked her hair. "I'm so, so sorry."

Mother pulled open the drawers of the dresser and sorted the contents into two tilting piles.

"What are you doing?" he asked.

She stared at him for a minute, her face expressionless, then returned to her stacks without answering. Underwear and socks in one pile, handkerchiefs and knit shirts in the second. A heavy sweater with the underwear, and three cotton shirts. Pajamas and robe with the handkerchiefs. David discerned no pattern to the split. A pair of broadcloth boating pants went with the sweater. At last, pointing to the first pile, Mother said, "Put as much as you can into the rucksack. You'll need to be wearing whatever won't fit. Find a box for the rest, I can sell it."

It was the first time all day she had spoken more than a single word or at most two, David was stunned to hear her accent was completely changed. She said "can" like "kin". She said "for" like "fur." And that odd grammer! Gone was the lilting cadence of French consonants, replaced by languid, drawn out syllables. The pitch of her voice was lower as well, as if the accent had lent effervescence to everything she said. Where had her accent gone? Who was this person standing here in Mother's skin? David's mind whirled with conflicting facts, and no answers came. He rubbed his eyes with the heels of his hands, pushing the tears back behind his eyelids. Oh God, he missed Father so much, the yearning burned him from inside out. "Mother," he ventured, "where are we going?"

"Home," she said in that strange voice. "I'm taking you home, please don't ask any more questions, I simply won't have you yapping at me all day."

She couldn't mean they were going back to Park Avenue; they didn't own the brownstone any more. Back to France? Mother had no relatives there, except a brother who had been missing since the war. Had he been found? David pretended this was the answer. Would he be going to school in Paris? That would impress his friends, but the language would give him a bit of a problem. He tried to remember his vocabulary lists, and all those practice conversations which had seemed so trivial at the time. "Bonjour mademoiselle. Je m'appelle David Vandenholm." Mother's absent French vowels mocked him.

Mother left with the box of clothing to sell, calling a brusque "I'll be back in an hour," over her shoulder.

David sat on the couch with his knees pulled up tightly under his chin, trying to ease the knot inside him at the thought of the unknown territory before him. He wished he could talk to Mother. He wished she would speak to him and stop looking at him as if she hated him. She blamed him for what happened to Martina. He blamed himself. It had been his responsibility to watch over Martina, not leave her alone with that ogre. He rubbed his eyes, ashamed he could still cry at his age, ashamed he wanted Mother so much when she didn't want him, that he didn't want to be the man of the family, and that he had failed so badly at the role. "Things will be better once we get out of here," he promised himself. "They have to be."

Through the night David tried to sleep, while the light in the living room remained on. He crept out to use the bathroom down the hall once; Mother was sitting in the chair by the window, staring out, with a cigarette smoldering between her fingers. The ash curled, long and gray, about ready to fall and join the heap scattered around the ashtray on the table by her elbow. She didn't move as he stepped into the room, so he stepped back and retreated to his bed.

The day was already warm when Mother woke him the next morning. Martina was sitting at the table, not eating, not moving, her comb poking out of her shirt pocket. David stared, astonished, at the food at his place: a small pile of dry toast, a bite of steak next to a half slice of roast chicken, a mound of wilted greens, a glass of milk, a fried egg. Mother's and Martina's plates were similarly encumbered. The door to the icebox stood open; the shelves empty.

"Wear your heavy boots." Mother had already dressed Martina in her rugged hiking clothes. They would be traveling steerage to Paris, of course, which wouldn't be very clean. David tried to imagine how disgusting it would be; he'd never known anyone who'd traveled steerage before. He realized he was now the poorest person he'd ever known.

David didn't look back when they left the apartment. It had been, after all, only a temporary stopping place. It wasn't home. He thought wistfully of the brownstone on Park Avenue. Who had bought it? What were those people doing now, in his bedroom, or in Father's study?

He didn't even look back when they left the hospital where Father lay, so still. He wanted to vow to return one day to rescue him, but it would be an empty gesture. He had failed Mother, he had failed Martina. He certainly could only fail Father as well.

They headed downtown. Mother led, with one hand on Martina's shoulder. The girl moved where directed like an automaton, coming to a halt when she wasn't being physically maneuvered. A peculiar sameness mirrored the way Martina and Mother were behaving, and David found it unnerving. He tried to concentrate on imagining what France would be like, trying to ignore the observation that they were not headed toward the piers. He was not surprised when they arrived at Grand Central Station instead.

"Three for Union Station, please," Mother said to the ticket clerk.

"Toronto or Washington?"

"Washington, please."

"Parlor seats?"

"How much are they?"

"$8.10, and 80 cents for the seats."

"Coach will do."

"Train leaves at 3:10PM. Track 4." The clerk shoved three tickets through the window to her. She tucked them in her pocket, took Martina by the hand and led her across the rotunda, eyeing the track numbers marked over the entry gates. David followed, a suitcase in each hand and the rucksack on his back. He felt like one of the colored porters who hovered around, waiting for work. He avoided looking at them, hoping they wouldn't be approached, but at the same time wishing they didn't look as if they had no money to waste on tips.

His feet tingled from the twenty-seven-block walk to the station, his fingers were cramped into their grip on the suitcase straps, and the lining of his hat was damp with sweat. He thought he recognized one of the boys from his class at Briarwood stepping up to the train a few coaches away and his pulse raced as he stumbled to move behind a pillar. Then the boy turned his head, the resemblance evaporating. David shut his eyes in relief.

The cheerless second-class carriage welcomed its passengers with hard, narrow seats and a floor smeared with the grime of a hundred shoes. Mother took a seat next to a window, guided Martina down next to her as the train pulled out of the station, up from underground and into the light filtering feebly through the glass. David slid into the seat across from them.

"Mother?" he ventured. "Where are we going?"

She turned to him, and in her face he saw such pain that he could only pull back, stunned. She reached out and put her hand on his knee for a minute, then pulled away.

David scrutinized the two faces before him, one facing blankly forward, no recognition in the empty sapphire depths, one staring fixedly out of the window, ignoring him. He said nothing more. The rolling farmlands of New Jersey reeled past him. Towns and stops, stops and towns. They passed fields bursting with dark green rows of early summer corn. Cows crowding around bales of hay, unbothered by the train streaming past, pulling at the air as it went.

At some point after they pulled out of the Trenton station he fell asleep.

"Last stop everyone, please watch your step as you leave the train," the conductor called as he came through the car. "Union Station, Washington. Last stop, ladies and gentlemen, please make sure you have all of your belongings."

David rose stiffly, shaking the pins and needles from his foot, which had fallen asleep after being pressed against the hard struts of the seat. He was sore, he was nervous, and he was hungry. He snuck a glance at his watch and found it was after eight in the evening. No wonder his stomach was rumbling so.

"Come along, stop your lollygagging," Mother snapped.

David lifted the suitcases and rucksack down from the overhead rack. Lollygagging? Around him people trundled toward the exits, loaded with carryalls and parcels. David carted their luggage himself, and followed, staring at the ground, and using Mother's feet as a guide.

Martina stumbled along at Mother's side, not looking around as she usually would have, not stopping or staring at the many things that would have caught her attention, not babbling her nonsensical stream of words, not even flinching or screaming when strangers bumped into her.

David's teeth started to chatter and he bit his lip to control it. He was trudging blindly into he knew not what, in the company of a sick girl and a silent mother. Everything had been so strange, so wrong, since Father's accident, and it would never be set right. Questions tap-danced around each other in his head. Where were they going? How could Mother have left Father behind? What was going to happen to them? They hadn't even eaten all day.

"Mother, do we have enough money for supper tonight?" he asked.

"Maybe," she answered, her voice sharp. "We need to find our train first."

Another train? David hadn't thought they would continue on from there. Each step of this journey was catching him by surprise. It was like playing chess against a superior opponent, with every move of his own only a defensive reaction to the previous attack. Well, of course they were going on from there. "It's not as though we can live in the train station," he scolded himself for his lack of thought. But on to where?

Mother marched across the rotunda to the ticket window. "How much is one full fare and two half fares to Charlottesville?" she asked. "One way, second class."

The man in the window flipped a chart over and ran his finger down a column of numbers. "Three dollars, forty cents."

"Fine." She counted out the fare one coin at a time, then passed the money through the window. "When is the next train?" she asked, as she carefully put the tickets into her purse.

The man put his finger back up to the chart and said, "Next train is 9:18 tomorrow morning."

Her head jerked up. "Nothing until morning?"

"Sorry, no."

Mother sagged. "Thank you," she said.

Charlottesville. Where the hell was Charlottesville? He savored the curse word in his head. David had the vague impression it was in North Carolina. Or was that Charlotte? He wished he dared to ask.

"Oh dear," Mother sighed, "I didn't think…," she trailed off, frowning. "I didn't plan for…" and once again her words faded to silence. She scanned the station again, but more slowly, less intently, less expectantly. With sloping shoulders, slouched like a completely different woman, she headed for a row of benches on the other side of the rotunda, pulling Martina behind her. She jammed Martina's suitcase under a bench and pushed the girl down onto the seat. "You stay here and look after your sister," Mother told David, "I'll see what I can find for supper."

David sat on the bench next to Martina, placed his arm around her unresponsive shoulders and shoved his own suitcase under the seat with the heels of his boots. He leaned into her just to feel her warmth, tucked his face down into her hair and shut his eyes. What was happening to him? On a journey to who-knew-where? On a journey without a destination. He felt untethered, unattached to the ground, or to himself, as if his arms would rise up of their own accord and leave the earth behind. With his eyes shut and his head down, the world slipped away, the buzz of voices and the rumble of trains faded into a cottony mist.

Hunger blended into the mist, mixed with the hum of the station and the ache of not knowing, not understanding where they were going. How did this happen? How had everything fallen apart so fast? The strangeness ate through him. Oh God, he wished Father were here.

"Here."

David opened his eyes and sat up to take the small sack from Mother. It lay warm and heavy in his hands. "What's in it?"

Mother did not answer. She took her own sack and sank down onto another bench a few feet away.

David opened the sack to find two buttered rolls, a sausage and two bruised apples at the bottom. The perfume of bread and apples rose up, and David's mouth began to water. He took one of the rolls and tried not to cram the whole thing in his mouth at once. It was stale, clearly left over from much earlier in the day, but it was food. He took the sausage and, more slowly still, in control now, ate half of the puny thing one single morsel at a time.

Martina twitched. David jerked around at her movement. "I'm so sorry, kiddo," he said, turning her face toward his. "Mother has brought us a lovely dinner." He took the other roll out of the sack, lifted her hand from her lap and curled her fingers around the roll.

Her hand thumped back into her lap, the roll tumbling onto her skirt. David caught it before it hit the floor and put it back in her hand, then raised the limp hand to her mouth, positioning the roll in front of her lips. "Come on, it's good food, take a bite."

But she didn't. David looked helplessly over to the bench where Mother was sitting, also not eating. He put his arm around Martina and raised the roll back to her mouth. "Come on, you have to take a bite."

Martina did not move.

Mother stared vacantly at the crowd shuffling around them.

David tried to shake off the panic that was surging closer, larger, and louder. "Mother!" he called out, and the volume, the fear in his voice startled him.

Mother turned her head. One eyebrow arched up in wordless question.

"Mother, I can't get Martina to eat."

One shoulder moved—up, down. "She'll eat when she's ready."

The crowd and noise flowed up against him, as if David were stranded on an island surrounded by pounding surf. He clung to the bench, clung to Martina. Mother had used her own shampoo on the girl; she smelled reassuringly like home.

His stomach grumbled and he eyed the food in his lap with lust. If Martina wasn't going to eat, he shouldn't let it go to waste. Besides, he was bigger than she was so he needed more nourishment. But the memory of finding her, huddled and hurt in the corner of the kitchen, stopped him.

He broke off a tiny piece of bread and butter and pushed it between her lips, crooning, "Come on now, honey, swallow one bit. You don't even need to chew, just swallow."

For a few moments more Martina remained passive, then her jaw moved and she chewed and swallowed, the muscles in her throat rippling. David felt a foolish flush of pride and rubbed her shoulder enthusiastically. He put another morsel of bread into her mouth and resumed his encouragement.

When she had finished the roll, he tore off shreds of sausage and fed her those, one at a time as well. Finally she stopped chewing and David, glancing guiltily around, stuffed the remaining scraps into his own mouth. He left the apple in the bag. Perhaps Martina would be hungry later, he thought, redeeming his guilt and feeling protective.

Mother was still motionless on the other bench. The urgency of the questions had temporarily receded in his preoccupation with Martina, but now they returned. Where was Mother taking them? His head spun with weaving, pulsating thoughts.

Martina's head dipped toward his shoulder, her eyes already closed. He shut his own and pulled her into his arms. She was warm and soft, and he could not understand why that man had done what he had done. How he could have done such a terrible thing. Wherever it was they were going, no one was ever going to hurt his sister again. He held her tighter. Including and especially himself.

The sounds around him eventually merged into a single buzzing hum. The lights behind his eyelids melted into the flashing images of restless, disrupted dreams. Each time he woke he checked first across to the bench where Mother sat, always unmoving, but always there. In spite of her unnerving changes, her unwavering presence reassured him.

Toward early morning, nearly six by the big clock on the wall, he woke at last with a dry mouth and a full bladder. He unfurled himself carefully from Martina, unkinking muscles tight from sitting upright all night. He was sticky, dirty, hungry and unhappy. He crossed to the other bench. "Mother," he said as he shook her shoulder gently.

She woke slowly and stretched disjointedly. Gone was her usual sinuous grace, that tight, feline flow that so characterized her, and it jarred David almost as much as the drawn, gray waxiness of her skin.

"Mother," David whispered, "I have to go to the restroom and I didn't want to leave Martina alone." He pointed toward Martina, still sleeping, her head bent over on her neck like a drooping sunflower. "Perhaps she has to go as well," he hinted politely, "before she has an accident."

Mother nodded once. "You go first. I'll take Martina when you're back, so you can mind the cases." There was that peculiar, flat voice again. It was slower, thicker, than she normally spoke, and the lack of accent struck David with a renewed sense of wrongness. He hurried away to the men's room.

"We're falling apart," he whispered to himself, splashing cold water over his face and neck. He wanted a hot bath, he wanted to dry off on soft, clean, freshly laundered towels. He noticed the chipped, black-streaked tiles of the public toilet and shuddered. "Father, Martina, Mother—all gone. And I don't know where I'm going either."

Father used to say, "Your mother is the strong one. I went sailing off to Belgium and I left her behind with two tiny children and no family to help her out. Why on earth I thought that was a good idea, I'll never remember. But she waved me off, with a smile on her face and her head held high." Father would be devastated to see the condition they were in now.

He'd been daydreaming too long – he rushed back to the

benches, heart pounding, half certain he would find Mother and Martina gone. They were all that was left to him in this strange, new world where everything loomed over him with ominous intent. *I miss Father,* he wanted to say, and he wanted Mother to wrap her arms around him and rock him in her furs and perfumes as she had done so very long ago, in other train stations, in that other world so far away. "We're all just drifting away." He wanted to fold himself into a tight ball like Martina and let the world, and the pain, pass him by.

The two stiff figures waited on the bench, four pathetic bundles tied with twine at their feet, like immigrants newly cast ashore in a foreign land. When they left for their turn in the restroom, he sank to the bench and covered his face with his hands. It was all he could do.

9:18 found them on their way to Charlottesville, which was apparently another city in Virginia. As she had done yesterday, Mother settled stonily in the hard, second-class seat. Martina seemed more alert than before, but David thought his imagination might be painting the picture he wanted to see. Perhaps it was only that he wanted so much for her to get better. He held her hand and played games with her fingers, wiggling them and crossing them back and forth over each other. She had loved that game when she was little. Mile after mile of landscape rolled past. To a boy whose previous experience with open country had been the train ride through the gorge of the Hudson River, overshadowed by the wooded heights of the Catskill Mountains, this endless, mildly rolling farmland was depressingly flat, broken only by the occasional stream or stretch of trees, tall and unidentifiable, slipping past sideways at forty miles per hour.

The clatter of the wheels against the rails went on and on, alternating with the irregular bustle of frequent stops. Once they sat idle on a siding for nearly an hour, until the jolting of cars and screeching of gears indicated a train coupling had been planned and was at last underway.

By the time they reached Charlottesville, it was almost four in the afternoon. The passenger area of the station was quiet and calm; it lacked the hurried panic of Grand Central or Union Station. Most of the people at the platform waited in groups of two or three to board, or huddled together saying goodbye to friends and family. In the distance, greater activity revolved around the freight being unloaded at the far end of the train. The station looked odd, but David couldn't put his finger on the difference until he walked past the shabby sign proclaiming "colored waiting room." As if a cinema picture had widened from narrow focus to panoramic, a multitude of black faces came into focus around him. David noted how carefully both white and black kept to themselves in isolated groups.

Mother hoisted Martina's battered suitcase and manipulated the girl's arms through the rope straps, then slid into her own. David followed along behind them with the rucksack and the other case. Mother took Martina's hand and pulled her toward the exit. Well that answered one question— apparently Charlottesville was their final destination.

The railroad district seemed to be predominantly industrial. Factory buildings lined the opposite bank of a narrow river and freight cars rested on sidings beyond the passenger station to the east. Soon the hard edges of the commercial structures gave way to small houses and pocket gardens, then to larger houses with larger gardens, then finally to a district of wealthy homes facing wide avenues leading up gentle, tree-lined slopes. Broad stretches of velvet lawn and hedges bending from the weight of white flowers hid behind intricately wrought iron gates. Like the train station, the streets of Charlottesville held none of the rush and clangor of New York City, they were sedate and dignified. A few cars passed, a few horse-drawn carriages, a few people on foot and one woman on a bicycle. Everyone stared at the tattered threesome invading their pristine neighborhood, calling out the occasional, belated "how-do" as they went by, the men raising their hats to Mother. David ducked his head and watched the sidewalk pass by underneath his boots.

They walked alongside the sweeping commons and beautifully proportioned buildings of a college whose sign proclaimed it to be the University of Virginia. The houses got much smaller after that, then disappeared altogether, and they were once more in rough country. Stands of scrappy trees laden with creeper and ivy and raspberry cane crowded the side of the tarmac, fuzzy leaves and long thorns reached out for them. The sun was beginning to head toward the horizon; David wondered how much longer they would be walking. Martina was stepping oddly, as if her feet hurt.

A battered red pickup truck, pitted with rust and laden with lumpy sacks, jounced along the road and drew up beside them. The driver pulled the shapeless, gray hat off his head and spread his lips in a grin with several front teeth missing. "Evening, ma'am." His grin got even broader when Mother turned her face up and he got a good look at her. The hairs on the back of David's neck rose. The world seemed to be full of Richard Biscaynes. "Can I give you folks a ride somewheres?"

"We're heading out to Sculley's Bend, if you're going that way."

The man coughed, and didn't answer right away. His eyes flickered, and it was a long minute before he nodded. "Sure," he said. "Sure, hop on into the back." He was no longer smiling.

Mother lifted her case over the tailgate of the wagon, and followed it with Martina's. The driver stayed on the high front seat, not offering to help. David couldn't think of a way to ask him, or reprimand him.

"David, you boost Martina," Mother called, "I'll lift." She

climbed quite expertly over the back barrier and reached down for Martina's hands. "Put her foot in the gap there in the boards," she instructed, "And balance her while I pull." Martina tottered, on one foot wedged tight, until Mother pulled her forward until she was hanging on her stomach over the tailgate, half in and half out of the wagon bed. "Release her foot, then climb in and help me pull her over so she doesn't get hurt. "

David eased his sore muscles as gently as he could over the top board and down onto the sacks. They were sitting on old, hard ears of corn, David thought, feeling the lumps and smelling the chaff. Mother signaled the driver with a thump on the back panel of the truck cab. The truck started up, the engine coughed a few times before catching, and they headed off into the darkening distance. Mother's face was set and closed; he knew it would be pointless to ask for more information, but he had a name now, Sculley's Bend, and he had a suspicion this would turn out to be the end of their journey.

The truck jolted down the dirt road, swerving to avoid ruts and holes. The sun cast long shadows across the fields bordering the road. In the distance long rows of trees were silhouetted against the darkening sky. They had the same short, gnarled shapes that decorated the train ride from school to home along the Hudson River Valley. They might be apples, David supposed, or some other kind of tree with a similar shape. The corn cobs shifted as the truck rattled around a sharp curve where a noisy stream tumbled over large, granite boulders and ran under a narrow bridge. Mother sat up and shook Martina, who had dozed off. "Time," she said brusquely to David. She knocked again on the back of the cab, and the driver slowed to a halt.

With their cases and Martina, they reversed the process of climbing in. Once safely on the ground, the driver nodded

curtly and headed off, leaving nothing but a cloud of dust
settling behind him. Mother wearily strapped Martina back into
her case straps and hoisted her own. Without looking to see if
David was following, she took Martina by the hand and led her
onto a dirt road, hardly more than a path, which branched off
the main road and ran parallel to the stream. It was hard to
imagine what kind of vehicle could ever navigate a road this
bad, but in the fading light David saw faint marks of tire tracks.
At least they weren't heading into completely empty woods.
Sculley's Bend must lie at the end of this path. It had to, his
feet wouldn't last much longer, and Martina had to be ready to
give out.

The road followed the stream, once in a while veering
away over a rise, leaving the water behind, only to fall back
again around the next curve. As they walked, the light faded
from the sky, bleeding away between the trees, leaving only
glimpses through the dense leaves to clouds smeared with
purple stain. The rutted track disappeared into the darkness
ahead. Water splashing on stones to their right guided them,
but Mother marched on without hesitation.

Around one more curve a few lights shimmered in the
distance. In the darkness, the square shapes of windows floated
in the air, seemingly unsupported by any visible structure.
Once the angular lozenge of a door appeared, waxing as the
door opened, then waning and blinking out. Mother led them
past the first house, a gray outline with pallid, yellow light
glowing in the window. David was startled to realize the light
was kerosene, not electric. He peered up into the trees for
power and telegraph poles, knowing he would not find them,
even in full daylight. The second house was the same as the
first, a shack with a tilting porch and a few steps leading up to
an old door.

The misty shapes of a half dozen identical shacks spread
out in the area across from the stream. David could no longer

see the road below his feet, but it had gotten grassier, softer beneath his boots. This was a path that cars did not travel often. A wide spot in the water opened up between the trees, glittering in the rising moon, and the road curved to the left in front of it. David felt his way along the invisible road as it slid up a hill, still following the shape of the stream, past another six or seven houses, until they reached a house nearly at the top of the rise. It was too dark to see anything more than the edge of the window frame as the yellow light spilled out. Mother turned in, leading Martina. David's shoe banged into the bottom step, impossible to see in the gloom.

"There are three steps here," Mother said. David lifted his feet, able to discern the dim outline of them by the change in the shadows. The stairs led to a narrow porch, and a door.

For the first time since the fateful night they'd gone to that concert, such a long, long time ago, Mother looked David straight in the eye, her face mottled in the dribble of light leaking from the window. She seemed to be angry, but when she grabbed him by the shoulders she whispered, "I love you David. Remember that. Remember that tomorrow morning, and the morning after that." Tears ran down her cheeks. "Promise me," she rasped. "Promise me you'll remember that I love you."

"I promise, Mother," David whispered, frightened at the sight of Mother losing control like this. Mother never lost control. "I love you too."

She held him tight for a moment more, staring at him as if she wanted to say something else. Then she changed her mind with a quick shake of her head, swiped at her eyes, stepped away from him and banged on the door.

He was numb to any thought, except that this was the end of the walking, the end of staggering, one foot in front of the other, hour after hour. He heard footsteps approaching.

"Who is it?" a voice called. A black woman opened the

door, wiping her hands on a dish towel, followed by a teenaged boy in a torn undershirt, craning to peer around her. "Who—". She stopped speaking when the three of them stepped into the sallow light of the room. The woman's face reflected lightning fast changes of emotions. "Well I'll be," she cried, "Our Carol Ann's come home from New York!" She flung the towel over her shoulder and came to them, scooping them all into her arms. David was caught off-guard, not only by the strength of her hug, but by his momentary feeling of calm in her warm embrace, before he struggled and tried to pull away. She crushed them together them once more, before stepping back and holding them at arm's length. "Now let me get a good look at y'all."

Mother stood trembling, tears running down her face. "Oh Rita, I'm so tired."

"Of course you're tired, sweetie, of course." Rita released David and Martina, and pulled Mother back into a surrounding embrace.

David tried to slow down the speed of his swirling thoughts.

The boy came forward and stuck out his hand with a crooked grin, one that seemed to take up his whole dark face. "How do, I'm Eddy. How long you gon' be visitin? You come down by train all the way from New York?"

"Hush now, boy," Rita swatted Eddy across the top of his head with the towel, flipped it back over her shoulder. "Let them catch their breath, they been a powerful long time traveling, you can see they just 'bout run right off their feet."

A door at the back of the room opened and an older man entered, one of the largest men David had ever seen. He would have towered over Father. He was broad across the shoulders, with a barrel chest and solid legs. His hair was still black, with only a sprinkling of white through it; his skin was an even, light brown. In spite of his height and width, he had incongruously delicate features, but his hands were huge. He walked toward them with a smile, then the smile dropped away. He stared, not moving for long time. "Hello, Carol Ann," he said at last. "Welcome home."

"Hello, Poppa," Mother said. With a tearful glance, drawing a breath that seemed to use every ounce of her energy, she staggered past the man to the door in the far corner of the room, where she stopped and turned around. "These are your grandchildren. I got 'em here, now I'm going to bed." She stepped through the doorway and disappeared.

David jerked his head up. All the aching and soreness in his body, all the numbness in his mind merged into a blur. For a few minutes all thought fled, and he simply stood where he was, one hand resting on Martina's arm. Poppa? Maybe that was an honorary title—this man couldn't be her father—this man was black. This was Virginia, not France. Mother was from France. She had an accent and a brother. She had white skin. She was white.

David stood, silent and confused. Another thought percolated through the sludge of his brain. *If Mother is black, then I am, too.*

CHAPTER 17

CAROL ANN

The copperhead snake snapped forward and a small life disappeared. *I blinked*, Carol Ann thought, *I let go for one split second and I was back where I started*. Only worse, because for a while she had danced on top of the world. For such a little while. *I'm not even Celeste Vandenholm anymore*. She'd had to sign those annulment papers and she hated herself for doing it. Her whole life was simply gone. Her arms and legs felt brittle, as if all the marrow had been scraped out of her bones, but the bones themselves had been left behind, hollow, unable to hold up her limp muscles any longer.

In the twenty years she'd been gone, the tiny bedroom had become a waystation for broken things: a chair with a missing leg, a lantern with no chimney, two baskets with torn handles. How fitting. Last night she'd needed to move a tabletop and three church bibles with torn spines before throwing a sheet over the straw ticking and collapsing like a felled tree.

She wished she could cry. Tears would validate this pain. Tears would signify true anguish, not this wafting cloud of despair, this nothingness she couldn't hold onto. These random, formless stabs of guilt had no dignity. Martina attacked, possibly raped, because of her own poor choices. David having to leave school. Peter sending his car over an embankment because he couldn't face her without money in his hand. Had she really brought him to such a desolate decision?

She heard Rita and Martina come in and settle down in the other bed, but she lay still and pretended they weren't there. She tried to imagine that the whole world had gone away, that she lived in a cloud, or that she was a cloud. Being alive hurt too much. At last she returned to the oblivion of sleep.

It was her bladder that woke her. Her eyes were gummy, her teeth were furry, her leg stung with pins and needles from where it had gotten caught by the edge of the bed and wedged between the wall and the mattress. Rita and Martina were already gone, even though the sun was barely high enough to poke through the cracks between the wooden plank walls. She stood up, discovering she had fallen asleep in her dress the night before. She put on her shoes and limped to the outhouse.

The smell was the same—sharp lime, fetid urine and feces, mingled with the musty scent of old pine boards. The wooden box with newspaper and catalogue squares sat in the same place it had twenty years before. The old planks were cool and familiar against the backs of her thighs, the view of dusty leaves through the bird-shaped holes Poppa had carved were unchanged by the passage of so many years.

"I'm Carol Ann again." And in that dark, quiet place of familiar, unwelcome stench, it became true. "Hello, Ocean," she said to the horse-shaped knothole just below eye level on the right-hand wall. "I'm back. I told you I would never see you again, but I was wrong." The speeding horse, which had carried her through her childhood to places she had never been, continued his infinite run, mane and tail streaming out behind. She traced her fingers over Ocean's rough edges. "Carol Ann is right back where she started from." She wanted to vomit. She wanted to hide there all day, but the close, odorous air began to make her head ache.

Rita stood at the big outdoor stove, exactly as Momma had always done, stirring a large pot of something cooking, talking quietly to Martina who sat immobile in a chair at the trestle table near the stove. Neither one turned around when Carol Ann came up, although Rita paused her stirring for a moment. Behind a wire fence to the side of the yard was a small flock of hens, scratching, pecking and clucking. Stupid creatures. To know one was to scorn the whole species.

She looked around for signs of Poppa, relieved to see he wasn't there. That was not a confrontation she was looking forward to, his anger and his disappointment in her would be intense and painful. She had done many things he would not be proud of, and he would not hesitate to school her on each and every one.

Carol Ann went to kiss her daughter, expecting and getting no response. She pulled a chicken feather out of Martina's hair. A dish of stewed apples and a spoon sat on the table. "Did Martina eat anything?"

"David got her to take a bite or so. She's not quite with us, is she?" Rita asked, still not turning around.

"She's always been that way." The words came out harshly.

"Mmm-hmm," Rita said. "Gathered as such."

"Where's David?"

"He's over to the church with Poppa and Eddy, setting up."

"Oh Lordy, it's Sunday." Carol Ann couldn't believe she had so completely lost track of the days. Was it only Friday night that she and David had gone out, leaving Martina and Richard alone? She felt the tears start to come, so she bit her lip and went into the house. She lifted an enamel mug off a peg on the wall and returned outside to pour herself a cup of coffee from the pot on the weather-beaten table. She didn't bother to hunt for cream, there wouldn't be any. Might not be any sugar either, these days. Certainly none to waste in coffee. She took a sip and gagged. Not even real coffee; she'd forgotten how bitter chicory was. Rita still didn't look at her when she came near, but kept her attention on the stew cooking in the big pot. So Rita was angry at her as well. Carol Ann slumped down at the table next to Martina and leaned over to give her daughter another kiss on the cheek. She had automatically taken the spot she'd grown up in, with her back to the house, near the stove so she could get up and help whenever needed. Poppa and the boys had sat across from her—farther away from the chores, tired out after a long day of their own work. Without any effort on her part she was tumbling back into that well-worn rut which had been such a struggle to climb out of the first time around.

"I missed you, Rita." Carol Ann willed her sister to turn around. "I wanted to tell you how it was."

"I missed you too," Rita said, without looking up, her back straight and stiff, her movements short, the warmth from last night an ephemeral moment.

Rita hadn't changed much at all, at least not from the back. Her waist was still tiny, her legs were still long, even if the skin on her brown arms and hands was not as smooth as it had once been. As she turned sideways to put more wood into the stove, Carol Ann saw the fine lines between her narrow, delicate eyebrows. Everyone had always said they looked so much alike, Carol Ann and Rita, but Rita's bright green eyes made Carol Ann's hazel ones dull in comparison, and Rita's high, arched cheekbones made Carol Ann's face flat. On the other hand, Carol Ann had been blessed with hair just that little bit softer and straighter, and such pale, pale skin. Carol Ann had no illusions: she looked white, Rita was stunning.

"Could you turn around and talk to me?"

"No." But she did. "What you want to talk about?" Her

query was brusque. Her gaze was fierce.

Carol Ann's thoughts tumbled, not landing on solid ground. "You're as pretty as ever," she said at last.

"Hmmph," Rita replied, turning back to the simmering pot.

"You are, you know. You were always the pretty one. You should have gone to New York instead of me."

"Hmmph," Rita repeated "Pretty don't get the water boiled."

Carol Ann burst into jagged laughter. "You sound like Poppa."

"It's true, though," Rita said sternly, her face suddenly jutting, thrusting angles. "You went off and we ain't never heard word one from you other than la-di-da letters and fancy talk about the big city. Sure, the money you sent was great, but don't you think Poppa might have like to hear 'bout his grandkids? Maybe even a photograph?"

She stepped up to Carol Ann and shook the wooden paddle, dripping gravy, close to her. "And how 'bout me? Think I would have liked you to come home once or twice? How you think I felt last night, findin' out my own sister been lyin' to me nigh on twenty years?"

Rita's voice whipped in fury. The muscles under her eyes pulled taut, narrowing her glare to slits. "Sometimes all you think about is your own self. Momma died and you jus' swan outta here, 'cause you don't want to be 'stuck in the mud'. Did you ever once think I didn't neither? Did you think about us once, the whole time you was in New York? Did you think of anything except your own self? Probably ain't nothin' wrong with your girl except she's hiding from you!"

Carol Ann pulled back as if Rita had actually struck her with the paddle. Martina scooted soundlessly away as Carol Ann bumped into her. Rita had never, ever been so vicious! She had never said a mean word in her life! Rita had always been the warm one, the gentle one, the one who welcomed the world with open arms and an open heart. The sisters stared at each other.

Then Rita's stern face collapsed with the suddenness of a dandelion puff in the wind. "Oh, Sister, I didn't mean it!" Rita dropped the wooden paddle onto the ground with a thud, and dropped onto her knees on the ground in front of the bench. She grabbed Carol Ann's arm through the thin sleeve and held on. "I'm sorry, sorry, Sister, so sorry." She wrapped her arm around Carol Ann's neck and pulled them together. "You know me, I open my mouth and frogs fall out. They don't fall out, they jump out. They leap out. They fling themselves out. They ..."

"Oh hush, you silly *couj'n*," Carol Ann said, hovering halfway between anger and forgiveness. And yes, guilt as well. Rita was partly right, Martina's condition was her fault. She should never have left her alone with that man. Rita's gently massaging fingers brought her back to the present. She absorbed the belated homecoming against her skin. "You weren't going to manage the stiff treatment for long anyhow," she said.

"No, no I weren't, was I?" Rita put her arms around Carol Ann and held her close, sniffling. "I'm glad you're back, even if you didn't want to come. I been missin' you all these years." She raised her head and inspected Martina, her face changing once more. "I am truly sorry," she said. "It musta been hard for you, 'specially after, ahhhh, your husband, umm, got sick."

"Peter," Carol Ann said.

"Peter." Rita nodded.

"Had an accident," Carol Ann prompted.

Rita nodded again. "Accident." She peeked sideways at Carol Ann, then quickly looked back down at her hands.

The breeze stroked her cheek, carrying the scents of field and stream she had missed for so many years. The two tall pines rustled softly, like silk against silk. Birds twittered, flit, rested. Sculley's Bend. "Go ahead, ask your question," Carol Ann nudged her sister.

"I didn't have a question," Rita protested.

"Of course you did. I haven't been gone so long I've forgotten who my sister is and what's plain on her face."

Rita looked up and then away, cautious. "I been jus' dying to know what it was like, being," she lowered her voice to a whisper, "white."

Carol Ann sat silently for several long moments. What was it like? "There isn't an easy way to answer that," she said at last. "Anything you want, anything at all, all you need is money, and everyone has money. At least they used to, before the Crash." She shut her eyes and the Park Avenue townhouse rose around her. "Electricity, soft carpets, jewelry, clothes, servants, the best doctors for Martina and the most exclusive schools for David." She smiled, her eyes still closed. "All of New York right outside my door, with no one to tell me where I couldn't go and what I mustn't do. No one to tell me I didn't belong in the center seats in the theater, on the arm of the most wonderful, the most handsome man in the room." She felt as if her heart had been torn in half.

"But on the other hand, I was always worried I might get caught," she confided. "The whole time I was pregnant I was terrified my babies would come out dark. It was worth the fear to have Peter and David and Martina, but I'll admit it was frightening at times."

"I'm not surprised you were worried," Poppa boomed from the doorway to the kitchen. Carol Ann and Rita spun around in surprise. Martina sat stolidly at her place. "A falsehood is always paid with guilty coin," he declared.

"I didn't deliberately decide to do it, you know," Carol Ann snapped. "I didn't wake up one morning and say 'I think I'll be white from now on.' The first time it happened was a mistake. A waitress in a coffee shop seated me in the white section."

"But you didn't stop her." He glowered.

Her jaw clenched. "It's hard to tell black sections from white sections in New York. I was already sitting down before I realized what had happened, and then I was too nervous to say a word." Carol Ann recalled that life-changing moment when she'd looked up and saw herself alone in an ocean of alabaster faces and blue eyes. It was a frozen drop of time, forever unchanging in her memory. "I kept thinking they'd make this big stink about how I'd tricked them. Drank me that coffee so fast I burned the roof of my mouth, and got my behind outta there."

"But you kept on with this outrage," he slammed his hand down on the table and Carol Ann jumped. "You kept on lying, layering one falsehood on top of the next, and building a mansion of deceit." Poppa was thumping his fist rhythmically against the table. Thud, thud, thud. There was something he wanted her to say, and she refused to say it. "You never even told your own husband. Your own son. Do you not see how lies just lead ever onward, to more walls between people who deserve your loyalty and integrity?"

"No, I never told them." The fear and guilt she had carried all those years washed over her again and she sagged against the table. She knew what had stopped her—the stillness that came over a person's face when you told them you were black, before they turned their heads away and chatted casually with someone else, leaving you to stand awkwardly alone, with your hands dangling useless at your sides. She would have died if she'd ever seen that look on Peter's face.

She tried to lighten the mood a little. "It didn't seem to be such a big lie. At first it was even easy. I told everyone I was French—put on Momma's Creole accent. I got a job as a receptionist in a law firm, and it turns out all those white city folk learn real French in school, not Bayou, so I took classes at night. I didn't want to lose my job. I had a good job, Poppa."

"So you found such lying to be easy and advantageous. Indeed, necessary. You merely enjoyed the fruits of those lies." Poppa's volume had risen, his face darkening with his anger. The booming frightened the chickens away from the edge of the yard, and the jays in the trees above fell silent.

The wall surrounding her own temper broke inside her. "Yes, I liked it," she shouted back at him. "I knew you would think it was wrong, but I didn't care!" She glared up at him in defiance as he towered over her, the years rolling away until she was a teenager again. Living a secret life had been exciting and dangerous and made her feel alive—like a champagne cork zooming away from the bottle. It had brought her Peter, David and Martina. But there was more to it than that. Being white on the surface had freed her from the confinement of her heritage, in a way the act of leaving home had not. She had been convinced that simply arriving in the big city would change everything, but the real move to freedom had needed that additional metamorphosis. It was as if she had stepped in to play a part on a stage and had melded completely with the role, casting her old self away.

"Repent, before it is too late!" Poppa shouted. "You ever fail to look to tomorrow, seeing only the pleasures and comforts of today." With a violent move, he whirled about and stalked away.

Carol Ann bowed her head as Poppa lectured. For better or for worse, or perhaps a combination of the two, she was back home. Home with giggly, rock-solid Rita who pulled laughter out of the air. Home with Poppa, who had lived his whole life by the word of The Good Book and followed a path single-mindedly straight and true. Here she was part of the fabric of life, in spite of the sins she had committed, in spite of the span of years that had elapsed. In exchange, she forfeited those years, and was once more the child she had been when she left, not the woman she had become while she had been gone. She dropped her face down onto the table, overwhelmed by exhaustion, defeated by the power of all the mistakes she could not undo.

CHAPTER 18

MARTINA

The lines come, the jagged lines come and come and come. The lines tear. I tear the lines. The general who smells like paint thinks he is a god but he is not. He thinks he can tear through the lines.

But.

He.

Can.

NOT.

CHAPTER 19

DAVID

David finished the meager and greasy breakfast while Mother shepherded a still silent Martina to the sink to wipe her hands and face, then led her outside where people were beginning to congregate for Sunday service, gossiping loudly as they sauntered along to the shabby little church at the end of the path, a tiny building haphazardly whitewashed, turning it from grey to grey. Each one was carrying a bowl or a plate, and when they saw him, Martina and Mother, they stopped walking, stopped talking, and gaped.

Then a voice called out, "Why just look here, it be Carol Ann, come home from New York!"

"When you get home?"

"How long you stayin'?"

"These your children?"

"What's their names?"

Bodies pressed in around them, touching, hugging. Gap toothed, or in some cases, completely toothless, grins fenced them in. Martina stiffened and David gently slid her behind him while Mother did her best to answer the flood of questions.

"Yo' girl, she a mite shy."

"This yo' boy? He got a powerful look of you, Carol Ann." A wrinkled raisin of a man shook hands with David.

"I'm Willy Hume. That's my truck." He proudly waved a hand to a rusted pickup truck parked at the bend where the drivable ruts petered out into un-drivable ruts. "It's a bit broke down right now, but nothing some fiddling and jiggling won't fix."

"I'm Miz Thackett, yo' momma used to watch my Shairee when she was a baby." A gnarled brown hand patted his cheek. "That old fool Willy is pure wrong, same as ever. You got the look o' yo' grandpoppa. You gonna grow into his size, too, you're a bog one already. You come home to Sculley's Bend for good?"

David didn't know how to answer that question.

"Miz Baylor, I'm Portya's momma." She pulled a cluster of little children toward her. "These here are my grands," she said. "Custis, Dorrie and Cupcake." Three scrawny children stared at the ground. Their too big hand-me-downs hung on their bony frames. Who was Portya?

"Mrs. Mills," a large woman enunciated. "I taught your mother in school, and I hope that she continued with her reading and education while she was away from us."

"Absalom Samuelson," one man announced. He was young, and fairly light skinned.

"Zebediah Samuelson," another said. "My momma thought we were gonna be first and last, but there six more after us." He laughed, and everyone around him laughed. He caught David's eye, and David felt as if there was finally someone here who might understand what he was going through.

More names, more faces, more questions.

"That be a right nice shirt you wearing."

"You come all this way from New York? How many days that take you?"

The voices blurred together, the questions became a string of beads, like a pop quiz at Briarwood. Just keep answering until there were no more questions.

David was overwhelmed by so many shades of black and brown. He was a marble stone on a gravel beach: smooth, pale and immovable against the surf and sand swirling around him. He'd never seen so many black faces so close, black hands, dark creases in dark faces. He stood tall and elegant in his button down shirt, rumpled as it was, against the ebb and flow of pale, cotton dresses faded to grey, trousers worn so often they were shiny at the knees and seat, cardboard belts and limp hats. Soft-soled shoes, little more than shapeless bags of leather with string laces. Bare feet.

The small crowd began to drift down the path to the shabby little church. "They ain't so many today on account of you come so late last night," Eddy whispered, "but just you wait till next Sunday. Whoo-ee'." He laughed. "Carol Ann Hammond come home from New York with her boy and her girl, well that just 'bout the most interestin' thing happened round here in ages."

"Vandenholm!"

"Huh?"

"Our name is Vandenholm," David snapped.

"Oh. Okay," Eddy shrugged. "Hey, I got a funny northern joke."

"Not on the Lord's day, young man." Rita interrupted.

"Yes'm," Eddy replied, but he glanced slyly up at David. "I'll tell you later," he mouthed.

More neighbors, those who didn't live right in the immediate cluster of houses by the river, came drifting in from the path that led away over the distant hill. More faces. More introductions. More smiles. More hands, more questions. There suddenly wasn't enough air.

Eddy took his arm. "You ok, Cousin? You gone all wobbly." He pulled David along with him toward the shadowed door of the church, moving people out of the way as he went. "They mean well," he whispered, "but they can be a powerful lot of yapping hounds, that's for certain."

David leaned gratefully against the wall, taking in a deep breath. His grandfather came out of the building and gave him a quick glance. "You all right, Grandson?"

David nodded. "Yes, Sir, better now." He just couldn't bring himself to call this man "Grandfather," or worse yet, "Grandpoppa."

Grandfather began to ring a small hand bell, practically no more than a school bell, and the tiny congregation turned and streamed toward them. He led the way inside the stuffy, but blissfully dim, interior.

Mother and Martina walked up to the front row of seats; David struggled to remain to the side of the aisle so that he could sit in the back, but Eddy pulled his arm again. "Family sits in front." Eddy had woken David early that morning and together with Grandfather they had arranged chairs in a few short rows, facing a small podium that looked as if it had been assembled out of boards left over from building some chicken coop somewhere. This morning David had wondered why there were so few chairs, now it looked like a full auditorium. Every eye was on him as he and Eddy walked down the aisle like a bridal couple.

David had been in crowds before. Over a million people had jostled and jammed each other along the Manhattan streets to see the helium balloons that Macy's sent up last Thanksgiving Day.

This was entirely different.

Grandfather stood up behind the podium and held up his arms. Silence fell. "Welcome brothers and sisters," he boomed. "As you know, our Carol Ann has returned to us, and brought her son and her daughter home with her."

Voices all around David called out "Praise be!" and "Yessir." He jumped with the suddenness of it.

"We rejoice in this day of celebration by opening our

service with the hymn, 'Come Ye Thankful People.'"

David reached for the hymnbook sitting between him and Eddy, but realized that no one else was.

"Come ye thankful people, come," Grandfather boomed out, a surprisingly pure sound from such a large man. The congregation around him burst into song and repeated the line, swaying and clapping.

"Raise the song of harvest home!" Grandfather sang. The congregation waited until he was done and then, once again, sang the line after him with their own rhythmic accompaniment.

"All is safely gathered in," Grandfather led, followed by the congregation.

In this staggered and awkward way they proceeded loudly through three verses about the joy of homecoming and safety. Did they not know the verse? Was this not in the book? This wasn't anything at all like services at the Dutch Reformed church at home.

David stared. Mother was clapping and swaying too. He joined in, making the sounds with his hands and his mouth, singing the tune, repeating the words, but not part of the congregation. A large, transparent bubble formed around him, walling him off from the rest of the world, like a sphere of unbreakable glass. He looked through its protective layer at the other people, and felt huge, ungainly, out of place. A large, white moth in the night. Mother and Martina receded into the distance, shrinking, merging with the crowd.

The heat pressed in, the air stagnant. Women waved small paper fans made of folded magazine pages, their brightly colored advertisements sliced into jumbled strips. Men quietly flapped their hats in front of their faces.

"Our next hymn will be "His Eye is on the Sparrow" from our book," Grandfather announced.

"One for the old folk then one for the young folk," Eddy

whispered, as the scant number of books were opened and shared between seatmates.

David hadn't a clue what Eddy meant.

The singing, dancing and clapping went on and on.

At last the sedate readings began. David began to relax. An elderly man limped slowly to the podium to read ponderously, word by word. "What man of you, having a hundred sheep, if he has lost one of them, does not leave the ninety-nine in the open country, and go after the one that is lost, until he finds it? And when he has found it, he lays it on his shoulders, rejoicing." He limped back to his seat.

Mother was called to read after that. The Parable of the Lost Son, of course. "I will set out and go back to my father and say to him: Father, I have sinned against heaven and against you. I am no longer worthy to be called your son."

Her stiff lips and flat tone indicated just what she thought of having to humble herself like this, but the verses held more truth than anyone in the congregation knew. Mother had sinned, and David had too. They had been starving, they had been desperate. It was time to repent. The words were appropriate. He was sure glad he wasn't up there next to her.

Mother finally sat down and Grandfather stood, raised his arms and waited for silence. A fly buzzed against the ceiling, and the swish of paper fans hushed through the heavy air. "Bring the fattened calf and kill it. Let's have a feast and celebrate," Grandfather called out. Beads of sweat slid down between David's shoulder blades. Grandfather's voice rolled over the congregation, rousing them. A chorus of "amen" and "yeah it so," followed his words.

"For lo, this child of mine was dead and now is alive again; she was lost and now is found."

"Amen, brother!"

"Yessir!"

Grandfather raised one finger. "Yet the Good Book

reminds us that there are two sons, and their father loves them equally but rewards them according to their repentance." Next to David, Aunt Rita snorted. "Even when there is cause for celebration, yet all of us are cleansed when we turn our eyes to the Lord Our Father."

"Say it, brother!" a voice called out.

"Amen," said another.

"And the Good Book tells us, 'Let not steadfast love and faithfulness forsake you; bind them around your neck; write them on the tablet of your heart. So you will find favor and good success in the sight of God and man.'"

"We celebrate today. We celebrate the safe return of our Carol Ann and her children, with the same joy in our hearts that we greet all of our loved ones with when they return home safe to us at day's end." Grandfather held his hand up, stopping the chorus of agreement. "In this way we are like unto our Savior Jesus, who celebrates each day with infinite love and joy in his heart, when any one of his sons or daughters returns home safe, whole, cleansed of the evil of the earthly world."

The sermon was endless. The congregation murmured and called out, the fans waved, the heat pressed down and sucked the breath from his lungs.

"Grandson, please come up and read from Corinthians for us,"

Eddy poked him. David sat up and looked around. That man, that Grandfather, was holding out his hand and Mother was nudging him. David nearly choked on his sudden horror. Speak? Here? In front of all these people? The glass bubble surrounding him shattered. How was he ever going to get through this? The walk to the podium took a hundred years. He looked down at the Bible before him, and put one shaking finger on the page. He should lean forward, clasp the edge of the podium and speak as if he was talking to each person one at a time. He had learned this in elocution class. Father had been able to do it wonderfully, even at a huge party, everyone in the room thought they had his undivided attention. "It's in the way you use your eyes," he'd told David. "Stand up straight, look a man in the eye, and he will be your friend and colleague for life."

The passage of text was a mile long. The words went endlessly on, from the page through his finger, out across his lips. He stared fixedly at the page, unable to raise his head even an inch, unable to quell the trembling of his arms. Afterward, he could only remember one line, "For we were all baptized by one Spirit so as to form one body—whether Jews or Gentiles, slave or free—and we were all given the one Spirit to drink."

At last, at last, the reading was over and David could stumble, his face scalding hot, to his seat.

"Nicely done." Mother smiled at him.

He turned away. Even looking at her made him furious. This was all her fault. He wanted that protective bubble of glass to come back, it had deserted him when he needed it the most.

At the end of the service they filed back down the aisle and out the door. David stepped out into the morning sunlight and sneezed. Grandfather, a few paced behind him, laughed, and then did the same when the light hit his face. David felt his own face freeze. Grandfather shook everyone's hand and chatted with each for a minute, exactly as if he were the Reverend Dr. Macloud at St. Nicholas, their church at home. Exactly as if he was a real minister.

The clustering, chattering gaggle surged around him once again.

"You sure is a good reader, them words come so smooth."

"You smart, just like your momma was, she was a girl."

"You such a good reader, you could be a teacher if you

wanted."

David could only stare across the chasm that separated him from these people.

The plates and bowls of food they had carried now sat in a lusciously tempting row on the table by the shadowed wall, waiting. David struggled to remember the last time he'd seen that much food in one place. He was about to take a plate when Eddy put a hand on his arm. "Family eat last," he said quietly. "We ain't nearly so hungry as some of them children nor old folk what got no work."

"I'm pretty hungry," David muttered, but he dutifully stepped back and took a look around, a more careful look, at the gaunt faces and covetous eyes. The children were clamoring to be fed, but waiting, straining forward like half-trained puppies. He'd had breakfast that morning—an egg, as well as bread and jam.

He had walked past a breadline with Father once, was it only just a year ago? "Some of those poor men haven't eaten for days," Father had said. "Maybe even longer. Thank God we're not lining up with them." At the time he'd wondered at the tone in Father's voice. Now he wondered if Father had already lost his job by that time, if their money was already nearly gone.

And still the gossiping galloped on and on. Eddy poked him in the arm. "What's the difference between snow men and snow women?" he asked.

David stared.

"Snow balls!" Eddy crowed. "It's a northern joke. We don't get too much snow round these parts, leastways not enough to build a snow man."

David smiled, bending the corners of his mouth.

At last it was his turn to take a biscuit, a plate of boiled green leaves leaking brown, greasy fluids, and a scant few forkfuls of some mysterious meat stew. He was hungrier after he'd eaten than before he started, if that could be possible, so he went back for more greens, in spite of himself, scraping the last few scraps out of the bowl.

At long last the neighbors who lived over the hill began to make plans to pack their dishes and head for their own homes. Once again David's hand was shaken until the rhythm became automatic, and the faces and names blurred into each other. Those who apparently lived in the cluster of shacks here at the river continued to chatter away at both he and Mother. Aunt Rita stood nearby, her arm protectively around the silent Martina. In the distance several men clustered around the carcass of the dead pickup truck, offering each other advice, taking turns leaning into the engine compartment, wrench in hand. At last the sound of tearing metal screeched across the clearing, a gasp of filthy soot erupted from the tailpipe, and the men cheered. The truck backed up, Willy at the helm, and carefully turned. Children and adults alike piled into the truck bed, carefully laying shabby blankets down before tucking their Sunday best clothes around them, and the pile of neighbors disappeared into the distance.

David went into the house—in the main room Grandfather was surrounded by men, all solemnly discussing some topic. He went into the kitchen, the women were clustered around the counter, laughing together. He went into the yard and found a scrabble of smaller children playing some game in the dirt. Eddy was at his elbow the whole time.

He went to the privy, there was someone there, and suddenly the world imploded. "I can't stand it any longer," he snarled. "I just can't live like this." The dirt, the poverty, the faces. The constant, intrusive questions, the dim interiors. "I have to get away from here!"

He leaped over the ditch that separated the yard from the path in front of the house and began to run, back down the path, back to the road, back to the known world.

He pounded down the road until his chest ached and his side twisted into stitches. His breath came in short gasps, wheezing in his throat, but at least it prevented him from crying. He wanted to go back to New York, back to Father. He did not want to spend any more time with this supposed grandfather, a complete stranger, a man he was supposed to respect because he was the local preacher. Who were they kidding? David wanted to reverse time and reclaim the life he'd once so blithely assumed would last forever. How could Mother do this to him? To Father? Everything was once so wonderful, and now it was complete devastation, smashed into shards that could never be melded together again. He'd been dreaming of going back to Briarwood, he'd been sure the money would eventually turn up, but even returning as a charity student wouldn't have been as bad as this—Mother had utterly ruined his chances of success at Briarwood. Even with the few colored faces along the walls of student photographs being singled out for honors, he could never survive as a colored student after having been the top of the heap. Never. His stomach tensed at the thought of what his life would be like if anyone discovered his secret.

No, not his secret. Mother's secret. He was white, by God.

He reached the road to Charlottesville which they had traveled only a short time ago, in a rusty truck whose driver clearly knew who lived at Sculley's Bend. He'd made them ride in the back and now David understood why. This is what life was like on the bottom of the ladder. You rode in the back. He paused at the ditch edging the road, confused for a minute about which direction to turn. It had been dark when they came in, but he was pretty sure they'd turned in from the left. The sun and shadows pointed the way, he turned to the right and resumed jogging, conserving his breath, it was a long way to Charlottesville.

From there it was another long distance to New York, in so many different ways. But he had a plan. Once he reached Charlottesville he would figure out how to jump a freight train like the hobos did. He wasn't sure if there were any hobos in Charlottesville, or where to find them, but he would solve that problem when he needed to. If that plan failed he could always work for the money to pay for a ticket home. It would take longer, but he was smart, and back in New York he'd run all those errands for the tailor on the corner. He knew how to work hard.

Of course, once in New York he'd have to start over again, camping rough until he saved enough to rent a room. He was certainly old enough to be on his own, and that would make Father proud. He pictured his Father lying so pale in his hospital bed, and thought of telling him how he'd left Mother and Martina behind. He would tell Father everything. Father wouldn't like it, but he would understand. He would approve. David smiled to himself. He refused to dwell on those days of hunger in the tiny apartment with Mother and Martina. He firmly put aside the thought of the meager pennies he'd made running errands in an arrangement that was more of a handout than a job.

He couldn't block out the memory of Martina, curled up on the floor of that squalid apartment, smeared with blood. The moment when he'd seen, and recognized, the severed fingertip in the puddle of blood on the floor came flooding back at unexpected moments of the day and night. He'd promised himself at that instant to always protect her, and here he was running away. He slowed to a walk. How could he leave Martina again? On the other hand, it couldn't be helped, even if he didn't much like it. He had to find work. Maybe he didn't need to go as far as New York, perhaps he should stay in Charlottesville. Yes, that was the smart thing to do. He could work, and yet he would still be near Martina. He started jogging again. For the first time in his life, he was taking independent action, he was standing up and acting like the man that Father would want him to be.

He didn't know how long he'd been moving, alternating between walking and jogging, but the sun was starting to slip below the tops of the trees when he heard the faintest sound of tires scrunching on the gravel in the distance. Ahead of him, a puff of dust drifted from around a turn and slowly grew larger. A sleek Chevy roadster approached rapidly. The car pulled even with David and stopped in a cloud of dust which settled on the shiny paintwork. The driver cranked down his window.

A man and a woman sat in the front seat; the woman leaning sideways across the man at the wheel to peer out at David. She was dainty and pale, with brown hair and a pink nose, as if she had been sneezing. She wore a boxy hat at such an angle David wondered why it didn't slide right off her head. The man was large, with red hair and sharp blue eyes. A hare lip twisted his mouth. When he spoke, his speech was lisping and high pitched, almost girlish. David tried not to stare. "Where you going to, son?" the man asked, "Can we give you a lift?"

"Charlottesville," David answered. "About how far is it?"

"Oh honey," the woman said, flapping a hand limply toward the road in front of her, "ya'll must be new round here—why Charlottesville is purely in the other direction."

David stared at her, stunned. "The other direction? I thought I was heading south?"

The man shook his head. "Pretty much due west, son."

David felt as if his muscles were turning to water. He couldn't keep moving like this. He'd have to turn around and start all over, and the daylight was nearly gone. He'd never get to Charlottesville today, he'd have to sleep outside with no blankets and no food.

The man scrutinized David intently. "You'd be Carol Ann Hammond's boy, then, ain't you?"

"Yes, I am," David answered. He narrowed his eyes. It would appear that news traveled fast in this community.

"Round these parts, we usually say 'Sir' when we're speaking to someone." The man didn't say "someone white" or "someone better," but they both knew what he meant. "I'm Marcus McKinley, I own most of the orchards round about here."

"Pleased to meet you. I'm David Vandenholm."

Silence stretched between them, and then the man laughed, short and sharp. "You are your mother's son, that's for damn sure. We rightly did miss her spunk when she took herself off to New York City." The woman in the passenger seat twitched, and squinted intently at the man. He slapped a hand on the window frame. "Jump on the back and hang on to the spare, we'll take you as far as the turn for the Bend, you can walk home from there. Tomorrow, you report to the orchard manager for work, tell him I sent you. Your cousin Eddy'll show you what to do."

"Are you offering me a job?" David asked, puzzled.

"Offering, that's a good one." The man chuckled. "Round these parts, we look out for our own," he said. "Ain't no call for Carol Ann's son to be going off to Charlottesville when there's apples right here what need spraying. And boy," he lisped at David, "don't be fooled by our friendly manner out here in farm country. Ain't no work to be had in Charlottesville, and that's a fact." It sounded like a threat.

David admitted defeat, he knew what he had to do. Running away had been a child's dream, short lived as it was. "Thank you," he said. "That would be extremely generous of you," he paused, then choked out a reluctant "Sir." After all, the man was his boss now, it had nothing to do with race or social standing. Anyway, it was only temporary, until he could manage to get back to New York, and get back to Briarwood.

Marcus McKinley indicated the passenger with a jerk of his chin. "By the by, this here's Mrs. McKinley, you'll be seeing her round and about." The woman looked up attentively. She angled her head to slide a small smile at David. Her eyelashes fluttered and the tip of her tongue showed pink against her lower lip. David was suddenly aware of how dirty and sweaty he had become on the old road. He nodded once. "Ma'am," he said, to be polite, then walked to the back to the car, climbed onto the trunk support and clung to the straps of the spare tire.

The car rumbled along the dusty road unwinding the route he had just traveled. If only his life could roll backwards just as quickly, just as directly, with nothing more than a cloud of dust to mark his passing.

CHAPTER 20

CAROL ANN

The torpid sludge that was life in Sculley's Bend seeped up from the ground and sucked at Carol Ann with every step she took. She dragged herself from the bed, where she didn't sleep, to the table, where she didn't eat, to the yard, where Martina and Rita were already up and working.

Rita lifted a huge glob of long strings out of the pot, studied it and lowered it back down slowly. Carol Ann identified the acrid fumes as soon as they hit her—sheep's wool and aniline dye. Rita was coloring yarn for her endless knitting. Here in the gray ooze of Sculley's Bend, it took sweat and effort to bring color into life. The air was scented with boiling dye and old grease from years of fat back pork. The call of orioles in the trees mingled with the buzz of bluebottle flies circling the scraps of apple still on the dirty plate in front of Martina.

Carol Ann had been so worried about David when he'd run off that night, and now that he was back and working in the McKinley's orchards, she still worried about him. Every day he came home and spent more and more time to himself, disappearing over the hill to some hidden corner of the field or around the bend in the river.

"Don't worry about the boy, he just needs some time to himself," Poppa said. But she couldn't help it, she worried.

Throughout the long, hot nights, all during the endless chores, part of her mind watched Martina, looking for signs that she would mellow and soften in the warm southern sun, part of her mind looped endlessly over what to do about David.

This morning the yard was quiet.

"Where is Poppa?" She called out to Rita, who was adding more wood to the stove underneath the huge pot of simmering yarn. She still had his anger to confront, and he would not be as easily won over as Rita.

"He's over t' the school."

"School? What school?"

"Poppa teaches school now. In the church, actually. About a dozen little ones from here in the Bend and round abouts. My Eddy would like to go, but he's got to work."

"Poppa teaches school? He's almost seventy!"

"When the Crash come, even before that really, the Kintersville Board of Education run out of money to gas the bus, so the Bend children gotta walk."

"It's more than five miles!"

"Yep, that so. The bigger kids can do it not much problem, but the little ones, they can't, so they were staying home. Why Portya Baylor's baby girl is barely gone six. No one to raise them up or teach them their letters, so Poppa took over and started the school. The big kids stay now too, and a few others what's closer to here than town. Board of Ed don't seem to care."

"I can't believe Kintersville is so poor it can't run the bus for its children." Carol Ann shook her head. "Times have sure gotten hard all over."

"Yeah, well, harder for some than for others." Rita snapped. She stirred the pot of dye and yarn with vicious strength. Acrid fumes drifted across the yard.

She had always been like this: quick to love, and just as quick to anger. Carol Ann waited without speaking. Her sister would finish without prompting.

"Damn Board of Ed's got enough money for the white school bus. How come it's always us what run out of gas money first?" Rita slammed back to the table and banged herself onto the bench. "Not to mention everything else. Black loans come due first. Black jobs get cut first. Even the Black speakeasy in Charlottesville gets raided before them revenuers even think to get going after the whites. Poppa always talks about how it's gonna be better one day. How the NAACP is sending our boys to law school and the coloreds finally going to come into their own. Huh!" She shook her head sharply. "I can't ever imagine how anyone could think whites would let blacks get on."

She gave a wriggle, like a duck shaking off water. She angled a sly look at Carol Ann. "I loved it when your letters came—all those exciting things going on! You were so generous with the money you sent."

Carol Ann waited, knowing more was coming.

"What's it like?" Her face lit up and she leaned forward, her eyes locked on Carol Ann. "What's it like on the other side for a change?"

Carol Ann drummed her fingers on the table as she thought. She wasn't sure she could explain it. At last she said, "You remember what that Frankie Wahl used to say about Bend girls?"

"Screw the pretty ones and beat the ugly ones with a stick." Rita made a spitting motion. "I'd bet most girls would rather'd got beat."

"Did he bother you too?"

"After you left, yeah, he used to sneak around me and try to make trouble." She spit again. "Didn't get far, the jackass, but carried on like that till my Michael come. But forget him, keep on telling."

"There was this one fellow named Wethersby Leffington-

Squires. Quite the name, isn't it? What were his parents thinking?"

"—heard worse," Rita said, then laughed as well. "Nope, don't guess I have. What a terrible thing to do to a baby!" She shook her head. "Terrible, terrible. So tell me about him."

"So Wethersby, he was so handsome, and quite taken with himself, let me tell you. He'd been sniffing around all the single girls, ever so nicely, such a gentleman. He used to kiss the back of my hand." She held out her hand like a duchess. "But wherever we were, the group of my friends, whenever we went out to dinner or a movie show, he'd always have his eye on the colored girls."

Rita frowned. "I don't like the sound of that, no sir."

"He told the other fellows they were good in bed. Cheaper and cleaner than a hooker, safer than a white girl cause they don't expect to marry you. Of course the fellows, they told us, and we all had a fine laugh." Carol Ann twisted her lips in humiliation at the memory, at her compliance. "I didn't want it to bother me. I tried to forget about it the way any other white girl would, but it got stuck in my head and wouldn't leave me alone. I felt it behind my eyeballs, every time I saw him." She rubbed her finger across the bridge of her nose. "It kept growing, and growing, until planning to teach him a lesson was all up inside me."

"Jus' so." Rita chorused, filling in the blank spaces as if she were in church.

"It was sheer luck, what finally happened," Carol Ann said. "I was at the grandest ball, oh Sister, I wish you could have seen the gowns, and the band, and the huge crystal chandelier. It was all so," she tasted the word, "luscious."

Rita sighed.

"I was dancing with a nice older man, this was before I met Peter, of course. He mentioned he was a senior partner at this famous, snooty law firm, which turns out to be the same firm Wethersby works at. Practically his boss, this man was. I didn't hesitate a minute, and said that Wethersby must be an excellent attorney if such a prestigious firm was willing to overlook his questionable hobbies. That's all I said, just 'questionable hobbies'. He never asked for proof, didn't doubt me for a minute. A woman of my standing clearly would not stoop to deceit. They fired him the next day. "Carol Ann smiled slyly.

Rita grinned back at her.

"I know it was abusive, I know it was wrong," Carol Ann said, "but I can't tell you how satisfactory it was, all that power on my side for a change. Getting even for all the Frankie Wahl's in the world." She paused to savor the memory. "Word got out and people laughed about it for a while, then it was all forgotten. We never did see much of poor Wethersby Leffington-Squires after that, he moved to Albany or Boston, I think."

"That's good," Rita said. "That's nice."

"Revenge by proxy," Carol Ann said.

They sat still for a minute, with only the quiet crackling of wood in the stove and the bubbling of liquid in the big kettle. Sun flowed through the trees and bounced off the curves of the pots. Martina sneezed, but did not otherwise move. Carol Ann reached out and wiped Martina's nose with a lace-edged handkerchief.

The "V" in the monogram caught her eye and stopped up her throat. V for Vandenholm, was that still her name, now that she'd signed those annulment papers? Was this still her handkerchief, now?

Rita reached out for the handkerchief and studied the fine lace edge, the sheer fabric, the silk stitching of the monogrammed letters. "Pretty." She rubbed the hem between her fingers. "Pretty," she repeated. She glanced at Carol Ann from lowered eyes.

Carol Ann raised one eyebrow and half-smiled. "Go ahead and ask your question, Sister."

"Why'd you come home for all of a sudden? It's fine to have you here, 'course," she tacked on hastily.

Carol Ann pushed her cup away from her and dropped her head into her arms on the table, her failures too heavy to support any longer. Her eyes burned and she teetered on the edge of tears, but couldn't fall over into the relief of weeping. She longed to go back to bed and sleep for a hundred years. A hundred thousand years.

She felt an arm around her shoulders and a hand stroking her hair. "It's ok, you lay yo' burden down, cause you safe to home now," Rita said. "You safe to home."

The words trickled like syrup through her, turned into meaning, and a dark and tight knot inside her broke apart. The sobs erupted then, a volcano of blistering pain. Wails ripping her throat. She was a huge, wounded beast in agony. She struggled in panic out from under Rita's arm and scrambled over the bench. She had to get this beast away from Martina. This pain, this noise, this wounded animal would frighten her little girl, she couldn't let that happen! She raced to the other side of the yard and collapsed in a heap under the big maple. Soft arms circled her once more as Rita took her back into sheltering warmth.

She sobbed until there was nothing left inside her. She sobbed beyond that, until she was so exhausted she couldn't inhale deeply enough to cry any longer. She listened to her breathing, gasping, slowing. She slept, or perhaps she merely dozed. When she woke Rita was still holding her, rocking her, humming softly, exactly as Momma would have done. She was vaguely aware that Martina had put her head down on the table across the yard, but wasn't crying or panicking.

"I left New York because I made a terrible, terrible mistake, and there was no way to fix it. I couldn't go back and undo the damage. I couldn't trust myself to take care of my babies, I couldn't trust myself to take care of Peter. No matter what I thought of doing, how would I know if that was the right thing to do? I came home because it was the only thing I knew for sure wasn't wrong."

"What mistake was so terrible, *cherie*?"

Martina was, um, almost hurt by this man I left her alone with," she whispered quickly. "She might have been, but she fought back. But I left her alone with him. I did that." She stuttered to a halt. She wrapped her arms tightly around herself and tried to remain composed enough to tell the dreadful tale.

"The poor little thing. How awful, awful for you. I were a mite curious what it was, but I never did think it was something like that."

Carol Ann inhaled, then told Rita the story of the night of terror and guilt. "When I came back," she continued, "he was gone and Martina was alone, curled up in a corner. There was blood everywhere."

"Oh Lord, how horrible for you. And for her. I hope you hunted him down and chopped his pecker off at the root." Rita looked like she meant it.

"Oh Sister, it was an endless nightmare and I couldn't wake up. I couldn't figure out what had happened. I kept telling myself I should wait to see Richard, to hear his side of the story, but I didn't want to. I wouldn't have believed him anyway. I kept seeing this image of him on top of her, and I couldn't even begin to imagine kissing him, or making love to him, or marrying him. If Peter—" She inhaled. "Died." A shudder shook her. "The worst part is, I believe he planned the whole thing from the first time he saw her, and I never saw it. What was a man his age doing passing time in a children's playground?" Carol Ann took another shuddering breath. "I should have been paying more attention, but I wanted him to be interested in me, I wanted tickets to the ballet and dinner out in swanky restaurants." She shut her eyes and put her head in her hands, reliving the worst night of her life. "It was all about what I wanted." She started to shiver, tremors running up her spine. "David tried to warn me, but I told him to be quiet." A stray sob escaped her. "He has every right to hate me."

Rita put her hand over Carol Ann's and squeezed gently. Carol Ann was surprised her skin was still so much lighter than Rita's; she felt as if the transformation she had undergone in New York those many years ago had completely reverted as soon as she'd arrived back in Sculley's Bend. "You did right, sugar. Whatever else, you trust that. You here now, where there plenty of family and plenty of help. Besides, been downright quiet here these last years since my Michael and my Sarah got the influenza and passed. Some excitement'd be good for all of us." Her tone rang with cheer, but her eyes shone with tears.

"Oh Rita, how terrible it must have been for you. No one should have to bury a child, ever. And Michael at the same time." Their paths had been so parallel, both losing husbands, and children as well, in a way. "How did you do it? How did you ever survive such torture?"

Rita wiped her eyes with the back of her hand. "You do what you got to. You pick up one foot and put it down in front of the other. Eddy was jus' five at the time, he needed me. When a baby need you, it mean you got to lock the pain away 'til you can have time to feel it. After a while it stop hurting so much and start being just sad, leastwise most of the time."

She pressed Carol Ann with a quick hug and jumped to her feet. "Come on, that coffee gonna be something strong by now. Let's get us a cup before it's nothing but char in the pot."

Carol Ann laughed weakly. "Oh heavens, Sister, that's your answer to everything, a cup of hot and black. Just like Momma."

"Well, it can't hurt, and it give the hands a thing to do. I know, I know," she held up her hand, palm out, to stop Carol Ann from speaking. "Momma used to say that too, but it's true nonetheless."

Carol Ann took her cup of coffee and returned to the table where Martina still sat, head down, motionless. She picked up one of her daughter's flaccid hands and strummed her fingers gently down her daughter's arm. How Martina used to love that. Carol Ann tried to tell herself there was at least a softening, a relaxation in response to her touch, but she was probably fooling herself.

CHAPTER 21

MARTINA

Sparrow?

Falling sparrow?

No lines here. No soldiers here. There are warm ones here.

Am I a sparrow?

Where are the circles?

Where is the general with the big hands sleeping now?

CHAPTER 22

DAVID

David paused to rub the muscles in the backs of his arms. He had been spraying pesticide for so long they burned from exertion, and blisters pebbled both hands. Short breaks did nothing to relieve the pain at all, they were sufficient only to let him concentrate on it.

The McKinley orchard stretched in endless rows. With the crash of the economy, David had been told, Marcus McKinley had been able to buy out several of the smaller farms surrounding his, and consolidate the properties. He must have nearly seven hundred acres, people figured, and more than enough cheap field hands and tenant farmers to work it. Now David was part of that bottom rung work force. Marcus McKinley owned all the land bordering Sculley's Bend, which added up to more apple trees than David had ever seen before, or ever wanted to see again.

He leaned his weight against the handle of the pressure pump in the steel canister, then lifted the hose over his head. Squirrels chattered as they jumped from one bough to the next, and insects hummed gently in the distance. The arc of drifting spray floated in and through the curves and contours of the twisted branches of the fruit trees. Sunlight glittered on the chemical drops, throwing a rainbow into magnificent prominence above him.

He hated it all. The pesticide stank. Under his feet, the thick clumps of weedy grass and the uneven ground attempted to throw him off his balance, while fallen sticks poked up into his trouser legs and gouged his skin. One day it had rained, and he was outside the whole time, his clothes chafing everywhere his body moved, mud splattering in his face and rain spilling down the back of his neck. Other than that day, the sun shone relentlessly in the broad, blue sky, burning every inch of exposed skin, which had peeled once and was now burning again. He carted manure to fertilize the worked-out hillsides, repaired six foot high barbed wire strands to keep the marauding deer at bay, and ripped out old trees with hand-wound winches, then cut them into firewood and fence rails. All this for thirty cents a day.

And then there were the mosquitoes. They bit and worried at the oozing scratches on his face and legs, and at the burned and chafed patches on the back of his neck. He rubbed himself faithfully each morning with handfuls of wild verbena leaves, a trick Eddy had shown him. The smell kept the bugs away for a while, until the sweat washed the herbs from his skin. But even when they weren't biting they were hovering, they buzzed and whined in a never-ending drone, so close to him he started to think they had actually drilled inside his skull. A song of insanity and rage composed specifically for him, with gnats singing descant and lazy bottle flies in the manure taking up the baritone harmony line.

"In the fall," Eddy told him, "the yellow-jackets, they're the worst. They settle onto the rotten ground apples, and they get drunk and ornery."

Delightful. One more thing to look forward to.

He hated the birds most of all, happily flying free and making excessive noise about it. Laughing at him from the treetops because he was stuck here on the ground. Trapped. Crawling around in the dirt like an earthworm. What would his friends at Briarwood say if they could see him now? Would they even still be his friends if they knew who he was? Over and over he imagined a scene with Chad—he could imagine the look on his face quite clearly, the expression of amusement and pity, of arrogance and condescension—as he, too, laughed at David. David knotted his blistered hands around the chemical sprayer and pumped the crossbar up and down.

"You gonna rip that handle right off," Eddy said quietly, walking up next to him. "You gonna pump that thing so hard, you'll be shootin' youself backwards when you open her up."

David glared at his cousin. He flexed the raw meat his hands had become and winced. How had he been brought so low? This mindless sweat and manual labor was beneath him, by God.

But he was a Vandenholm. He was going to come though this trial, he would rise above it. One day he would look back on this and laugh. He would get his feet under him, he would surround himself with beautiful women, dripping with diamonds. He would take them to the opera, to the ballet, spoiling them with special events and lavish gifts.

"Hey Cousin, you gonna keep staring at nothing or you gonna start spraying again?"

With a sour grimace at Eddy, David yanked on the hose end of the sprayer and held it up high among the branches of the next apple tree in the row. Eddy lifted the heavy iron rod to hold the hose in position, and opened the valve. A curtain of insecticide filtered down, splattering a sheen of milk white foam on the round leaves. David jerked the hose down and marched toward the next tree without waiting for Eddy to catch up.

"Don't you ever get shut a being angry?" Eddy asked mildly. "Seems to me a fire hot as all that oughtta just burn itself right out, soon or later."

"What's it to you if it does or it doesn't?" David muttered.

"Ain't nothing to me one way or t'other," Eddy said, and hauled the wagon loaded with chemical tanks behind him, as David walked away with the sprayer. The donkeys were being used to haul trees for new fencing today. "Just being friendly, is all." He stopped, slid the leather strap off one shoulder and adjusted the cotton padding underneath the harness. His dark brown skin was chafed into crimson welts across his chest. David looked away while Eddy pushed the strap back and lifted the steadying rod into place. David raised the hose nozzle into the next tree and triggered the rush of spray across the ripening fruit.

He should give Eddy a break from pulling the heavy wagon, but he'd be damned if he was going to let this place win. He might be stuck here, but he would run off again before he allowed himself be shackled into a harness to pull a cart through the field like a gelding. He looked at the patient resolve of Eddy's square jaw and the bunched muscles under the sweaty skin. Worse than a common farm animal. Worse than one of the donkeys. David wrenched the hose and canister, dragging them to the next tree.

"I don't see how you can stand it here," David said. "I don't understand why you put up with this life. You could move north, you could head up to New York where Negroes aren't treated like this."

"Never thought about it much," Eddy said. "Got me an uncle in Chicago, oh! I guess you got one too," he swiveled around and grinned David. "Yeah, Uncle Seaver, he yo' Momma's and my Momma's brother, the one between 'em in age."

"Hnn," David grunted. One more thing he hadn't known. All the years of lies, how Mother must have laughed at his ignorance, not telling him about herself, her other family. Not even her real name. Cousins, aunts, uncles, a grandfather, all holding fast to a wealth of information, and relishing their many chances to flaunt it before him. Was Mother keeping even more secrets from him? Did he actually have a huge family scattered around the country?

Eddy was still babbling. "Anyways, Uncle Seaver, he says, one Saturday night uptown, you ain't never want to be white." He stuck out a brown arm, "not like I'd ever have a choice, not like Uncle Seaver and yo' Momma."

"There's more to a city than nightclubs and jazz halls," David said. "Not that your Uncle Seaver would know about that." David pumped the sprayer handle. "There are libraries, stores and restaurants. Concerts. Cars. Skyscrapers." He paused. "Things are different. They," he struggled to find the right word and failed. "Permanent," he said eventually. "Things in the city are built to last. They're solid and steady. Everything doesn't move around all the time, like this." He waved his arm at the trees, their thousands of leaves chattering and dancing, the grasses in the distance flowing and bending in the breeze. "Everything here moves and moves, and it's all so small." He shuddered. "Like the whole place is made out of little mice."

"Little mice! That's right funny, that is." Eddy laughed, his face gleaming. "You funny to be around. Little mice! But like as may be, I don't mind. Anyways, ain't no jobs in New York nor Chicago, and I got me this job right here. Momma and Grandpoppa, they need me."

David fumed. This wasn't being needed, this was being trapped inside a life that didn't fit him. This was being used.

The wind gusted in a new direction and David inhaled a lungful of insecticide. He knew from experience it would make his fingers tingle for the rest of the day. This place and everything in it was toxic in one way or another.

CHAPTER 23

CAROL ANN

The days blurred into each other. Two weeks. Or was it three? Life would continue on forever, exactly like this until she was old and dead. Until Peter was as well. Yesterday she had refused to speak to anyone and had gotten out of bed only to visit the outhouse. Today, she decided as she tugged at the thin sheet, she would do the same.

"Oh no, you most certainly will not," declared Rita. "You will get your behind outta bed this minute. You will put on clean clothes and you will make your bed. Then you will come out to the yard and eat some."

Carol Ann rolled over and faced the wall.

Rita's hand connected with the sound of a small thunderclap. Carol Ann's buttock stung from the force of the blow.

"Now I said, you just get yourself outta that bed." Rita had never sounded so ferocious. "You got a daughter what needs to eat, and you got a son what needs you to set a good example. After that, them onions down by the back fence gettin' mighty thick, time to split them up."

The bedroom door slammed open and shut.

When Carol Ann arrived in the yard, Rita was chopping carrots with Martina cuddled next to her, shelling peas with the delicacy of a fine artist. Sunlight bounced off the multi-colored curls and the delicate planes of their faces. Carol Ann walked to the stove to pour herself a cup of bitter chicory. Canning jars gleamed as they steamed clean in a large kettle.

"I hate splitting onions," she said.

"Yep, you always did. But it's what need doing," Rita replied.

"Why are there so many onions?"

Rita put her hands on her hips and affected Momma's Creole accent. "I put zem in cause your Poppa, *bien sur,* he like zem, and zey grow like that because God, *le bon Dieu,* He like zem."

Carol Ann pushed a smile at the imitation. "I do the accent better, but you sure have the hip wiggle down."

Rita laughed, and the sound of it carried the echo of many memories, much laughter, flowing between them with the years. A touch of warmth. Carol Ann finished her chicory and led Martina out to the muddy back garden. "I can't believe I'm back here doing this again," she muttered. Along the way, she picked up a short stick and snapped the end to make a sharp edge.

On her knees among the rows of onions, she jammed the stick into the first cluster, then gouged her fingers into the warm earth, following the path of the stick. She found the thin, white bulbs of the onion sets and yanked them out of the ground with such force the cluster sprang away from her hand and the tiny bulbs separated, the stringy grass tops falling over in a tangle. "Damn, damn, damn!" Now the stupid things would take even longer to replant. Next to her Martina began to breathe heavily, frightened, causing Carol Ann to halt. What had she been thinking, indulging in a tantrum like that in front of Martina? She slowed down, reaching for the onions more gently.

She took the clumps of dirt in her hands and showed

Martina how to break the onions apart. "The size of Poppa's hand," she said, and held out a sample. "When the sprouts and flowers grow in the spring, they eat from the fat winter bulbs. In the summer, after they're all done flowering, these skinny roots can be separated." How many years ago had she first received those instructions? Who had taught her? She couldn't remember. Had it been Momma? One of the older children? Maybe Seaver, with his sharp looks and quick jokes, or Leon, long dead on a battlefield in France. Or even Rita, beautiful, smart, funny Rita, still knitting sweaters in the house she'd grown up in.

Martina didn't say anything, but carefully broke off a clump precisely the right size. She hadn't spoken since she'd been attacked, but she was moving again, and eating a little, and there was clearly a softening, a loosening in her that Carol Ann hoped was a sign of healing.

"Very good, honey," Carol said. "Put the clumps here, we're going to dig them back in the ground when we're done." She showed Martina where to lay down the clusters.

So many things were different, but so much was still the same. The tang of onions, clay and earthworms in the garden. The mumble of the creek in the distance and the rustle of pine trees along the road. The slick feel of her sweat as she wiped beads of moisture off her face. These things would never change, she knew, and clung for a minute to the thought that this wasn't so bad, perhaps, after all. Looking back on her life over the months since Before the Accident, when Peter had been by her side, she could honestly admit there were worse things than standing still. She stood up and bit the spade into the dirt, preparing a new home for the split onion sets.

She'd always called this cluster of shacks at the end of the rutted path her home, but it was just a word. Wasn't home where she had lived with Peter for so many happy years? Where her children had been born, where her life had taken root, even if the seed had first sprouted here? The question preoccupied her throughout the morning as she and Martina moved slowly along the row of onions in the warm corner of the garden, and hovered in her mind all afternoon.

Periodically she looked down the rows of vegetables and sighed. So much work to be done, hour after hour, day after day. By the time they trudged back to the house at the close of the afternoon, they were dirty and tired. Carol Ann was comfortably satisfied with the work of the day, but looking forward to stopping for the evening. "I done the onions," she called out, as she and Martina came into the yard. "And weeded the tomatoes and runners."

There was no answer. Glass jars filled with carrots and peas glowed a pattern of jewel colors in the late afternoon sun. The pots on the stove sat clean and empty, except for one in which a meager slab of salt pork lay soaking in water. Carol Ann grimaced. Fat back wasn't bad, although it was slimy on the tongue, but salt pork was so awful it didn't matter that there wasn't much of it to share. Times were hard indeed if Rita was planning salt pork twice in the same week. Carol Ann seated Martina at the table with beans to snap, wishing she could sit with her feet up, a cool drink at her side, and soothing cream to rub into her hands. But there was more to be done, of course. She retrieved the flour canister from the pantry and the yeast sponge from the windowsill and beat together a batch of biscuits to take down the salt of the meat. Voices echoed nearby, just as she slid the finished biscuits out of the temperamental wood oven.

"Well hi y'all." Rita came around the corner of the house. "Bread smells good. Your biscuits, they always were the best. By the by, we got us a few more sitting down to supper."

Three children trailed behind her, so ragged and dirty it was nearly impossible to tell if they were girls or boys. The youngest and the oldest, or at least the shortest and the tallest, kept their eyes on the ground, while the middle one glared out at the world from beneath a solid mass of grimy curls. He, or she, looked to be about eight.

"This here's Custis," Rita stroked the head of the middle child. "Here's Dorrie, and this Geraldine, but we call her Cupcake." Rita reached out and touched each head in turn. "They'm Portya Baylor's kids. She's late back from work tonight, so best we put on extra greens."

"She gettin' drunk and turnin' tricks," Custis said.

Carol Ann blinked.

"Ain't gotta feed us, we got vittles t'home," the boy declared. "We can fend for our own selves." He put his arm around Cupcake, who lifted a hollow-cheeked face to her older brother in sheer hero worship. She was starving, but she would die before she would betray her brother's pride. Dorrie, the older sister, hovered nearby, her fists clenched in silent misery.

Rita pretended she hadn't heard. "Y'all head on out to the pump and wash up, you babies. Reverend come home any minute now, and supper be on the table right behind him." She handed Dorrie a towel and gently shoved her and Cupcake toward the pump.

Custis stayed put and looked his mutiny out of large, dark eyes and square-set shoulders. He clearly wanted to stay; his eye kept straying to the pot on the stove. He could be convinced with the right words, but Carol Ann remembered how strongly the need for independence tore you in half. She recognized her own rage and frustration in his stiff back and out-thrust chin. It was hard to be so powerless in a world full of traps waiting to bring you low. If David had been like this she could have talked to him. Perhaps she might have told him her secret and not sprung it on him the way she had, but David had never been powerless. He had always been one of the powerful, part of what she had been hiding from. Yes, she thought, I was afraid of my own son.

"You know," she said, sitting on the bench at eye level with the children, but talking as if to Rita, "Since David's working all day, I miss him an awful lot. It will sure be nice to have a few other children around in his place until he gets home."

"You don' mean that, you jus' saying it," Custis said, but he hesitated in his refusal of the meal, which smelled enticing in the steam from the stove. Even salt pork was delightful when you were hungry enough.

"I do mean it," Carol Ann said. "A house is so quiet without babies around."

"I was thinking that very same thing myself when I laid eyes on these three as I was coming on." Rita took the towel back from Dorrie as the two girls returned, and handed her a wooden spoon in its place.

Carol Ann followed her lead and acted as if the decision had already been made. She busied herself with cleaning the table and laying out plates and cups, keeping Dorrie and Cupcake busy and giggling, while Rita occupied Custis with taking down and winding the straggling skeins of yarn from the clothesline.

The sun was well set when more footsteps rounded the house.

"This here's your boy coming now, then?" Dorrie asked.

Eddy and David came up from the woods, walking together, Eddy smiling at the pleasure of an evening to relax, David nearly staggering, shoulders rounded and pace slow. She may have forgotten what it was like to work from sunup to sundown, but David had never known. She wanted to wrap her arms around him and protect him, but he was so far out of her reach. She bit down hard on her lip to trap the words, the pain, inside. He pointedly looked away from her and she felt as if the temperature had dropped ten degrees. How long, she wondered, would this winter chill last?

The children looked up as the older boys entered, and Cupcake flung herself at Eddy's legs. With a laugh, he scooped her up and held her upside down, blowing raspberries against her neck. Dorrie crept up for her own hug, and even Custis hovered closer to the merriment and Eddy's charm.

As if a dinner bell had rung, the children started to orbit the table, waiting for the food to be set out. Carol Ann turned Martina to face straight forward.

"What wrong with her?" Cupcake asked. "She drunk?"

"No, of course not," Carol Ann said, startled. "That's my daughter, Martina. She has something wrong with her brain."

"She look like she drunk," Cupcake said. She studied Martina intently. "She look like she one drunk and sad nigger, 'cept she a white girl."

"Hush, Cupcake," Dorrie commanded. "You being some rude now."

"Well that what Miz Agnes say when Momma look like that," the little girl muttered.

"Well it still rude," Dorrie answered. "She might hear you. 'Sides, I guess she ain't rightly white, is she?" She glanced quizzically at Carol Ann for confirmation.

"It's all right," Carol Ann interrupted. "It's rude but it's true—she does look drunk and sad, but she's not, it's her bad brain. And she does look white, doesn't she?" It felt odd to be talking so openly about drinking and whoring, about skin color, about Martina's problems. She was so used to hiding her problems, and her secret, from her society friends. Here she could say or do anything at all; it would make no difference. In a way, this was a freedom of its own kind, with her own kind.

She glanced at David, who looked as if he would explode from the anger and misery he was holding inside. She wished she could do something, say something, but she couldn't. It was coming, she could tell, and her skin prickled with tension.

David's fury would erupt, and God only knew when.

Eddy jumped over to her side. "I got that plate for you, Aunt Carol Ann," he said, relieving her of the biscuits. He broke off a tiny piece as he ferried them to the table, and she swatted his backside with her dishtowel but he just grinned. David's glare caught her and she stopped.

"Hey there y'all," Poppa called out, startling them. "Looks like we have some folks visiting — how nice! I was thinking to myself on the way home, a hot meal with kin and neighbors would be a fine thing tonight." He beamed at the children, but Carol Ann noticed that he didn't even look at her. Some things never changed. Poppa could forgive in church, but not in the kitchen. If only he and David could see how much they resembled each other, and not just in their height and strong build.

"Custis, you've been reading so well, I think you should fetch the Bible and read the blessing tonight," Poppa said.

A shy smile broke out through Custis's clouds, and the dinner decision was put to rest at last. Custis, no longer the prideful and protective brother, but simply an eight year old boy once more under the magic of a compliment and reward, shot off to the other room on Poppa's heels, presumably in search of the Bible. "Oh no you don't, young sir," Poppa said, "No one touches The Good Book with dirty hands. You know where the pump is."

Custis grabbed the soap and towel and darted away, while the smaller girls proudly held out their already clean hands. Everyone took seats, and Custis, now clean and damp, stumbled through the intractable language of the 45th Psalm, which concerned the virtues of honorable women and daughters. Of course. Carol Ann was tempted to stand up and walk away, it had been too long a day to put up with even one more slap like this.

"Amen," they chorused.

"Excellent work, young man," Poppa said.

Custis glowed.

Cupcake was still staring at Martina. "How come she don't talk none?"

"I suppose she doesn't want to talk right now." Carol Ann hoped Martina would start again soon. She hoped David would as well.

Cupcake nodded with the wisdom of six years. "Yep, drunk and sad, poor ole nigger white gal."

"Young lady," Poppa snapped, "we do not use language like that at this table or anywhere else."

Cupcake looked puzzled, but clearly knew enough respond with a quick, "Yassir."

Custis leaned closer to Carol Ann. "Does your boy got a bad brain too?"

"Oh no, he's as smart and shrewd as you are," she told him. At the other end of the table, the bench squeaked as David fidgeted.

"Then why don't he talk none?"

"I suppose he doesn't feel like it either."

"What that mean, shrood?"

"Shrewd. It means you can figure out what people are really up to, and when they're lying. It means knowing how to take care of yourself, when you have to."

"Shrood. That's a good word, I like it." Custis leaned casually against the table and kept his eyes straight on her for only a moment before politely looking away.

David leaned toward Eddy and whispered something through tight lips. Eddy looked startled, then laughed quietly. It might have been at Custis's expense, but even David was learning to fit in.

Rita and Dorrie huddled at the other end of the table, heads close, nodding together over a shared bit of story. The night was warm, the darkness blanketed the trees, and the air was scented with the perfumes of childhood summers. Carol Ann discovered she was glad the children had stayed. If only in this one way, Sculley's Bend was better than New York. Portya Baylor, off to Kintersville getting drunk, escaping on her own path out of the Bend, knew her children would be in good hands. Perhaps better than when she was around, Carol Ann thought, looking at their gaunt faces, as they sopped the last of the juice from their plates with bits of biscuit.

Nostalgia overtook her. So many nights had finished just like this, when she'd come in from cleaning houses in town. The light in Momma's kitchen window after the long walk in the dusk had been a soft and golden welcome. Momma would be waiting, occasionally Poppa and Rita would be home already, but Seaver and Leon were always the last ones back, eating quickly and heading back out, in a hurry to spend a few hours with their buddies before turning in for the night.

Cupcake fell asleep and slumped sideways, toppling against Martina, who reached out and poked her hard in the shoulder. The smaller girl woke with a jolt. "Hey!" she said. "What for you do that, huh?"

"Sparrow," Martina shouted, and everyone turned to stare.

"Sparrow," Martina repeated, just as loudly.

"Oh, Martina," Carol Ann cheered. "Sparrow, sparrow, yes indeed!" Her heart leaped with the joy of this moment. Nothing else mattered, Martina was talking again.

"That's my honey bee," Rita said proudly.

David applauded. His face lit up with his love for his sister, and relief, as deep as Carol Ann's own, that Martina was coming back to them.

Martina didn't say anything else, but when Carol Ann took her hand to stop her from poking Cupcake again, Martina relaxed and nodded her head. Carol Ann caught David's eye, and they smiled at each other briefly before he remembered his anger and deliberately turned away. The children went back to their dreams, sated and comforted.

For better or for worse, she would always be Poppa and Momma's daughter; she would always be Rita's sister. This stunted corner of the planet herded people like hogs, with no future and little past worth remembering, but she would always be able to arrive on their doorstep with no warning, and find food, a welcome and the warmth of wood smoke and family. She thought of Margery and Helen, she could only dimly recall how she'd braced herself to ask them for help. It had happened so long ago, to another person, in another life.

She gave in to the magic of the summer night. For the first time since Peter's accident-or-deliberate-act, Carol Ann took a full, deep breath. Her failures would return to torment her tomorrow, but tonight it felt as if the soft air reached all the way into her soul.

CHAPTER 24

MARTINA

The big one says there is only one God. He is watching all the birds. Make a loud noise so he will know the people are joyful and he will not be angry. The other mother one puts her arms out and makes the good circles come.

CHAPTER 25

DAVID

A man astride a gleaming chestnut gelding rounded the end of the row of apple trees and charged toward David, hooves thudding on the hard ground and leather stirrup straps slapping the horse's solid flanks. Ray Torrence, the orchard manager, rode at speed until he was nearly on top of him, then wheeled the horse around with a sharp word. He was a short, stocky man with a broad chest, thin white eyebrows, a face flushed an angry shade of red and, according to Eddy, a temper to go with it. Without thinking, David stepped back a pace from the reach of the shiny leather boot hovering just at chest level and mere inches from his face.

The man laughed. "Ain't got much nerve, do ya, boy?" He took a large, white handkerchief out of the pocket of his striped shirt, wiped his forehead with a delicate motion, then tucked it carefully away.

The handkerchief was grey and grimy, David noted, and the movement artificial. What at poseur.

"Miz Amelia needs help moving furniture," Torrence said. "You boys get on up to the big house and finish spraying after."

"Yazzur, Mister Torrence," Eddy said, slurring his words together and staring at the ground.

David shot him a glance and stood up straighter. "All

right," he said crisply, looking Torrence in the eye. He bowed slightly, enough to be visible but not obsequious.

Torrence leaned down slowly, staring back at David. He tapped a loop of the reins against the pommel of the saddle. "You got one bad attitude on you boy," he said. "You goin' to have to do better'n that." He blinked once. "You hearin' me, boy?"

David stood steady, his thoughts racing. He should not to be treated like this, he was white. Not that there was any excuse for treating blacks this way either, of course. If Father were here, he wouldn't have to put up with this treatment. On the other hand, he needed this job. Mother needed the money he brought in, Martina needed to eat, and Aunt Rita kept feeding the neighborhood. Of course he certainly didn't begrudge those children a decent meal, but still, sometimes it felt as if all of Sculley's Bend depended on the pittance he earned.

"I'm speaking to you," Torrence said very slowly, "hear me, boy?"

"Yes," David said, lowering his gaze. "Sir." His skin burned under the streaks of dirt and sweat. His hands gripped the chemical pump so hard the rivets gouged into his palms. It didn't matter, he told himself, what anyone thought of him. It didn't matter how they treated him, this summer wouldn't last forever. He would figure out a way to get back to Briarwood with his dignity intact, then he would forget about them and never think of them again.

"That's better, boy. We'll make a good nigger out of you yet." Torrence sat up in the saddle, brushed the dust off the neat creases of his work pants and returned the way he had come.

Eddy shook his head. "You crazy, David? You gonna get yourself fired for sure, you keep up that smart mouth, and whipped on top of it, most like."

David glared at him. "It's not right. He shouldn't talk to us like that. We shouldn't have to stand for it."

"That man's a snake and a mean one at that. Best just to bend with the way the wind blowing, one day to the next."

David turned on his heel and stamped through the trees toward the McKinley's house. "Come on," he called over his shoulder. "We've got furniture to move." It made a break from the endless spraying, at least, which needed to be done every month, over and over, across all the acres of apples.

Amelia McKinley was not as young as David had thought when he'd first seen her in the car the night he'd run down the road, but the way she was looking at him out of the corner of her eye captured his attention. Her doll-like, white hands drooped as she pointed out the boxes to be carried up to the attic, the dressers to move from one side of the room to the other, as if her wrists weren't strong enough to lift the weight of her fingers. She certainly wasn't the sort of woman David had ever thought twice about, but when she stood with her back to the windows, David saw the curve of her breast through the backlit cotton of her blouse. He watched her as she moved in front of the light, and when her angled eyes caught his with an intriguing fierceness at odds with the rest of her demeanor, he didn't look away as quickly as he could have.

"Now tell me why I haven't seen you here before?"

"I've just come from New York."

"New York, hmmm." She said Noo Yaawk, slowly, in a breathy way David found himself listening to, in spite of her dull hair and limp hands. "I never been to New York, it must be simply fascinatin'!" Her voice lowered at the end, as if she were sharing a secret with him. "You surely know all sorts of things a simple country girl like me don't."

Her fierce gaze caught his eye once more. Then her face softened, her eyelashes fluttered, and she smiled, lips parting just enough to show tiny, crooked teeth and the tip of a very pink tongue. She flirted with the skill of a dancing bear, David thought. She wouldn't last ten minutes in the same room with any of the girls he knew back home. Somehow that vulnerability made her more attractive instead of less.

"You don't look all that simple to me," he replied, smiling back at her. "Ma'am," he added, but this time with a little laugh in his tone, acknowledging the distance beyond formality they had already traveled.

"You know," she said in that soft, almost whispering voice, "you don't much look like a colored boy." She said "colored" in three syllables, drawing each one out. She stepped close to David as he shifted a chair to its new position.

"My father was white," he said, inhaling her light, flowery scent. When had he last smelled perfume? He caught Eddy frowning and mouthing something. "Ma'am," he added.

"Oooh," her eyes opened wide, as if he'd said a tremendously shocking thing. He had, he supposed. "I heard tell of things like that happening in New York. Why I'd say—"

Marcus McKinley's footsteps preceded him long before he arrived. His heavy boots thudded solidly on the wooden steps at the front of the house and continued their march across the porch and down the hallway. He stepped into the sitting room where they were, and his girlish high voice, pitched to be heard over the clatter of farm machinery and men, filled the corners of the small space. "I told you to wait upstairs until I got here." He sounded stern and humorless as he stood in the doorway, scowling at his wife. His eyes were cold above the deformed shape of his hare lip.

David quickly turned back to the box he was nailing shut. Best not to let The Boss catch him shirking. Oh no, couldn't let that happen. Amelia was now peeping at her husband from those angled, sly eyes. What did she see in him, with that hair lip and lisp, and those boorish, arrogant manners?

"These boys? Why they've been purely gentlemen through

and through." Amelia laughed. "No need for me to stay hiding upstairs like an old auntie."

"We'll speak of this later," The Boss replied. "And you," he said, turning.

David found himself on the receiving end of a level, unsmiling blue gaze. "Sir?"

"You've a look of your grandpoppy, and your mother as well, leastways a bit. Right fine girl she were, she were young."

"Yes, Sir." David was surprised, but of course they would have all known each other in the years before Mother had come up to New York.

"Fair skinned for sure, but that don't make no never mind. You tell her I said how-do." Marcus McKinley put his hand out for the hammer David was holding. Slowly he rolled up the sleeves of his shirt and drove the rest of the nails into place with a single blow each, the muscles in his forearm rippling. He laid the hammer back on the top of the box. "Heard you got a sister too, that right?"

"Yes, Sir."

"I like to know what's happening on my farm."

"Yes, Sir."

A moment's pause filled the room as The Boss studied David, making sure his message had been received.

"You boys get on back to the spraying. Anything else my wife needs here, I'll call you."

"Yessir, Mister McKinley," Eddy said, sprinting for the door.

"Yes, Sir," David said, moving away more slowly. He wanted to look back at Amelia McKinley, to prove a point, he wasn't sure what, but he didn't dare.

"You best be staying clear o' her," Eddy said quietly as they left the house and returned to the orchard. "Mister McKinley, he ain't a easy man, for sure. Busted a man's arm 'bout a horse once, don't see him taking too kindly to man nor boy setting eye on his woman."

"She was after me, not the other way around," David said.

"She white," Eddy said, "and she married to the Boss."

"So?"

"You colored." Eddy frowned.

"She's not all that pretty," David said. "Not nearly as pretty as the girls I know in New York."

"You was white in New York. The rules, they're different here."

"So if I do anything with her it will be my fault, merely because I'm black?"

"You ain't talking about stepping out for real, is you?" Eddy whispered, looking around to make sure no one was nearby. "You ain't never talking 'bout for real nothing with Miz McKinley, is you?" His words ran together, the more agitated he grew. He stopped walking and stared at David.

David stopped as well. "I thought we were talking about her flirting with me? What are you talking about?"

"You casting your eye on her," he said, aghast. "You talking smart to her."

"So she was just playing, it was harmless." David shrugged. "Although I dare say I could have her if I wanted to," he lifted his chin and glanced away, striving to appear casual and sophisticated.

"Playing!" Eddy said, his hands jammed into his armpits and his elbows flapping up and down. "You a colored boy now. It ain't, you ain't," he choked to a halt. "It ain't allowed!" He walked away so fast he was practically running.

David caught up to him and trotted alongside. Eddy was still frowning and worrying his hands against his ribcage. "This is really serious, isn't it?" David asked. "They wouldn't fire me, would they?" He might complain, but in reality he needed this job.

Eddy stopped short, his eyes wide. "Fire you?" he

stuttered. "Fire you? Boy, Mister McKinley ain't gonna fire you he finds out you making sweet talk with his wife, he gonna kill you."

David stared back, horrified, his disbelief dying stillborn. "You're kidding," was all he could think of to say.

"He string you right up in that there tree and you be dead, dead, dead." Eddy's words ran together in a breathless stream.

"But—"

"He hang you up your Momma, she gonna cry for weeks and weeks and months."

"But it's illegal." David managed to say.

"Ain't illegal here. Ain't illegal to lynch a uppity colored boy. Not uppity boy what cast eyeballs on good white lady what be married to the Boss." His accent slurred the sounds into a barely comprehensible gush. "What illegal is mixing blood, like a colored boy making time with a white lady." His breath came in short gasps.

"Take it easy, don't panic."

"You my cousin," Eddy shouted. "You family!"

A tongue of anger flared inside David. He wasn't family. He was white. This was all a huge mistake, a nasty prank that had gone on too long. "Well calm down," he said sharply, "I'm not going to do anything stupid." But even as David turned on his heel and continued down the path to the orchard, as he picked up the chemical sprayer with his tired arms and blistered hands, his mind revolved slowly and strongly around the glimpse of her breasts against the light.

Darkness caught them walking home; the last row of trees had taken extra time because they ran out of insecticide and had to retrieve another canister down from the farm shed. A blare of sunset, streaking the sky with colors. A gold so bright it looked like fire, and a blue so rich it had infinite depth.

"Like the soul of the Lord," Eddy said.

"What?" David stumbled over a rock in his path. How did Eddy walk barefoot all the time?

"Looking at the sky when it so big like that I think of the Lord. I think the soul of the Lord is like that, jus' goes on and on and never run out of forgiveness and loving kindness."

"That's a beautiful thought," David said, trying to put sincerity in his voice, understanding Eddy was offering him a truce. Soul of God indeed. A sunset was the result of the perceived distance of refracted light. He opened his mouth to say so, then shut it. What was the use?

"Grandpoppa would sure take on happy if I was t'go for a preacher. I guess I will, for him, you know. Me, I'd go study engineering if I could. If we ever had the money."

"An engineer?" David tried to keep the scorn out of his voice, but couldn't. "You need a lot of time in school before you become an engineer."

"I know, I'd need to finish high school, and college, and then there's apprentice years. I met an engineer once, down Charlottesville, he told me." Eddy shrugged. "Weren't saying I were gonna be one, just saying I'd'a liked to." Deep darkness settled down over the path and David lost the sense of where Eddy was; he couldn't tell if Eddy's voice was coming from far away or right next to him. "All those buildings you seen in New York City, I seen pictures. All those towers scraping up to the sky," his voice got low, and vibrated with feeling. "Imagine being able to build one like that. Imagine looking at a building stretching all the way up to God, and being able to say to folks 'You see that skyscraper, that's mine. I done built it with my own two hands.' Yessir, that would sure make a body feel big all over." He sighed. "Yessir," he said softly, "being an engineer must be about the best job there is." He fell silent, suddenly, as if the words had simply run out.

David could have said something about the reality of work crews and architectural design, but he had a feeling that

Eddy knew more than he did about dreams that would never come true. He regretted his earlier scoffing. They walked on in silence, stepping carefully in the darkness, the ground invisible under their feet. The yellow lights of kerosene lanterns from the Bend houses were barely visible in the distance, and the sky above the horizon turning silver with the rise of the moon.

"Welcome, boys," Auntie Rita said, as they walked through the door. "Supper be out in two shakes, now you're home."

Mother sat nearby, mending a gray shirt. Her hair was an unkempt frizz around her face, the hollows under her elegant cheekbones were dark shadows, her lower lip was just the same broad shape as her sister's. David stared at her, wondering how he had lived with her all these years and not seen what was suddenly so unmistakably clear. Alsace indeed, he sneered. Try New Orleans, via Sculley's worthless Bend. Had Father known? Had they both been lying to him his whole life? He glared down at the rough floorboards beneath his muddy shoes. Everyone here kept telling him he looked just like his grandfather. Did all his friends in New York suspect what he had just learned?

Grandpoppa was wrapping twine around the broken leg of a chair, his forehead wrinkled in concentration. He looked up at Eddy and David and smiled. David felt anger surge forward again. This bucolic scene, this homily of how to be happy with no money, hid the reality of long hours of backbreaking labor, food scavenged from the bogs and fields, and worst of all, deceit and lies.

"Our friends, they be joining in for supper again tonight." Aunt Rita pointed her chin at Custis, Dorrie and Cupcake playing quietly together at the table with Martina. "I like a big group, it's a party." She smiled at David, not waiting for a response, which was fine with him, since a room full of black farmhands and whore's children, eating the food his sweat and blood provided, didn't seem like a party to David. They had eaten here every night for a week now.

"Go wash up, y'all, supper's setting on."

"Washing, washing!" cried Martina, rubbing her hands across her face.

"That right, honey, you washing your face good." Aunt Rita beamed, and wrapped her arm around Martina's shoulders in a quick hug.

"Bee, bee, honey bee!" Martina shouted.

"Oh sorry, sorry, child, I done forgot. You a honeybee, you. Don't shout."

Martina nodded. "Honey bee," she said, more quietly. "Bee bee."

David smiled. Martina was so happy here, at least one good thing had come out of their arrival in this dismal hole. The little mite, his baby sister, deserved something good to come her way. He shut his eyes, mortified at the memory of how he'd failed her. He wouldn't fail her again. He shook himself out of his reverie.

At the pump, he removed his shirt. Bared to the waist, he and Eddy bowed low under the stream of cold water, then scoured their hands and faces with thin cloth and homemade soap. The hard, yellow bar had crackles running the length of it, streaked gray veins full of accumulated dirt. David hated even to touch the slimy thing, let alone wash with it. "God, I miss real soap," he said.

"Don't let Granpoppa hear you taking the Lord's name in vain," Eddy said. "Not over soap, leastways."

The dinner ritual was equally unpleasant. It began, as did every meal at this table, with a pious sermon by Grandpoppa. Tonight's topic was on the subject of pride, and not overstepping one's assigned place in the fabric of society. "When Solomon, son of the wise King David, tells us in Proverbs of the six things that God abhors, what does he state first? The first of all the things that God abhors, the most grievous wrong you can do to the Lord, who gave us all life, is turn a proud look on your neighbor."

Aunt Rita winked at him and he lowered his eyes. Clearly she was trying to make him feel better, and he wanted to appreciate the effort to help him fit in, but it fell on him awkwardly. These farmhands were not his real family. A lump rose in his throat and he wanted to cry. Father would have understood how awkward and out of place he felt. David tried to picture Father in this setting. What would he do? What would he want David to do? Be strong, make the best of it, and set a good example. Well, he would try.

David sat up straight and closed his eyes, as if concentrating on the homily. He said Amen in a clear and slow voice, nodding his head graciously. He served himself quietly and neatly, last. In contrast to the rushing hands and spoons, he knew his outstanding manners would be noticed. Father would be proud. He carefully took potatoes mashed together with slimy okra, a portion of old, stringy carrots, and biscuits in thick gravy, bypassing the fried greens, smelling suspiciously like the skunk cabbage growing at the soggy river-edge between the weeds and the algae. He held his mismatched fork and knife as he would the heaviest Oneida silver, ate and chewed as slowly and quietly as at an ambassador's banquet, and ignored the fact that there had been no meat for almost a week.

Father would say something generous as well. David nodded to Aunt Rita. "This is simply delicious," he said.

Custis watched him for a while out of his eight-year old eyes, then nudged his sister. "Mistuh High n' Mighty—". He stopped short as Rita's arm shot out, faster than David would have thought possible, and her wooden spoon bounced off the side of the boy's head. "Yow," Custis yelped, putting his hand up to rub the bruise, and turning to glare at the perpetrator.

When he saw where the blow had come from, he dropped his gaze.

"*Met de l'eau!*" Aunt Rita said severely, eyeing Custis and shaking her spoon.

"Yes'm," Custis said.

David flushed, embarrassed that his effort has been so misunderstood. He replayed his words, and realized how clumsy and insincere they sounded. The multiple conversations swirled around and past him. He stared at Mother, bent in serious discussion with Poppa. He watched Aunt Rita, as she put food on Martina's plate, stroking her on the cheek, and pushing a wayward curl out of her eye. Eddy and Custis laughed together over a shared joke. He tried not to be paranoid and recognize that it wasn't necessarily about him.

The minute supper ended he slipped out of the cabin into the cooler air of the summer night. Let the others help with the stupid dishes. The moon was bright and high, casting silver across the leaves of the oak trees, their branches shivering in the sporadic breeze. The drone of the crickets was loud and steady, and in the distance he heard the splashing of the stream as it turned the corner around the rocky bend, and followed gravity downhill toward Charlottesville. He wandered upstream to the dead tree he and Eddy fished from, and clambered out along the broad trunk, deep into leafy green secrecy. It was astounding how much light the moon threw down. Usually it was impossible to see past his fingers in the darkness of the evening, now he could practically read by the shimmering light spilling around him. He leaned back, resting against the solid support of the biggest upright branch. It was so peaceful here, so calm, and he'd never been lonelier in his life.

Soft singing roused him. Peering through the branches, he saw a figure moving toward the creek, aimlessly, easily, at the sandy edge a few feet away. It was Mother, singing! Since when did Mother sing?

He was about to call out to her, when she slipped out of her blouse and reached for the buttons on the side of her skirt.

David froze in place. He could barely see anything except her silhouette, but his imagination was more than sufficient to the task. His mother was going to bathe naked in a stream! She was going to take off all her clothes, outdoors, and paddle about in a muddy stream bed, in the dark of a summer evening in the middle of some God-forsaken shanty town in this backwater part of the country. He shut his eyes, as he had when he was little, and counted to ten so that she wouldn't be there when he opened them. But she was, floating on her back, the ripples from every small movement ringing about her in waves of silver moonlight and black water. Her shoulders and breasts cleared the surface as she stood up, stooping to drink from her cupped hands. Drops of dark water splattered back into the creek with tiny sounds, mixing with the hum of the crickets.

David watched in horrified fascination, unable to look away. Right before his eyes, his mother was turning into a different being altogether. She was no longer fully human, this creature who wandered by moonlight, naked, drinking from her paws like a muskrat. Even the way she moved, the new, fluid grace that replaced her old taut snappiness, testified to this change.

Anger, quick and bright like fresh, scarlet blood, burst forth. She had no right to do this to him. To become one of them, stranding him alone. And if she thought he would follow her, she had another think coming. He was not colored. Never.   Black, mixed, mulatto, negro, mud, mongrel. He crossed his arms over his chest and dug his broken, filthy fingernails into the skin of his tense, tired arms. Never, never, never.

CHAPTER 26

CAROL ANN

Carol Ann did not leap eagerly off the hard mattress each morning, but with the passing of one muggy, placid day after the next, it grew a little easier to resist rolling over and dropping back to sleep. The spark was still missing, the emotion of joy just a memory of good times in the past, but renewal was starting to trickle into her dormant recesses. In the garden each afternoon, her toes dug into the ground with a steadiness she hadn't felt since the night in New York when Peter had skidded over an embankment, and she had been ripped so violently loose from her moorings. She was content. Yet her serenity rested on a foundation of guilt. How could she feel this way when Peter was slowly dying so far away? She imagined herself sitting by his side, stroking his golden hair back from his face. Was anyone cutting his hair now, or had it grown long and straggly these past months? She had abandoned him to hide here in the past. Her only solace lay in knowing his father was taking care of him now that she was gone. She had done the right thing. Of course she had.

The heat had been increasing for days, the air pressing like lead weights as the sun arced high overhead. Carol Ann and Martina took burlap sacks and headed for the shade and cool of the woods to scavenge for wild yams along the swampy edge of the creek. The leaves on the trees hung limp and dark;

the briar roses sprouted full and thick on their thorny vines. The air was hot on her skin; Carol Ann sighed as it moved across her face.

"Come on, honey," Carol Ann said to Martina. "We can stick our feet in the water and cool off." They headed for a place above the curve in the creek where it first started to broaden out and slow down. Here it was still narrow enough to move swiftly and deeply, but wide enough to provide enjoyable swimming. Each year, the heavy spring rains and runoff piled gravel onto the mud under the trees; in Sculley's Bend they called this spot "The Beach."

Funny how after all this time she still thought of beaches as being rocky edges bordered by clear, rippling water. She went to the ocean when she first arrived in New York, before she became white. Afterward, of course, she scrupulously avoided the fierce sun because it browned her way too much and too quickly. The damp breezes also blew her carefully straightened hair into tighter curls than fashion allowed, or that white women had.

Here in the creek of her childhood, the water danced over the smooth, shining rocks, its never-ending susurration freely offered and easily taken. When she'd come out in the darkness that night, she'd thought about how much Martina would enjoy the chance to swim. She would bring David here as well, if they could ever overcome the brick wall currently between them.

Carol Ann led Martina to the water's edge and took off the girl's shoes and socks, as well as her own. They sat on the rocky edge and stretched their feet out into the flowing coolness of the creek. Carol Ann pointed out the sights to the passive girl, crumbs of pleasure fighting their way through the sadness, grief and worry for her dear, damaged child. "See, honey, there's an oriole, and that's her nest." She pointed to a straw bag dangling from the limb of a tree. "She had her babies in there, back when it was baby bird time." Would she and the children still be here next spring to see the babies again? Carol Ann refused to think about that.

"And those little bugs in the water over there are water skeeters, see how they go skeetering by? If we're very quiet, maybe we'll see a few deer come out to drink. They used to stand right by that big tree." She pointed to the huge trunk growing out across the edge of the creek and curving upward, lower branches dipping to create ripples along the surface. "That old thing has been there since I was a girl. It's the old man of the creek, watching over all the fish and children to keep them safe." The words of the old folklore flowed, echoes of her mother's voice chiming softly in her ears.

"Safe," Martina whispered, and Carol Ann smiled, holding her daughter and resuming her monologue.

The mindlessness of her own babble, the murmur of the creek, the smooth sounds of the wind and the water together, lulled Carol Ann into a half-waking, half dreaming, place. She lay back against a stray clump of soft clover, inhaling deeply, feeling the scent of the white flower balls seep through her from the outside in. She stroked her hand lightly over the tops of the flowers and watched them bend down and spring back into position as her palm passed by. A door opened up inside her, to a place of stillness she had not been to for a long, long time.

Martina wriggled next to her, then struggled to her feet and lunged toward the deeper water. Carol Ann jumped after her, but Martina had clearly been planning her path, for she sprang nimbly across the first few rocks in the shallows and stepped unhesitatingly into the current. It only rose to her knees at that spot, and through the clear water the smooth stones of the streambed were visible.

Martina stared down at her toes, then crouched to touch them.

"No, no, Martina, you'll get your clothes all wet," Carol Ann called out. "Don't sit in the water."

Martina plopped herself down with a tremendous splash and kicked her legs out in front of her. She slapped her hands down on the surface and scared the delicate insects out of her way.

Carol Ann surrendered with a laugh and sat on a sunny rock nearby, feeling the heat soak upward through the thin cloth of her dress. She watched Martina play. Ah well, clothing would dry. "Come to think on it, that water do look mighty refreshing and this rock is purely cooking the backs of my thighs," she said, imitating her mother's Cajun lilt.

She stepped carefully across to her daughter, sliding through the mild push of the current. Bird-song and water-splash enveloped them. The creek breathed its cool mist into her face, and she became part of the air, and part of the river, with her feet solidly planted in the rocks and the mud. She sat down in the water behind Martina and wrapped her arms around her. The light material of her skirt floated at first, but quickly soaked through and sank down to settle underneath the surface, fluttering gently. The scrap of lace on the hem rippled a patterned dance; a mesmerizing waltz of repeats and variations. Martina put her hands in the water at her sides and fluttered her fingers back and forth. "Seaweed," she said.

"Yes," Carol Ann said, trailing her own fingers through the water and watching the reflected sunlight flicker across her skin. "Seaweed."

A few nights ago she had snuck out to swim in the moonlight while Martina and the children dozed, while Rita and Poppa sat quietly in the lowering light. The water had been as warm as a kiss, like velvet flowing over her skin. She had wanted Peter so much; wanted to share the night with him. She pictured him here, his smile gleaming, his arms around her, supporting her as they made love in the warm current. Perhaps if she had told him, that dream might have come true one day. Now it never would. How could she have left him alone in a hospital, surrounded by strangers, fed by a tube? Yes, his father had the money to buy the best doctors, but all the medical treatment in the world couldn't rebuild a life that no longer existed.

David, too, was a problem she would need to solve, sooner or later. The whole country may be sliding into poverty, one failed bank at a time, but the solution didn't lie in dropping out of school. She would have to find a way to convince him to return. If he refused to go to Briarwood, there had to be a few good public schools in New York, or even New Jersey.

She knew she should have the courage to face her mistakes, but right now all she could think of was how thirsty she was for the cool water against her skin, and for the soft song of the creatures in the summer day around her.

Martina leaned her head back on Carol Ann's shoulder, and together they looked up at the swiftly flying wisps of cloud. It was about belonging and owning, she thought. If you were owned by one life, you couldn't belong to another. She had belonged to Peter and he to her, in spite of the great deception which had fueled her freedom. Like a fence keeping out predators, that lie had protected her from being owned by Sculley's Bend. "Down here we're safe," Carol Ann said. "Up there we fly free, but we can get hurt. Down here we belong, but we're rooted in the mud. I don't know which is better. I wish I did."

The next day rain came down in sheets, the sky draping the trees like washing on a line. Carol Ann and Rita worked indoors, canning the first of the apples and last of the peas to put by for the depths of winter. Between the rain of the summer day and the steam rising from the pots on the stove, Carol Ann thought she might stay drier if she stood outside in the middle of the yard. "I hope David and Eddy aren't getting too wet."

"They won't melt."

Something in Rita's tone alerted Carol Ann. "They'll be working in one of the barns today, surely?"

Rita snorted. "You been away a long time, Sister."

Carol Ann grimaced at her own naiveté. Well, Rita was right on both counts, they wouldn't be coddled with indoor work, and they wouldn't melt.

Martina, set to the task of shelling the peas, was quietly babbling to herself at the table.

"She's looking some better, I think," Rita said, seeing where Carol Ann's attention had gone.

Martina was intent over the bowl of peas, her fingers moving quickly and confidently at the simple task. She was like a Vermeer painting, her lips red from strawberry jam at breakfast, her skin pale and smooth, her bright auburn hair picking up glints of copper in the thin light washing over her.

Carol Ann smoothed a stray lock of hair behind the girl's ear.

Martina's gaze flashed quickly over Carol Ann, pausing somewhere near her left ear. She smiled, like an angel coming to visit the lesser mortals. "Hello, Mother," she said, then returned to her task without waiting for an answer.

Carol Ann thought her heart would stop. Grinning hugely, she struggled not to overact and throw her arms around her daughter, knowing that would be exactly the wrong thing to do. "Thank the Lord. Thank the Lord. I was so worried she would never come back from what that monster did to her." She danced over to Rita and hugged her instead. "She's talking so much more than ever, and so much more clearly. She's happy here, Rita."

"So you see, you did do the right thing. Cities are complete whirlpools—all the hustle and bustle. It's a wonder how you put up with it. One day in Charlottesville and I come scalding back here like a jackrabbit with its tail afire."

Carol Ann laughed. "You get used to it. You come to start moving as fast as everyone else, so then slowing down is kind of like sleepwalking."

Rita pushed a curl off her face with the back of her hand, leaving a russet streak of stewed apple skin on her forehead, which she proceeded to rub into a broad smear. "That how you feel now? Like you're sleepwalking? Will you be needing to get back to the city soon?"

"I don't know. I wish I did. I miss Peter so much. I fall asleep thinking about him, wondering if he's still alive." Her thoughts took over. Perhaps there's a letter or a telegram from the hospital already on the way. Had his father taken him home to care for him? Can I keep him alive if I pray more? If I believe more?" She stopped and rubbed her hands over her eyes. "I wish, I want, I hope. New York was so alive and here everything is stagnant. But in the end, New York was so frightening. I don't know how to go back, and I don't know if I want to stay here. I don't know how to fix this mess."

Martina suddenly stood up at the table, interrupting her train of thought. "Privy!" she announced.

"All right then, off you go," Rita replied, without looking up from Carol Ann.

"Raining," Martina said. "Wet."

"It's all right," Rita said. "You can go anyway."

Martina stood up but didn't move toward the door, biting her lip.

Carol Ann quickly moved to her, and took her by the hand, trying to lead her to the privy.

Martina ignored her while she struggled with the thoughts in her brain. "I'll...get...wet," she said, each word separated by a short pause. A look of anguish scrunched her face.

Rita came around the table to them, took Martina's

shoulders in her hands and looked into her eyes. Martina's eyes caught for a second, then slithered away over Rita's shoulder.

"Rain won't hurt you, sugar," Rita said.

"You gonna be right safe."

"Right safe," Martina said. "All wet, right safe." She stood for a minute, wrapping one of her chestnut curls around a finger. Then she visibly relaxed, and happily tucked herself back into her repeating word pattern, whispering "right safe, right safe, right safe," as she stepped out the door.

Carol Ann stared after her, amazed. "It's like a miracle. Do you know how hard Nurse Savener tried to make that much progress with her?"

"I think she just needed to know there no more monsters out there waiting for her." Rita smiled at her niece. "She left all the monsters behind in the city."

"I didn't realize how frightened she was. It must have been terrifying for her, locked into her own world with no way to make sense of all the noise and confusion. It's obvious now that she's so much calmer, but I guess I was too wrapped up in how terrible it all was to think about how terrible it all was." Carol Ann sank under the rush of guilt. "That didn't' even make sense. Lord, but I'm a terrible mother!" She dropped her head into her hands.

"Don't be a goose," Rita said, coming over to sit close. "You're a fine mother, but you had a down spell. You had your own healing to do."

Carol Ann threw her arms around Rita and held her tight.

"It's gonna be all right now," Rita said, patting her sister on the back. "You'll see."

Martina returned with her clothes properly, if not quite neatly, in place.

"What a good girl," Carol Ann said, pulling her daughter into the circle of her arms, Rita holding them both. They held each other in silence and love.

"Well those apples ain't gonna can themselves," Rita said at last, breaking away and returning to the stove, surreptitiously wiping her eyes.

"Your father would have been so proud," Carol Ann whispered.

Martina nodded. "He's asleep," she said, then immediately began wringing her hands.

Carol Ann reached out to still them. "Yes, he's sleeping. We're safe here without him, aren't we?"

"Right safe," Martina replied. She sat down beside the bowl of peas. "All done, all open."

"Seem like there's more going on inside that girl than comes out," Rita observed. She took the bowl of shelled peas away and put a basket of runner beans in their place. Martina immediately began snapping off the ends as if she were racing toward an invisible finish line. "Only have to tell her something once. And she sure do love her daddy."

"He loved his children more than I can tell you. In his eyes, they were both perfect." A memory tugged at her. "One time, he punched a man who called her a retard." She shook her head. "That was the only time I ever saw him lose his temper."

"I knew from your letters he was a wonderful man."

"He spent hours teaching them to swim, to play chess." Carol Ann shuffled the scraps of green beans into a row of lopsided, green pawns, separated by ragged checkerboard boundaries.

Martina twitched. "Yes yes yes!" she shouted, staring at the table. She grabbed more beans from the bowl and rapidly placed them in starting rows on the makeshift chessboard. She grabbed one of the original pawns and advanced it forward.

"Okay, *cherie*, okay," Carol Ann soothed. She moved a bean from the opposite side forward and then started to laugh. How was she ever going to keep the pieces straight once they were all in a muddle in the middle?

"Yes yes," Martina said. She moved another bean in the distinctive L-shape of a knight, then settled quietly back onto the bench. Apparently she could tell the pieces apart with no trouble.

Carol Ann took a handful of apple slices from the bowl and put them in front of her. "You've lost so much and I can't make it up to you," she whispered, so no one could hear, "but I'm going to work as hard as I can to try." She moved a bean she thought was a bishop diagonally forward. Which beans had been in which starting positions? Martina didn't complain, so that must have been right.

"Hey, Rita, is that old chess set still around somewhere?

"Oh, sure," Rita said. "No one's played for years though, might be a few pieces missing."

"You used to be an excellent player."

Martina moved a bean to the side.

"I'm a mite rusty, that's for certain."

"Martina won't care. Poppa could make replacements for whatever's missing. He seems to be getting on with her."

Which beans were which? Well she was safe with one of the pieces still in their original starting position.

"All of The Bend is taken to her, she's a dear soul. Absalom Samuelson, he making her a doll, he said."

"She'd like it if you played with her. Peter used to play every night we didn't go out. Maybe he wasn't very brave, but he was kind, and so gentle." She smiled. Whatever other mistakes she'd made, she had done well in loving him.

Martina quickly knocked one bean off the board and replaced it with another, identical bean.

Carol Ann tried to swap her castle bean and her king bean, but Martina squeaked. Okay, that move wasn't legal. One of the encroaching beans must be the queen or a bishop. She moved the castle one square sideways. Martina pounced on the board, pinched Carol Ann's king and dropped it at the side of the board, placed her own bean in that square, then sat back with a thump.

Carol Ann laughed. "I guess I lost that game, but at least it was a quick death."

Rita slid in next to her. "Why'd you say he weren't brave? He married a black woman and left his father for her, didn't he? That took some doing, I think."

"He didn't know."

Rita guffawed. "Oh, of course he did, you *couj'n*."

"No, he didn't. I never told him."

"That why you think he was so weak, because you thought you were putting one over on him and he weren't man enough to figure you out?"

"Well yes, I suppose so," Carol Ann said slowly. "I think you're exactly right."

"But he did know. I bet his old rich daddy found out and told him. That's what they fought about."

"I never knew what they fought about."

Rita laughed again. "See! Why else wouldn't he have told you? You should have guessed. What else do a boy and his father fight about, right before the boy gets married?"

"The old man is one right nasty buzzard. He said he told Peter, but Peter didn't believe him."

"Peter loved you, that were clear as daylight from your letters. Maybe he didn't want to believe it."

A new thought rolled over inside Carol Ann's head. Peter was not the type to shy away from unpleasant news, but he would hide it from her. "He was waiting for me to tell him. He was going to play it however I wanted, for however long I wanted." She looked at Rita with wonder, puzzling over this novel concept. Peter strong? Strong enough to pretend ignorance for two decades and love her just the same? That would be wonderful, if true. Maybe he hadn't deliberately taken his car over that embankment. As Rita said, a man who loved a black woman enough to defy his father and marry her, this was a man with a streak of courage in him. Maybe he didn't leave her alone on purpose after all.

She would never know for sure, and it didn't matter, but just the thought made all the difference in the world. She rubbed her hands up and down her arms, feeling the warmth of her own comforting touch, and smiled.

CHAPTER 27

MARTINA

The other mother is a General! Each night when the sun goes to sleep, the armies battle and win. But the angry gods do not come, the good circles come and the one God keeps all the sparrows right safe to home.

CHAPTER 28

DAVID

The next time Amelia McKinley summoned David and Eddy up to the big house, she was waiting for them at the top of the stairs. "I believe I only need one of you today," she said. "Eddy, you can go on back to the orchards, that would be purely fine."

Eddy threw David a horrified look.

"Run along now," Amelia said. "I just need some curtains shifted, one of you is plenty strong."

With another beseeching glance, Eddy left.

David went along with Amelia's ruse, and pretended he was unaware of any posturing, although his palms had started to tingle as soon as he caught sight of her, precisely when she slanted her eyes at him and touched her tongue to her top lip. When she stumbled, and fell against him in the narrow upstairs hallway, with her face conveniently turned up to his, he kissed her eagerly and whispered her name into her limp, brown hair, his erection alert and pressing hard into her thigh. He tried to pull it away from her before she could notice it, but when he did so, she arched her hips into him, pursuing. She stroked his shoulders through his sweaty shirt. He shouldn't be doing this, he told himself, because she was a married woman. But he raised his hands to her breasts, curving them over their shape in delight as she pulled down the straps of his overalls and slid her own hands over his hot skin. He throbbed against her, and worked hard to concentrate on not losing control. Think about mathematics, had been the advice the seniors at Briarwood had given each other. He was finding that instruction more difficult to follow in reality than theory.

"You're so beautiful," he breathed, and at that moment she was. With her eyes heavy with lust and her cheeks and lips flushed hot and rosy, she glowed with an excitement that lent her a radiant beauty.

"So are you," she said. "You the prettiest colored boy I ever did see."

"I'm not colored," he snapped, and pulled away from her. Then she slid her hand over his erection and he decided not to make an issue of it. When she closed her fingers tight around him, he forgot about it altogether.

"Ah, if only they could see me now," he thought, not precisely sure to whom he was referring. Chad and the other students at school, of course. Steady Eddy. Well, perhaps not Eddy, given how upset he seemed to get, even at the thought of a little harmless flirting.

They staggered, one step at a time, toward the guest bedroom, Amelia stepping backward, David hunched over her like a lunging wolf, nearly overbalancing and plunging them both to the floor. By the time they reached the bed they were already naked. David was sweating in rivulets that left streaks in the dirt on his face and neck. Amelia fell back across the covers, pulling him down on top of her, mewing soft kitten sounds of lust.

The act of lovemaking wildly exceeded all David's expectations. Sure he'd kissed a few girls before, sneaking into the garden at a country club dance, in a dark corner at a busy party, but he'd anticipated awkwardness and doubt. He'd been waiting for Amelia to call a halt to the proceedings, or for Eddy to come back and interrupt. But there was no uncertainty, no hesitation. He was confident in the strength of his legs and arms, muscled from his work in the orchards, and he knew each movement to make, as if he'd been born for this one moment. His mind and body merged into one beautiful, victorious whole. He gloried in his prowess, and smugly watched Amelia wriggling beneath him, her face twisted and her eyes shut, tendrils of hair escaping their pins and tumbling away from her face as they rolled, skin to skin, across the bed.

He hadn't been prepared for the thrill of sensation all across his body, of hot breath and cool sheets rucked up around his knees and elbows, of soft skin in his hands, his mouth. He hadn't expected the explosive release of orgasm, so different than his fantasies, so different than his solo efforts. He felt as though he'd been flung into the air, to ride slowly down from the peak of the mountain to land at last, gently, on the delightfully crumpled sheets.

Amelia rolled away from him and pulled her clothing back together. He watched her through a haze of dreamy fog and the sound of the ocean in his ears as blood rushed to cool his overheated senses. He smiled lovingly at her flushed face, framed in sunlit, tousled curls.

"That was the most wonderful thing that's ever happened to me," he said.

"Hurry up, you stupid boy. Get dressed before we get caught," she hissed.

Her words shook him back to reality like a rock hitting the ground. She was right, her husband could come in any time. They could not jeopardize their love like that. He pulled his shirt and overalls back on faster than they'd come off, carefully not looking at her. He didn't turn around until he was dressed, and when he did turn, it was to discover the room was already empty. What they had shared was special and he wanted to see her smile at their secret. He picked up a box, to look busy. He wondered if what he'd done showed in his face, and struggled to appear unchanged. By the time Eddy returned, David had shifted three boxes into the attic, but Amelia was still safely ensconced upstairs, hidden from view.

David's world came alive that day. His skin puckered with goose bumps as he moved. He woke to a new awareness of his body, his legs flexed inside his overalls as if bands of iron ran through them, and his tongue touched his lips with a bruising sensitivity. His penis switched back and forth between sleeping quietly against the side of his leg, and then tingling and swelling up as it recalled where it had traveled that afternoon. His other senses had become more spectacularly alert as well. The trees grew greener, the leaves more distinct. The drone of insects even had more texture; he could hear the cicadas joining in a separate rhythm from the crickets in the grass and the bees in the clover. The flowery scent reminded him of Amelia, and he crushed some under his heel and inhaled, feeling his erection return. When Eddy wasn't looking, he tilted his pelvis forward and shut his eyes, recapturing the soft, encompassing depths of sensation. He knew his mind wasn't on his work, but honestly, how much attention did you have to pay to weeding rows of corn?

He was only vaguely aware of approaching hoof beats. The whip cracked sharply in the air right by his ear. He jumped, sweat breaking out cold on his neck, his heart thudding wildly in his chest.

On the great, glossy chestnut horse Ray Torrence stared down, laughing. "You sure are one jittery piece of not quite white trash," he sneered. He cracked the whip again, but this time David was ready and stood his ground. Torrence snarled like a feral beast, deprived of his fun. "I been watching you, boy. You pick up the pace here or I gonna miss next time." He kicked out, connected solidly with David's chest, vaulting him backward into the dirt, and rode away without looking back.

Eddy raced over to help him up. "You okay, David?"

"Yeah." David coughed and rubbed his chest. There would be a bruise there in the morning.

"He's a mean rattler. I don't know what got him on your back, but you watch out for him," Eddy warned.

David nodded. "We had better get back to work before he returns." Moving was painful at first, but as the rhythm of moving through the rows of young corn took over, the stabbing faded to a dull ache. Thoughts of Amanda seeped back into his brain. He didn't want to leave before he had seen her again. He tried to think of an excuse for going back up to the house at the end of the day, but eventually gave up and set off with Eddy in the lingering twilight. He glanced over his shoulder at the big house as they walked.

"I don't like this, no sir, not one bit," Eddy snapped. "I don't like the way you two buzzing round each other. Least you could do is keep your own eyes on the road, and not let the world know what's what."

"I don't care if they do know," David said, but he shivered. Even through the haze of his lingering pleasure, The Boss wasn't going to sit quietly while another man seduced his wife. It was adultery, and fornication was a sin, no matter how you sliced the bread. And she was so much older as well. He shook off these thoughts. No one was going to find out. Only he and Amelia knew, and she would certainly never tell anyone. He fixed his eyes on the path leading back to Sculley's Bend.

Martina met them in the yard, running to David, flinging her arms around him, then pulling away to spin in dizzy circles, only to race back again. "Oh Lord Jesus is a rock in the weary land!" she sang, the tune perfectly on key, her words clear and certain, her voice loud, her face raised to the sky.

"She sure do like to raise a hymn," Eddy said.

David hugged her to him and laughed. "Come on, Tina, let's go get us some greasy greens, shall we?" David took her hand and they walked together. At least this place had been good for her.

"Greasy, greasy, greasy!" Martina sang out. "A shelter in time of storm!"

Mother watched with wide eyes as he came to the dinner table, smiling, with Martina tucked under his arm. "Hello there," she said, and David heard the hesitation in her voice, waiting for him to make a snide remark, or turn away without speaking. But he didn't feel angry at her any longer, it was as if Amelia, with one simple, natural act, had pulled all the bitterness and all the anger out of him, and left him clean and new. Reborn. Maybe not what Grandpoppa had in mind when he used that word, but just as effective. He smiled at the thought, and settled Martina in her chair.

He straightened up and found Mother still watching him, but she swiveled away quickly when he caught her eye. *She's afraid of me!* David thought in surprise. *She thinks if she does the wrong thing, I'll be mad at her again.* A wash of tenderness filled him, and he remembered the day of Father's accident, when he'd come home from school and couldn't comfort her. He moved to the other side of the table and put his arms around her. She slowly reached to hug him back, and sniffed a little.

He patted her on the back, and as she pulled away at last, he smiled at her, and winked. "All better now, *cherie?*" He purposely asked in that way, much as she used to ask him when he was a little boy.

"All better now," she repeated, but when she stepped away from him a frown crossed her face. She didn't look as if she felt better at all. All through supper she kept sliding her eyes to study him when she thought he wouldn't notice. Maybe his afternoon showed on his face after all. He didn't care.

Anyone at Briarwood Academy who thought an hour in Master Levasseur's French class was a long stretch of time to endure, had never been freed from his virginity in the afternoon, then spent the evening surrounded by people he couldn't share his excitement with. It was odd how the mind could split straight down the middle and follow two paths simultaneously. One part of his mind moved through the boredom of routine activities: eating, washing, playing quietly with Martina. The other part returned to the spare bedroom in the big house, where Amelia lay under him, moaning and clinging, beads of sweat glistening as they traced thin paths down the white skin of her breasts.

He envisioned her so clearly she was practically real. Her smoldering eyes, her pink tongue, the scent of flowers that clung to her hair. He would see her tomorrow, she would call for him to come to the house, to the bedroom, and they would once again roll in each other's arms, sharing joy.

At last the interminable evening was over and he could escape to the back porch where his mattress lay next to Eddy's in the evening air. He jiggled and fidgeted. He wanted to bounce his hips up and down, or roll onto his back and bicycle his legs in the air. He was bursting with the need to tell someone, to share his excitement and his anticipation of tomorrow. It had been so long, so awfully long, since he had looked   forward to a new day. "Oh Amelia, you've changed my life!" He fell asleep with his pillow clutched to his chest and the image of Briarwood students staring at him with an envy too powerful to conceal. "Someday it will happen to you too, and then you'll understand," he told them with a grin. "Someday."

CHAPTER 29

CAROL ANN

Carol Ann stood at the pump, rinsing away the mud and dirt of the garden, savoring the bite of the cold water on her skin. Today had been a day of serenity. For the first time since she'd come home, she had been able to look back, without loss, without pain, with only love. Peter had known the truth, and this new knowledge brought her peace. She stretched her arms high in the afternoon sun.

A truck growled far in the distance. She stopped, and waited while it churned closer, up along the creek road. She swallowed a mouthful of water from her hands. Rita came softly out of the house behind her and Poppa came striding from the woodshed, where he'd been repairing school desks. A wood-paneled farm truck with three people in the cab turned up the road and skidded to a stop in front of them. Gravel crunched as Mary Mae Thacket, Portya Baylor and Willy Hume tumbled out.

"What is it?" Rita asked, stepping toward them.

Willy Hume glanced over his beefy shoulder as if making sure no stray eavesdroppers lurked there. As the owner of the only truck in The Bend, he was often present when critical events occurred, and the years of being the bearing of tidings both good and ill, as well as the guardian of secrets to be kept, had left him with a permanent habit of suspicion. "We should talk inside."

Poppa nodded, and led the others into the kitchen.

Rita stepped over to the stove and began to spoon chicory into the coffee pot.

"Y'all sit, please." Poppa pointed to the chairs around the table. They all shuffled into seats and stared at each other, no one breaking the silence for a moment. Then everyone began to speak at once.

"All right," Poppa held up his hand. "Let's hear one part at a time. Mary Mae, why don't you start?" She seemed to be the most agitated of the three.

Mary Mae was as tiny and quick of movement as Willy was stolid. She was so upset she had difficulty catching her breath. She rubbed her weather-beaten face briskly with one hand as if scouring the dust off her thoughts. "Trouble coming," she said, her mouth puckering over the words, her voice barely loud enough to be heard. "One of the field hands been making time with Miz Amelia."

"No!" Rita gasped, her tone low. Silence descended as they all stared at each other. "No," Rita repeated, her voice a near silent plea.

Mary Mae and Portya nodded. Rita shut her eyes and moaned quietly. Carol Ann felt her muscles stiffen in response to the news. All those years of hiding a secret from the world had taught her one thing—if you're going to do something so stupidly dangerous, for God's sake, don't get caught.

Mary Mae nodded, her head jerking in tight motions. "Trouble coming for sure."

"Yep, there gonna be something tonight," Portya Baylor stuttered. "One o' the town men was visiting Mother Ruey Belle's, ah," she stumbled to a halt, glancing sideways at the big Bible visible on its stand near the door.

Poppa put his hand on hers. "It's all right, we understand." Prostitution was in there, but Carol Ann doubted

Portya read well enough to know that.

"One o' the girls overheard the men talking. Mother Ruey Belle let me off early so I could come tell you. And thenst I found Willy, to drive me."

Mary Mae started nodding. "They passed me on the road, I were coming to tell you. Miz Amelia, she were in town telling Miz Stafford who came to visit, and my Lizzie, she was in the room and heard the whole story. Miz Amelia was telling Miz Stafford that one of the boys had his way with her." Mary Mae's old hands knit together as she spoke, and her fingers worried at the frayed cuffs of her black dress. "She said she fought like a bobcat but was no use. There was this big ole bruise right up on her arm." A sad scrap of lace trembled on the brim of her straw hat. "We come right over to tell you, Reverend."

"They won't be coming until after sundown. If we act quickly, we have time to get Sheriff Whitten in from Rayleigh. He's a good man, and he doesn't like mobs." He looked around the table. "Do we know who it was?"

Mary Mae and Portya both chorused no. Willy shook his head, his face blank. Carol Ann kept her own face even and smooth, but she knew who had done it as surely as if she had seen the act with her own eyes. David had found a way to release his anger, to vent his sense of being caged among strangers. That's why he'd been so very happy last night. Her breath grew tight in her throat and the edges of her vision turned dark. He was in danger now, her David. She struggled to drag air into her lungs, and the voices around her spoke through a buzz in her ears

"Don't know," Mary Mae said. "My Lizzie just said it was one of the field hands."

"Maybe there's time enough to head this thing off," Poppa said, "but we need to move now." He stood and thumped his hand on the table, softly. "Willy, you and I will drive to Rayleigh and find the sheriff. The rest of you tell all the boys to get to woods, just in case."

Rita stood as well, and went to the pantry. "I'll pack you up a brace of sandwiches," she said.

"Don't have time," Poppa said. "I'm sorry, Willy, we're going to have to skip a meal tonight. Every minute counts." Carol Ann exhaled, trying to appear completely only objectively concerned, tried to find a hint of the reassurance she'd always held as a child, that her big Poppa could overcome any enemy, vanquish all nighttime fears.   But this was too big, too evil, even for Poppa.

"Yes sir," Willy said, the first words he'd spoken. "I'd say so, yes sir." He stood as well, and the two large men created an immediate bulwark against all the evil beginning to marshal itself against them. Ridiculous as it was, Carol Ann felt heartened.

The women stayed in the kitchen after the men had gone out. The engine of the old pickup roared to life with a squeal and a metallic clattering of machine parts, then settled into a disconsolate rumble. The chunking of shifting gears punctuated the noise, then the truck rattled down the old dirt road, taking the cacophony with it.

The kitchen rang with silence.

"Could be Muckie Williams, he think what he got be so special," said Portya quietly, rubbing her fingertips against each other. "And believe me, it ain't." A tense laugh rippled through them.

"He too smart," Rita said. "Nobody can say Muckie ain't smart."

"All the boys are too smart," Mary Mae said. "They all know better."

Carol Ann pictured David as she had seen him leaving that morning, his shoulders square and his hips moving smoothly, more balanced under him, walking the way a man walked, not a boy. She saw his fair, white skin, and now recognized his unshakable air of privilege and entitlement.

"That Miz Amelia, she making this whole story up. Ain't no man no color gonna look twice at her bony behind," Portya said. "That woman is a snake."

"You're right, she's pure poison," Rita agreed. "I worked up at the big house one Christmas. She's like a mean old barn cat, lying so still then wham! she bites you the minute you ain't looking." Rita pursed her mouth in distaste. "Slapped my face once, she did, for not moving out the way quick enough. Said I was trying to make The Boss take notice."

Portya sniffed and shrugged. Her breasts jiggled under the fabric of the thin blouse. "Huh! Like you'd want that scraggy lip white man. Well I hope you just threw down your apron and walked out."

"Something like that," Rita said.

"Not really!"

"You never!"

Carol Ann looked at her sister and tried to guess what exactly had been said.

"Don't matter none," Mary Mae said. "Don't matter she lying or truthing, them white men gets ahold of this thing."

The fear of the cars and guns and flames at night resurfaced.

"Not for this one thing," Carol Ann begged Rita. "Surely they won't come for this one thing."

Rita shook her head and made a spitting noise. "Depends on their mood. Things have gotten worse here since money started getting so tight. Marcus McKinley, he's a good man with a sense of honor. He ain't gonna do nothing till he's sure. And Sheriff Whitten, he'll do what he can. But them other hotheads, Torrence and his boys down the hill, they get enough juice out of that still, no telling what they aim to do."

The afternoon crawled on, one minute at a time, as the

women waited for Poppa to come back with the sheriff, for the boys to come home from the orchards, for the children to return safe from the fields where they had been picking grubs off the ripening fruit.

"We should go get them," Carol Ann said. "We should find the boys and bring them home now."

"Best not to," Mary Mae said. "Best not to be running all over looking for them, no telling where they are. They'm be home soon, we got to pray they come before Torrence and his gang."

"And we don't want anyone knowing we know something's coming down," Rita added.

Rita set them all to shucking and hulling baby green corn for relish, but it wasn't enough to keep their minds off the time running out. Carol Ann's head began to throb, as if in league with the clock on the wall.

Martina was the only one unaffected, and Carol Ann was glad that the young girl could sit quietly in the corner, singing hymns, growing louder until someone hushed her, then getting quiet again, until she forgot began to get loud once more.

As the last of the sun trickled away through the leaves, throwing the long shadows of branches across the road and yards, shapes moved on the other side of the bridge. Carol Ann squinted, barely breathing, to make out faces. Black or white? David or Torrence?

Rita shouted "Praise be, it's the boys," and raced off to meet them.

Carol Ann followed her, and caught up as they crossed the creek. "Thank the Lord," she whispered, flinging her arms around David, who was too surprised to push her away.

"What's wrong, Momma?" Eddy asked as Rita grabbed him.

"Someone been making time with Miz Amelia, and there be trouble coming tonight. You got to get out into the woods,"

Rita said in a rush, pulling Eddy along to the house. "We gonna try waiting for the sheriff to get here, but if that takes too long, you got to be ready to head for the woods."

Carol Ann caught David's sleeve and prevented him from following. "We need to talk," she mouthed.

He turned a proud, smiling face to hers.

"Oh, God, it's true, isn't it?" She didn't wait for an answer. "Oh my God, you are such a stupid, ignorant boy! How could you have done such a selfish, dangerous thing?" Fear and fury roiled through her veins like a volcano erupting. He was so smug, so proud of himself, and she didn't know which was worse, the danger or the spoiled brat he was behaving like. He didn't have any idea how dangerous his actions had become, and he didn't think the rules applied to him. David—rebellious, headstrong, white—of course he would pick precisely this path to show his scorn.

She shook him as hard as she could. "David," she whispered, "you have to listen to me. They're going to come for you now."

"Nonsense," he said. He pulled away and smoothed his shirtfront with an infuriating air of calm rationality. "She wanted me as much as I wanted her."

She grabbed his shirt in her fist again. "That's besides the point. She's white and you're black." She knew as soon as she said it, that it was exactly the wrong thing to say.

David yanked his sleeve free from her hand and marched, head high, straight to the house and inside. The plank door slammed shut behind him.

Carol Ann followed behind, hugging herself tight. She took a breath and tried to think calmly, logically, tried to think her way through to a solution. As hard as she'd tried to raise David right, his temperament since he'd been a little boy was to lash out when he was angry, without ever understanding that the consequences of his tantrums were often worse than the lack of the toy he'd initially been so angry about. Sometimes she thought he'd inherited the worst of both his parents, and her impatience mixed with Peter's sense of entitlement, was not a combination that would carry him far in life.

Her own lies hadn't helped, she admitted to herself. What David had done was in reaction to what she had done. In his mind she was part of the problem and could offer nothing in the way of its solution, not even the reassurance that she'd once felt as trapped and out of place as he did now. She wanted to bang on the lean-to door, shove it open and confront him with his culpability, but her arms tingled with impotence. On the other hand, why did he think that motherhood meant she owed him her soul? Her secret had been her own, not her son's truth to command.

She bowed her head and recited a benediction. "Oh Lord," she prayed, "protect him from himself until I can beat a lick of sense into him. Keep him safe and let all this blow over. And please, Lord," she added, "let nothing happen until the Sheriff gets here to protect the rest of us."

The grinding of the old truck engine had Carol Ann running out to greet it. Rita, Martina and Eddy were already waiting out front, with Mary Mae and Portya. Others were coming up the road.

Absalom and Zebediah Samuelson crouched in the back of the truck, staring balefully over the wooden sideboards. Two other younger men that Carol Ann didn't recognize crouched beside them. When the truck stopped, the Zebediah leaped over the boards and Absalom and the others calmly followed. Poppa and Willy Hume climbed from the cab.

Poppa looked tired, with gray circles under his eyes and in the hollows of his cheeks, and a softness in the dark flesh of his face, a slackness in the muscles, which made him look old. But he stood tall and calm, and when he held up his hands for silence he radiated power. The voices stilled. "I've talked to Sheriff Whitten and explained the situation. He'll be here as soon as he can get word to his men."

"And if he don't get here soon?" someone called out.

"Then the boys got to run. We have Willy's truck."

Rita grabbed Willy's hand. They could come for him just for helping out. "Thank you for saving my son. You a brave man," she said.

Poppa scanned the men in the group. "Whoever did this, it would be best if he comes forward now. The sheriff can protect him better, the more time he has."

Everyone glanced around at each other, but no one stepped forward.

"This ain't right," Mary Mae said. "Ain't never been right."

Poppa held up his hands for silence once again. "Now we all know this is serious and it can get out of control mighty fast, but if we stay calm it will be better for everyone. The sheriff's on his way, I'm sure he'll be here in plenty of time. He'll tell us what's real and what is just talk."

"It don't matter what's just talk," Zebediah snarled, "if they got the chance to come after one of us, they will. I say we do something about it for a change." He picked up a rock and flipped it from one hand to the other while the chatter of discussion and argument rose around him.

Carol Ann wanted to voice her agreement. Even the black leaders in Washington were starting to stand up to injustice. But this was David, her David.

"I got kids to mind, I don't want them night rollers all over the place for who know how long!" Portya Baylor said.

"I say we stand up to them for a change!" Zebediah repeated.

Carol Ann watched as everyone shifted ever so slightly away from him. They did not want a confrontation, they were going to lie down and take whatever was dished out to them. Even Poppa justified this passivity by labeling it prudence, calling for the need to stay calm. The lack of power shuddered through her. Sweat broke out and chilled on her arms, her forehead. This was why she had left for New York once before. Not only the violence, not only the mud and grime and endless work. Not even the chance to be white in a white world, but the chance to taste a little power for once. If it weren't for David she would quickly join the fight, but she so needed for him to be safe, and a fight was not safe. This fight was never safe.

Poppa leaned forward. "You're right, it doesn't matter if it's only talk, but it might change over to action at any time. I know it, you know it, and Sheriff Whitten knows it, which is why he's coming with his men." He paused once more and waited for everyone to stop whispering. "But it's also true that if we actually hurt someone, Torrence and his boys will come back tomorrow night with half the town, and they won't stop at only frightening us. If we stay calm and sensible, we will come through this night without harm." He held up his hands for silence again. "A gentle answer turneth away wrath."

Zebediah Samuelson opened his mouth as if to continue arguing, then crossed his arms over his chest and stared sullenly at the ground.

Poppa nodded approvingly, and Carol Ann marveled at how even in this situation, Poppa rose up to become father to all of Sculley's Bend. He smiled gently, seeming to solidify into the energy and purpose of his preacher persona, and held his hands out above the heads of his flock. "This is the time for patience and prayer. I expect you act with sense and restraint, both tonight, and tomorrow when you go back to work. That's all there is to say on this matter. If anyone would like to talk to me privately, I will be in the church." He looked around the assembled faces, looking for guilt, Carol Ann thought. But he wouldn't find it, because David was still out behind the house. A gust of wind rose up and slapped her in the face.

As Poppa walked away, slowly and steadily, moving with the weight of the congregation resting solidly across his back, Eddy caught her eye, his indecision and fear written plain.

Carol Ann moved close to him and put her hand on his shoulder. "It's all right, Eddy. I'll talk to Poppa, he'll talk to David. We'll make sure he's safe."

"I told him," Eddy whispered. "I told him he best not be casting his eye on Miz Amelia, but she done called him up to the big house. She done it."

"I know." Carol Ann rubbed Eddy's arm lightly, trying to reassure him. "I know you did the best you could, but David, well, he has to do things his own way sometimes. He doesn't know the rules here, doesn't understand how it all works."

"They're going to kill him, ain't they?" Eddy asked.

Carol Ann put a hand on her stomach, pressing down on the surge of nausea. "No," she said. "No, no. Nothing's going to happen to David, we'll all make sure of that. You get out into the woods now."

She watched him go, wishing she could simply order David to go with him. If anything happened to David, she would sink into the ground and stay there this time. Of all the failures she had been responsible for, this would be the worst. This would be the one that would rend her in two.

Poppa sat in the front pew, bent low over the Bible on his knees. One hand moved back and forth across the rows of verse and his lips worked silently over the words. Carol Ann grappled with what she wanted Poppa to tell David, what he needed to know. This wasn't New York, he needed to know that. He wasn't white any longer, he needed to know that too. So many things she wanted to tell him, but she couldn't. All she could do was hold her breath and vainly try to block out the image of him hanging from the branch of a tree with a thick, white rope around his neck.

She stepped quietly down the aisle to join Poppa in the pew. They sat together, side by side, for a few minutes, while Carol Ann clenched her fists and watched the dust drifting through the late afternoon light that slanted down from the narrow opening high up in the walls. "I'm so frightened," she whispered at last.

Poppa reached out and covered one of Carol Ann's hands with his own. "The Lord also will be a stronghold in times of trouble, and those who know His name will put their trust in Him."

"You always have a verse to recite, Poppa. You always find words in the Good Book that fit."

"The strength of our Lord is easy to find words for." He paused. "It's not as easy to find the same strength and goodness in the people around us in this world," he said. He glanced toward the door, as if Torrence and his men were already there.

"You have the gift, Poppa, for saying things so people will understand." Carol Ann glanced sideways to see Poppa watching her patiently. "You know how to say what each person needs to hear." Even if he did shield himself in endless quotes. She gripped her knees, knowing she was floundering around in her own words. "I'd like you to talk to David," she said at last.

"Why, Daughter?" His tone was calm, but the muscles standing out on his forearms told a different story. Carol Ann swallowed hard, and sweat broke out across her forehead. How could she tell him his own grandson was the one who had brought this trouble down into the helpless community of Sculley's Bend? She sat for what seemed like hours, debating what to say, her thoughts flickering one after the other, faster than she could control them.

Tell him, he needs to know.

Don't tell him, this will all blow over.

Tell him, he's the only one who can help.

David will never forgive me if I tell, but he will get hurt if he doesn't understand how things work.

Tell him, because otherwise tonight David will get killed.

Murdered.

She breathed heavily, and wrapped her arms around herself, rubbing at the stiffness in her neck and shoulders. "He doesn't want to hide," she whispered, not looking at Poppa, her cowardice winning out. "He still thinks he's white."

She heard him start to ask a question, a clarification perhaps, when the sharp inhalation signaled his sudden understanding of what Carol Ann had failed to say. She shut her eyes and bowed her head, bracing herself for the wave of thunderous anger about to break over her. She deserved it.

Poppa stood slowly, heavily as if he were lifting the earth into the heavens. Carol Ann watched his shoes as he moved to stand directly in front of her. "How could he?" he bellowed. "Does he not understand what trouble he has brought down on us? On all of us, not only himself?"

"No!" Carol Ann shook her head rapidly. "He didn't understand what he was doing." She looked up.

Poppa glared down at her, his gray eyebrows thickening over his shadowed eyes. "How could you let him do this? What were you thinking?"

"I didn't know. I didn't have any idea. You think this is all happening because I didn't raise my son right? Because I'm an unfit mother? " Carol Ann looked away, shunning the intimacy of eye contact.

"That's not for me to say. But your ignorance will not help him now," Poppa snapped. "'Vengeance is mine', saith the Lord, but He does not always protect us from human retribution." He started to say something else, paused, then slammed the Bible down on the seat next to her. "This is how you raised him, and this is the result."

"Poppa!" Carol Ann reached out for him but he stalked away, putting the pulpit between them. "That's not fair! I didn't raise him to hate blacks!"

"Ye reap what ye sow!" He thumped his hand down hard on wood and Carol Ann jumped. He leaned forward, glowering, his skin flushed and his mouth hard. "You run off north and hide yourself away white, get yourself a white husband and white children because it's easier than being black. Well now, girl, you're finding out how hard it is to take the easy way out."

They glared at each other through the haze of their anger. The pause allowed Carol Ann to regain a fragment of her control. Think of David. "I know you're mad at me but this is too important. This is David's life we're talking about. He has to be made to understand what can happen. He cannot do anything dangerous or stupid tonight." Fear beat against Carol Ann like huge moths with heavy wings, buffeting her with blows she could neither see nor defend herself from.

She wanted Poppa to talk to David. She wanted to beg Poppa just to reason with David, to convince him to hide, be safe, to not stand out for once in his proud life. Yet even as she tried to frame the words, she knew they were wrong. To David, Poppa was not a wise, respected community leader. He was simply an old black man who could not possibly understand how he felt, who exaggerated the danger that could come to him, a white boy. She didn't want to take on this crucial task by herself. She dreaded the responsibility, the dire consequences of not convincing David to stay safe, to lie low. And yet, she knew she had to.

Poppa seemed to sense her change of direction. "You have to do this." He walked back from the pulpit and sat down next to her.

Fear disoriented her thoughts and roughened her voice. "I don't know how to break through to him, he's still too angry to listen. This is so important. He needs to understand he can't do whatever he wants, that he has to hide tonight, not get caught. Not say anything he shouldn't." She put her hand on his arm, feeling her tension mirrored in his muscles. "Tell me what to say, Poppa."

"You will find your own words." He put his arm around her and for a minute she felt the warm shelter it provided. "You will find the path, Daughter, and so will he." It occurred to her that he had retreated from "daughter" to "girl" and back again, and still had not once called her by name since she'd come home.

She walked slowly from the church to the house, listening to the crickets, watching the last indigo of the evening sky fade. The sheriff would be here soon; she would have to convince David to accept his protection. What could she tell him? She rehearsed her words as she walked to the lean-to, where she found David lying on his bed, staring at the ceiling in the dimming light. She tapped gently on the rough planks of the door and stooped to enter.

"I know you're still angry with me, but we need to talk." She sat down on the edge of the worn mattress and David slid away from her. "Do you understand how much trouble this is going to cause?"

David rolled to face the wall.

"Look at me," Carol Ann snapped, grabbing a fistful of shirt material and pulling him toward her. David turned his head only enough to stare at her with cold eyes. "Do you really understand how much has changed? Do you really understand you're on the other side of the fence now, and it's not even the fence you think it is?"

Confusion fluttered for a brief moment in David's eyes.

"This isn't New York. This isn't a simple question of black skin or white skin. This is about power and no power. They have it. We don't. If they decide to come riding down here and hang you up in a tree, and Poppa too for supporting you, and maybe a complete stranger, just because they bumped into him on the way, they could do it, and they would get away with it. Do you understand? Do you really understand how isolated we are here? That's what this is about." She spoke rapidly, her voice low, her eyes glaring. The fist holding his shirtfront clenched hard. "This is the truth of this world, David, they can commit murder, and no one will even blink."

David looked startled for a minute, then his eyes retreated back into their sullen depths. Carol Ann leaned forward, grabbed his shoulders and yanked him to a sitting position, shaking him hard. "Use your head, for crying out loud." She was practically shouting now. "Are you willing to die for nothing more than an afternoon's roll in the hay?"

"Don't you say that!" David shouted back, breaking his silence at last. He pulled away from her hard, and tumbled off the side of the bed. He stood to leave but Carol Ann leaped up and blocked the doorway.

"Listen to me, you stupid fool. You think she's special? That she's the one you've been waiting for all your life? Don't be ridiculous. You like the idea of getting even with me for bringing you here, for being black. And she's using you as well. She's stuck here, the same way you think you are, stuck away in an old apple orchard, with a deformed farmer for a husband, who doesn't pay enough attention to her, for the rest of her life."

"You're wrong!" David refused to face her. "You don't understand."

"Go ahead and shut me out, but I'm telling the truth. You think she's too fine to tell anyone? Ask yourself, what good is revenge, or even true love, for that matter, if no one knows about it?" Carol Ann shook her head and shut her eyes. "Don't be a fool, David. She had to tell someone, and now McKinley and his men will come down here after you. Your only chance is to talk to the sheriff when he gets here."

"Never," David shouted. "You're wrong!" She thought she heard him mumble, "it's our special secret," but she wasn't sure.

She started to argue more, then stopped and reached forward to touch his hair, streaked with blond from his time in the sun. He would never show his black heritage. "I love you, David. I love you and I don't want you to get hurt. I don't know what I can say to make you understand how dangerous this situation is."

David's muscles rippled under his shirt as he breathed. His eyes were still angry, but his lips trembled like a boy's. "You lied to me, you lied to Father, you lied to everyone we knew. It was all a lie, and now here we are!"

Carol Ann bowed her head. How on earth could she respond to this accusation, this truth. "I wish I could give you an answer that would make it all better, but there isn't one. I didn't mean to poison your memories of your childhood, and I hope one day you'll realize that the good times were real, not imaginary. I loved your father so much, and one innocent lie led to another." She sighed. "It's so much easier to let things slide than to be brave and tell the truth." She paused. "It will be hard to sacrifice your pride and tell the sheriff what you did, to ask for his protection when he comes. I know just how hard it will be, but it's what you have to do."

"If you could do it all over, would you tell the truth?" David challenged her.

Time seemed to slow down. How often she had asked herself this question. "It's not as easy as that. If I hadn't been passing, I would never have met your father. Then I would never have had you and Martina, and I wouldn't change any of that for all the truth-telling in the world. And no matter what else you think, you know that's no lie."

They stood there in silence for a long time, leaning against the wall, but Carol Ann thought the silence was calm for the first time in a long while. Then slowly, as if his arm was rusty with disuse, he reached out and put his fingers across the back of her hand. Tears trickled unheeded down her cheeks. "Oh David, I do so love you. Please don't do anything stupid. Please."

In the distance a dog barked.

Willy Hume's pickup fired to life.

The rattle of vehicles barreling down the road at top speed, gravel clattering, grew closer. Sheriff or Torrence?

The sound of barking grew louder.

Carol Ann leaped to her feet, pulling David with her. They raced for the road, for the safety of the pickup.

Just as they arrived, the engine coughed, choked and died.

Carol Ann flung herself against David and wrapped him in a tight embrace, holding him close. Against her chest she could feel his hammering heart beat echoing her own fear. He clung to her as he had when he was just a tiny little child, and a single, gasping sob escaped him.

CHAPTER 30

MARTINA

The gods have come! They are here! Where is Jesus-our-one-lord? Make the circles come! Too much noise! Too much light! The gods are so big, no one is safe. Where are the circles? Black feet devils. White bodies angels. Screaming! Dogs barking. So many dogs barking. So loud! Why did they use the door?

CHAPTER 31

DAVID

David lay face down in the bed of the pickup truck where he'd been thrown with Eddy. When he tried to rise, a heavy foot jammed into the small of his back and knocked him flat. "You stay put, boy. We had enough trouble outta you niggers." He couldn't identify the voice, and the anonymity made the words all the more menacing. Sweat trickled sideways across his forehead. He bit his lip with the effort not to throw up and tasted blood. These men had arrived before the sheriff, grabbed him, and now he was going to die. The front of his pants clung wetly to his thighs, and the flat, dull odor of someone's feces washed over him. He didn't know or care if it was his own.

He shivered and tried to brace himself with his hands, so his face wouldn't bang so violently against the rough boards as the truck dove into each rut in the road and then leaped out. In spite of the bright lantern light, from his position he could see nothing but a pair of feet—Eddy's, perhaps—and the torn denim of the overalls above them. The truck stopped, boots thudded and scrambled. The weight of another body, and another, hammered against him as two other men were forced onto the floor. Their fast, frightened breathing joined with the others; David caught the occasional word or grunt from their captors.

His brain swirled with the effort to block out the endless loop of his guilt.

He recalled scraps of his motivation as he lay with Amelia: anger at Mother for all her deceptions, at Father for abandoning them in his own way. Thoughts of revenge for the many wrongs, to bring pride and strength back into his impotent days. He remembered his smug satisfaction at the idea of everyone knowing what he'd done, and who he'd done it with. Amelia couldn't have told. She wouldn't have. Maybe she didn't love him, but she wouldn't have slept with him and then let their secret out, knowing this would happen. Someone must have seen them.

The white-robed arm holding the lantern moved, and the pool of light slid away, leaving David in darkness as thick as glue. He knew he ought to be thinking about escape, but his fear cloaked him as heavily as the darkness, and he curled in on himself, trying to hide.

Betrayed. He wanted to say "again," and his thoughts skittered from Mother to Amelia to Father, traveling around and around in a tight circle. But in this hour, so close to dying, honesty came over him. His own stupidity had betrayed him. Whoever had said "death organized one's thoughts" had been wrong. His mind stumbled like a wounded bear.

He had been angry, so angry, with Mother for the very same things he had done, and now he would never be able to tell her he was sorry. He had made such a dreadful, fatal mistake, and as a result men had come for him in the night, grabbed him and dragged him to the truck before he knew what was happening. He would not be able to tell Mother he loved her, and that was the worst punishment of all. She would never know he now understood, perhaps only a little, of what it meant to be caught up in the wrong world, in the wrong skin, trapped. He'd had the slimmest glimmer of what it might have been like for her, coming so young, so gullible, to the roiling cauldron that was New York, not knowing the rules, not knowing the people, doing whatever was necessary to survive.

Eddy gasped a shuddering, terrified breath, and David's mind did clarify. He would die tonight, but the others did not need to. He began to look for an opportunity to create a distraction so they could escape. He tried to roll enough to get a better view around him, earning himself another kick.

When the truck stopped David didn't immediately react. If he lay still and made himself hard to deal with, they would focus on him and the others could run.

"Out, out," a voice shouted. Movement rocked the truck, and boots crunched hard across the planks of the truck bed, dispensing kicks. The rumbling of additional trucks rattling down the road and revving their engines created a backdrop of sound. Headlights coming up and over the bumps and dips in the road sent ribbons of yellow light crisscrossing the legs and boots within his line of sight.

"Get your black asses down here." More shouts. More thuds and grunts.

David felt a boot thump into his ribs. A hand on his collar pushed him off the back of the truck and onto the hard dirt. He fell, landing hard on one knee, began to rise, then limply dropped back to the ground. Perhaps if he could stay down long enough the others would have a chance to run. But more boots connected with his ribs, and more hands grabbed his arms and hauled him to his feet. Not nearly enough time.

In the light from the lanterns and truck headlights that completely encircled them, David saw there were the six of them from the Bend. Next to himself and Eddy stood Absalom and Zebediah, who also hadn't hidden well enough or soon enough, and two of the other hands David didn't know as well. He thought there were nine white-robed men, but there might have been one or two more in the shadows, he wasn't sure, all holding shotguns or hunting rifles. If he created a commotion now, the others could run, but they'd get shot in the back. He stood up straight and stared at the white ghosts, one at a time. They would hang him tonight, for his own sins, but he would stand tall before them. He tried to think of an appropriate speech to deliver when the time came, but all he could think of was "I regret that I have but one life to give for my country," which didn't seem at all right. In spite of his determination to stand tall, shudders wracked his arms and legs, his whole body.

Next to him Eddy stood, shoulders hunched, teeth chattering. On his other side Absalom mumbled a nearly inaudible prayer. He smelled his own sweat. "Tell Mother I love her," he leaned toward Eddy and whispered. "Tell her I'm sorry."

Ray Torrence, his voice clearly recognizable, stepped forward and drove the butt of his rifle into David's stomach. "Cut that yappin', boy!"

David doubled over and inhaled sharply as pain and nausea caught him. With an effort of will he rose slowly upright.

"I'd hit you again but I don't wanna slow you down too much." He turned to call over his shoulder to the other men, "We gonna have us a right ole coon hunt tonight, ain't we?" The men all around laughed and waved their guns in the flickering lantern and yellow car lights, sending bizarre shadows leaping and dancing across the ground and upward against the leaves of the looming trees.

"Go ahead, boy, run." The orchard manager poked David with the butt of the gun again, hard enough to make him stumble backward a step. "You run, nigger. I like a little," he paused, and the black eye holes in his robe swiveled malevolently toward him, "foreplay." The audience roared their amusement and Torrence broke his stare and turned back to his friends and laughed with them.

"Stop that." Another voice intruded, sharp with command. A tall man stepped forward from the side of one of the trucks, into the glare of the headlights. "We're here for justice, not to play games."

The rest of the men shuffled around, and the sound of their boots scraping in the dirt caught David's attention. Someone coughed, and it seemed to be the signal for an outburst of voices.

"Ain't fair, we here to go hunting," one man muttered.

"Don't see why we can't have both. Nothin' wrong with sport and justice at the same time," another said.

"That's right, we come to have us some fun."

The tall man put up his hand for silence, and waited until he got it. "I said we're here for justice. We'll do what needs to be done, then we go home." The high pitch and the lisp from the twisted harelip identified Marcus McKinley under the sheltering costume.

"But Boss," Torrence protested. "The men come for the night. We rounded up all them there, not just for turning around and going straight home." He stepped forward and pushed Absalom in the stomach with the flat of his boot.

"Step back and step away," McKinley ordered.

"We're not on your nickel now, Boss. If we want to stick around and enjoy ourselves we damn well can."

"You're on your own time, but you're on my land, and these are my workers. You want to play stupid games, you do it somewhere else, with someone else's hands."

McKinley and Torrence stared at each other, and David's breath clogged in his chest as he waited for the outcome, alert for his chance. He dared to peer sideways, looking for an opening to let the others run. His jaws rattled and his teeth chattered so loud he was sure everyone there was be staring at him. Patience, he schooled himself. This is like fencing, wait for them to let their guard down. If he moved now, if any of them tried to get away too soon, it would certainly start a full scale shooting and they would all end up dead. His only hope was to pray that Marcus McKinley was a strong enough leader to keep his men in line.

"I said, step back and step away." McKinley's voice was cold, smooth and restrained. David was terrified.

Torrence snarled softly but retreated a half pace. As he turned he swung out with an abrupt, vicious movement and knocked David in the chin with his rifle butt. Bright lights flashed in the backs of David's eyeballs. For a few seconds the trucks, the trees and all the people danced through splashes of purple and green, and the ground twisted upward toward him. He put a hand on Eddy's shoulder to steady himself, and clung tightly until stability returned. Under his fingers Eddy was shivering, and he let go before his cousin's fears unseated his own attempts at cool control. He covertly surveyed the area once more, desperate to map out a strategy to give the others an opening to freedom.

Marcus McKinley walked out of the direct glare of the headlights to the passenger side of his truck. He opened the door and leaned in, then reappeared holding Amelia by the arm. He dragged her forward to face the crooked row of terrified farmhands.

Her back was to the headlights so David couldn't see her face, but he guessed from her cringing posture and the way she leaned away from her husband that he had been hitting her. Her hair was down, straggling back from her face in tangled disarray, and one sleeve was torn at the shoulder.

"Which one," McKinley asked loudly. "Which one raped you?"

She curled away from him and her voice came out in a whine. "I don't know."

He shook her, hard.

"I can't tell, it's too dark."

"Bring those lanterns over here," McKinley called out.

She hadn't betrayed him after all, was David's first thought. She could hardly have mistaken him, with the lights from the trucks shining directly into his face. He'd been right all along, they had been seen, or more likely heard, by some eavesdropper. Amelia was haloed by the headlights, looking like an angel, and David's heart filled with warmth.

Then she raised her arm, a torn strip of sleeve hanging down, and pointed directly at him. "That one," she said clearly into the silent circle of men.

David absorbed the blow of her treachery and stood up straight in front of the accusing finger. This was his fate. Had Father felt like this when he'd been staring down the barrel of a German MG 08 on a blood soaked field in Belgium? Had he been doused in this flood of hot sweat, racked by this unstoppable shuddering, startled by the cool, crisp focus of his thoughts? Eddy had been right as well, Mother would cry and cry and cry. He would not break down before that pointing finger.

McKinley stared into his wife's face and shifted his grip on her arm. "You sure about that?" he asked, speaking in dark, measured tones.

"Course I'm sure," she snapped. "That one," she repeated, stabbing her finger into the air, then dropping her arm and hugging it across her waist. She glared up at her husband.

Marcus McKinley stared at her until she lowered her eyes. "I'm asking you one more time, if you're sure."

Amelia nodded, and seemed to hug herself tighter.

It wasn't until McKinley raised his gun and sighted along the barrel that David realized she hadn't been pointing at him, but a few degrees to his right, at Eddy. He called out a shocked, "Wait!" but it got lost in the rifle blast that knocked

Eddy out of the line and onto his back in the dirt.

In falling, his cousin flung out his arms as if welcoming the bullet which tore through him. The yawning hole in his chest shone black and wet in the yellow light, and in the echoing hollow after the blast, David heard nothing, not even his own screaming. He tasted warm vomit in his throat, in his mouth, saw it splatter on the ground, and its odor mixed with the stink of burnt gunpowder. He would never forget that smell.

He fell to his knees to cradle Eddy in his arms, refusing to admit it was already too late. The eyes were wide, staring at the sky, seeing nothing. Blood spilled over his hands. He was shocked at how hot it was.

Footsteps crunched the leaves next to him, and he peered numbly into the black eyeholes of a white hood.

"You tell his Momma I'm right sorry I had to do this," Marcus McKinley said. "He was a good boy and didn't deserve to die this way." The eyeholes stared at him, bottomless and soulless. "Did he?"

David shook his head, signaling his understanding of the warning in the words. Any thought he'd had of heroically confessing the truth died in the glare of reality; a confession would not undo this night and would only serve to get him killed just as swiftly. He looked past McKinley to where Amelia had been standing and saw her climbing into the truck she had arrived in, a bright lantern centering her in a pool of light. From her safe circle she turned back to the scene in the dirt, and smiled.

The whole night seemed to freeze. She had peeled the skin from her face and revealed a hideous skull smirking beneath the human mask. "I own you," the smile said. "I won."

Revenge is no good if no one knows about it, and neither is power. Mother had been right. He was literally, living proof of

Amelia's power, and they both knew it. Then her husband stepped between them, one arm raised, and slapped her across the face. When he moved away, the skull was gone and the ordinary, limp woman had returned, servile and defeated.

David knelt in the dirt as hot tears rolled down his cheeks and dropped onto his hands. His thoughts blurred into a haze of anger and despair, of pain and grief. All the poetry he had learned in school about death and dying seemed pointless, insufficient to capture this engulfing anguish. Only one phrase made sense to him, weaving through and around all his thoughts. "Thus he died for my sins." A core of fury, rigid and bitter white like a pillar of salt, formed in his gut.

Over his shoulder voices rumbled in a fog of meaningless noise.

"Shoot 'em all."

"Coon hunt."

"Goin' to get my dogs outta the truck."

"Y'all stop that and get on home now."

"Ain't no fun."

"They gone now."

"I said get on home, you too."

"Praise the Lord, it all over," a voice said. "David, it all over now."

"David, Torrence an' his boys, they gone now," another voice said. "We got to get home now, in case they get drunk and come back."

David grew aware these last voices were addressed to him. He didn't know how long he had knelt in the dirt but the trucks were gone, the clearing in near darkness, lit by only one lantern. A bat swooped in close to them and veered off.

Two of the field hands were already gone. Absalom and Zebediah crouched next to Eddy's body, resting their large, knotted hands gently on him. Zebediah reached out, closed the staring eyes and wiped the thread of black from the side of Eddy's mouth. "He were a good boy, Steady Eddy were," he said. "This ain't right, it just ain't right." His face was a knotted mass of clenched anger.

"A smart boy, fixing to grow up a preacher jus like his Grandpoppa," Absalom said.

David heard the words, and struggled to frame thoughts around them, but all he could think about was Eddy's blood, cooling so quickly on his skin.

"Lord, you take good care o' this boy, he a good boy," Zebediah demanded. "You take him into your palace and give him all what a boy should have."

"Amen," Absalom answered.

Maybe it was his fault, his hands absorbing the heat from Eddy's blood.

"Give him new clothes, all white clothes, and chocolate to eat."

"Lots of good food," Absalom added.

David and the other men knelt together in the clearing, shoulder to shoulder. David could no longer distinguish whose hands were whose.

"Amen," Absalom said.

"Amen," David whispered, joining in. He felt his one word rise up from that core of anger inside him, on a current, moving away from him, pulling him to someplace new.

"Give him shoes that fit his feet like velvet and a soft pillow on his bed," Zebediah said.

"Amen," David and Absalom answered.

"Give him rest, Lord. Give him a chair to set in and nothing to do but sing with the angels all day long."

"Amen."

"Lord, give him peace," David said. Silence settled over them as they knelt in the tiny island of light. "The soul of God is up there," he whispered to Eddy. "You said you could see

Him above you in the sunset." If there was a God, David wanted Him to watch over Eddy now, as now one had watched over him in life.

"The Boss left us a lantern so's we can get home," Absalom said.

"Well ain't that mighty nice of him, considering he just up and killed Eddy," Zebediah sneered. The mood of prayer shattered.

"Most times he a good man, Mr. McKinley is," Absalom said.

"How can you say that?" David demanded. "After what he did?"

Zebediah nodded fierce agreement, but Absalom shrugged. "Weren't his fault Eddy were sleeping with Miz Amelia. I don't say rape now, but was something, sure. Man's got a right to protect his woman."

"A man has a right to due process of law," David snapped back. He should speak in Eddy's defense, but common sense silenced him. There was plenty of time to confess later, if Mother thought it was the right thing to do. He would be able to apologize to her now, he thought bitterly. Now that it was too late for Eddy.

"Theres laws and then there's laws," Absalom said. "We best be getting on home 'fore one them pateroller peckerwoods take it in his mind to come on back."

David choked down the argument he was about to make. This wasn't the time to argue, they still weren't completely out of danger.

"We can build a stretcher outta shirts and them branches," Absalom said.

"Anyone know where we are?" David asked. "How do we get home from here?"

Absalom looked around the clearing. "We just down the road to the old cider house, ain't we, Zeb?"

"Think so," Zebediah said. "Look like this road ain't been used in a while."

"We ain't far then, no more'n a couple miles, mostly."

David remained in silent vigil next to the body while the Samuelsons found suitable fallen branches. He pulled off his shirt and rebuttoned it around the poles. They lifted Eddy gently and laid him on the stretcher, then David stepped to the back and took hold of the poles. "I don't know the way home, you two take turns carrying the front and leading the way," he commanded.

"It be a mighty long way to carry," Absalom suggested, stepping up to the front of the stretcher.

"I'll manage," David said. The rough bark bit into his palms and he rocked the weight from one hand to the other, settling his grip. On a somber three count, he and Absalom lifted the stretcher. Eddy was surprisingly light, and David knew he would get no heavier, no matter how many miles they had to walk. Time slowed down, strength flowed in. "This is for the times I didn't pull my own weight," he told his cousin. The trees rose tall at the edge of the light, seeming to bend over and toward them, as if threatening the little group. The flickering of the lantern moving ahead of them gave the illusion of movement to the still body, and each time his eye caught it, David felt a stab of hope and resulting despair.

Had the few minutes he'd spent with Amelia been worth it? No, no, and yet again no, on so many counts. He had sacrificed Eddy for a chance to show the world how important he was, which in the end meant nothing more than a peacock's superficial display of make-believe power. Eddy, dead so young, because his spoiled, ignorant cousin refused to believe the rules applied to him.

David continued his march down the old road, never stumbling, never relinquishing his task. This was his penance: to carry the burden of Eddy's death, until he found justice for this night's tragedy. How young and melodramatic that declaration sounded, but the hot, hard knot inside him made it more substantial than mere words.

They reached the edge of Sculley's Bend and crossed the plank bridge. Oblongs of light widened as doors opened and people came pouring   out to meet them with voices calling, questions beginning. By the time they arrived in the churchyard everyone in the Bend, even the children, had assembled. David saw other neighbors from farther away, they had rallied to help care for the community in any way they could. Aunt Rita raced toward them, her face a jagged tear of pain and denial, and they paused as she grabbed Eddy's shoulders and shook him, screaming meaningless phrases into his deaf ears. Mother's figure leaped into sharp focus, swaddling Aunt Rita in her arms, leading her away. David and Absalom resumed walking. Grandpoppa beckoned to them from the doorway, and they mounted the steps and proceeded down the aisle to rest the stretcher across two chairs that had already been set out, waiting.

Aunt Rita followed them, and flung herself onto her knees before her son, and buried her face in his hair. With gentle fingers she stroked his cheeks and lifted clinging bits of grass off his neck.

Mother came up behind him and hugged him ferociously tight. "Oh David," she whispered. "Oh David."

Grandpoppa bowed his head and placed one hand on Eddy's forehead and the other on Aunt Rita's. "The Lord is my shepherd," he began, and broke off with a huge sob. He took a handkerchief out of his pocket and held it over his face. "I can't, oh Lord, I can't." He sank to his knees and moaned. "Take me instead, Lord. But not this one, not this one."

The congregation fell silent. All through the church, the cries and wailing faded. People shifted uncomfortably in their seats.

Grandpoppa looked up for a minute, staring straight at David.

He knows. David burned with guilt and shame. He recognized his own despair mirrored in the old, sad man before him and knew the words "this one," had meant, "why this grandson and not that one?" He might someday make some puling, pitiful reparation for all the wrongs of this night's work, but he could never take Eddy's place in this man's heart, or any other heart.

Martina crept quietly up the aisle and knelt down next to Aunt Rita, leaning sideways to rest her head on Rita's shoulder. She put her hands out to touch Eddy's chest where the bullet had torn it apart, and when she felt the stickiness there, she pulled them back. She studied them carefully, then took the handkerchief from her pocket and covered Eddy's chest with it.

"Cousin Eddy," she said.

"Yes honey," said Aunt Rita, sniffling.

"Cousin Eddy is in God's home now," Martina said, and Rita, with loud, rasping sobs, flung her arms around the girl, who screeched and slid backward, but then awkwardly returned the embrace, patting the older woman's back with a mechanical rhythm.

David gazed through the dim, kerosene lighting, at the tiny church with its spare wooden benches, at the black faces, at the tears and pain etched into those faces. He was the cause of this misery. He studied Grandpoppa, the leader of this desolate flock, himself so lost, at Aunt Rita, wretched in her own agony, at Mother, so torn between protecting him, glad that he was alive, and grieving with everyone else. He felt the force of his guilt like water silently building up behind a weakened dam. He wished himself capable of returning a measure of comfort, of peace, to this community he had so damaged, but only words came to him. How he longed to be a man of warmth, of charm, as Father was. He yearned to have more skills than dry education, just this once. But in the end, all he had were words, and few though they were, he offered them. This time, for the first time, he would stand up and speak at the right time, for the right reason, because it was his responsibility to do so. Forever onward from this day forward, it would be his responsibility to do so.

He stepped in front of the pews and turned toward the watching faces of the small community. He stood up straight, and tried so see each and every face, to show each and every one of them he was ready to shoulder his burden. He bowed his head over the body he had carried out of the forest, over the death he had created. He spoke strongly and his words rang though the night and the congregation. "Warm summer sun shine kindly here," he began. "Warm southern wind blow softly here." He wanted to reach out and touch Eddy's arm, but he did not. "Green sod above, rest light, rest light. Good night, dear heart, good night, good night."

CHAPTER 32

CAROL ANN

It was too beautiful a day to bury someone you loved. The sun shone golden behind a curtain of haze in a sky washed with turquoise and lapis; a little rain had fallen during the very early morning, suffusing the air with just enough moisture to take the edge off the heat and keep the dirt lying still in the road. The flowers and trees, rinsed of their habitual coating of dust, filled the eye with color and life. But not the heart.

Carol Ann put her palms over her eyes, puffy from a night of sobbing. Hearts in Sculley's Bend were wrung out and empty today. She didn't know what to do, where to go. She could barely breathe for thinking about what Rita was going through right now. It felt like even the house had caught its breath, that it was sitting still and stiff, holding all the pain in tight to itself.

Martina hadn't left Rita's side for a minute the previous evening as they sat vigil over Eddy's body in the church. Rita hadn't seemed to mind, leaning against the girl for support. Martina's bed had been empty when Carol Ann woke up, almost certainly she and Rita had slept in the church as well. Soon the women would begin washing Eddy, oiling his skin and hair and dressing him in his best clothes. Praying over him, for his soul to wing fast to everlasting peace. Carol Ann left the cabin to search for Poppa and, indeed, several women with bowls and clothing folded over their arms were heading down the path.

She found Poppa in the shed; the sound of sandpaper scraping against wood led her to where he stooped over the nearly finished coffin. There was such tenderness in his hands and movements, as if he were soothing Eddy himself. Each board showed the loving care of his meticulous shaping, each one nestled as straight against its neighbor as palms pressed together in prayer.

Tears seeped down the dry riverbeds of wrinkles in his cheeks, along the gullies of his nose, into the valleys of his mouth and chin. A drop splattered the surface of the pale wood before him, a minute later one fell on the back of a hand so slowly smoothing the clean surfaces. He made no attempt to wipe the tears away.

He was such a large man, he had been such a large man, and now he was collapsed down inside himself. Like Peter, she thought, no more than an empty shell. Everyone around her had crumbled, and she had been part of bringing this tragedy, this disaster, down on all of them. She had raised David to think he was entitled to the best of everything the world had to offer, without the need to consider the price. She had been living a lie, and she had brought him into that lie with her.

"You were right, Poppa," Carol Ann said. "There are things I can't run away from. It's time for me to step up and take a stand." She had run away from Sculley's Bend, she had run away from Peter's condition, she had run away from dealing with Martina's attack and thrust her into Rita's arms. She had even run away from her own self, her own race, her own skin.

She stepped forward and put her hand over his. "I'm sorry, Poppa." In those words she meant all the things she should have said over all the years. I'm sorry for leaving you behind and running away to New York when Momma died.

I'm sorry for keeping David and Martina away from you. "You must be so ashamed of me."

"No, not that." Poppa stopped working the wood. "You flew toward the sun, as any young bird does."

"But you've been so angry at me. So disappointed."

"Angry, yes. At your lies, your deceit, at your haughty manner. I was disappointed that you kept so distant from us. But ashamed? Not for one minute, Daughter."

"I've been ashamed enough for both of us," she confessed in a whisper.

He held his arms out to her then, tears fresh on his face and hers, and she dove into his embrace and buried herself there, inhaling the scent of his sweat and sawdust. She welcomed his forgiveness, and it her made her burden a little easier, but only a little. Perhaps that was the way of it. Healing would come little by little, over time, with patience and hard work. She sneezed as the sawdust tickled her nose, "I love you, Poppa," she said, because it was the only thing left to say.

At last Poppa took a shuddering breath and pulled away. "The sheriff, he went home last night, but he be coming round again soon," he said, turning back and putting his hands gently on Eddy's coffin wood, his face caving in on itself once again. "Someone need to make sure there ain't gonna be no trouble come from us here." He picked up the planer and began coaxing long, ghostly curls of pine off the already smooth surface. He looked like each movement was a struggle.

Carol Ann watched the dust dancing in the sunlight angling through the gaps between the planks of the shack walls. She swallowed, gripped her courage, and raised her chin as she had seen Momma do so many times. "I'll talk to the sheriff, Poppa. You do what you need to do here."

"There be folks wanting to talk back, and not be so still and sweet. Robey Watkins will be wanting to fight loudest, and maybe this time that be the right thing to do."

"I'll talk to them, Poppa. I'll make sure no one starts anything we're not all prepared to finish." She sincerely hoped she'd be able to live up to those words.

"Thank you, Daughter," he whispered, a sound like a used up balloon. "Thank you."

Carol Ann took one last look at him, then walked back into the sunshine, blinking in the sudden brightness. The glimmer of an idea took hold. A long ago forgotten article in the Times, Peter and their friends arguing amicably at a dinner party while the women discussed fashion. The rights of factory workers? She hadn't paid much attention, other than to make sure, from her position as hostess, the argument didn't turn acrimonious. The rights of employees. Yes, that was it. A woman had sued some petroleum company because her son had fallen from a rickety scaffold at work. Loss of comfort and companionship, they'd called it. The details were coming back to her now.

They would need a lawyer, but back in New York she knew lawyers. Good ones. They would need money, and back in New York she knew women who spent their entire day raising funds for worthy causes. Carol Ann squinted into the middle distance, seeing nothing, focused on her growing confidence in the path that stretched sure and straight before her.

This early in the morning the sun spilled into the churchyard at a sharp angle, painting long streaks of light and dark across the backs of men moving to put tables out under the two huge sourgum trees in the side yard. Just visible behind the church, David, Zeb and Abraham were clustered together, their digging rhythmic with the bending and straightening of their backs, the swinging of their arms and tools.

Oh David, what could she say to him? He had been devastated yesterday when he'd returned with Eddy's body. He'd had the pride, the arrogance ripped so violently out of him, leaving behind the loving, caring, but unspeakably wounded boy, turning rapidly into a man. Last night had inflicted a gash that would never completely heal. She hoped it would not putrefy, she hoped the budding strength, the growing courage, she'd seen when he spoke his benediction was truly a measure of the way the young tree was stretching straight. She would tell him how proud she was, and how she shared his guilt for her contribution to this tragedy. She hoped that would be enough for now.

People were appearing at the crest of the hill, dressed in their somber dark clothes, carrying pots and baskets. One family after another trudged the dirt path to the church. Willy Hume's truck chugged slowly up the narrow road, lifting an elongated cloud of dust. Carol Ann was soon surrounded by a sea of weathered brown faces and sad smiles as neighbors and friends clustered around, touching each other gently, pressing bowed heads to stooped shoulders, defeat and impotence smothering them all. She smoothed down the wrinkled blue cotton of her dress, fingered the frayed edge of a hole near one of the flowers in the pattern, and nodded stiffly as the mourners passed her.

Under a hat newly garnished with black paper carnations, old Mrs. Watkins looked like a brown wren hiding in a bramble bush. "Robey come early, he over there toting tables. He was thinking to talk to the Reverend before service."

Carol Ann put her hand on the woman's shoulder. "I think we got to leave Poppa alone till he ready. Meanwhile, if folks want to talk about good ways to make this right, that would be a fit thing to do."

"But your Poppa," the older woman twittered, and then stopped. "You right," she said, her voice suddenly soft. "Your Poppa, he need to be in the dark for a while, he hurting now." She turned toward the western side of the church, where early morning shade still lingered and the ground was still cool, not yet baked in the heat of day. The older men and women had begun to congregate there, and Carol Ann moved slowly toward them.

She nerved herself for the task ahead; she'd never tried to guide a group before. To have her first time be so important was daunting to the point of overwhelming. She clenched her fists with determination. She had told Poppa she would do this.

Most of the men were talking, all at the same time, their voices low and fierce, the overall buzz harsh and insistent. They crouched in the shade while the women stood against the wall, listening and nodding or shaking their heads. They didn't say much, only now and then repeating a word or phrase, but Carol Ann knew their single words carried weight. She slid in next to them. She knew these people—from church, from her childhood, they had been her parents' friends, one and all. But she didn't know their stories, she couldn't comprehend what they'd lived through, some of them were old enough to have come up as slaves. They never talked about those years. They didn't talk now. They whispered. They nodded. They gestured.

"Sheriff be here soon," Robey Watkins said. "We got to tell him what happened. We got to tell as how Mister McKinley done shot Eddy down with not one word." He rubbed his fist across his forehead, his myriad wrinkles deepening with his scowl. "Like the good book say, 'Happy is the one who pay you back according to what you done to us.'"

"Nossir," Micah Branch said. "We can't do nothing. Everyone working McKinley acres gonna lose their jobs." He was the oldest person in the group, well into his eighties, Carol Ann thought, perhaps old enough to have fought in the war. Had he been forced to fight for slavery? She'd never heard him talk about it.

"Ain't nobody gonna do nothing," Robey said. "Rows still gonna need spraying and weeding tomorrow. Apples still gonna need picking come fall."

"Y'all know what gonna happen," Henry LeClerc said. His Georgia accent was still heavy, even after half a century in Virginia. "We make a ruckus we gonna get done up good," he said. "They be coming down on us all like the hounds outta hell."

Murmurs of agreement met this pronouncement. Carol Ann was glad there wasn't wholehearted agreement to strike out for justice. Or revenge.

"I agree with Robey, ain't right," Willy Hume said loudly. "Fella can't shoot someone just like that and then just walk away smooth like butter and cream."

A few heads nodded. Carol Ann was surprised. She'd have thought Willy would be arguing in favor of acquiescence, on the surface he seemed so mild mannered.

"What gonna stop them from doing it only this one time, just cause they can?" Robey asked. "That ole Torrence, he and his boys getting worse and worse. They ain't got no money for town no more, so they come loadin' for us."

"Doctor Sweets up north in Detroit defended hisself against that white mob what wanted to run him outta town. Law up there said that ok. Time's is changing for us all," Willy said.

Carol Ann blinked, surprised, she'd forgotten about that trial.

"Don't wanna bring down more trouble," Micah Branch said. He hunched his shoulders, his elbows poked out as if he was protecting the people behind him from this incoming danger. "They gonna say Eddy, how he attacked that sweet and pure Miz McKinley. Them good ole boys ain't never gonna see one second of a courtroom. We be poking at the lion for nothing." Several people nodded agreement, mostly the older members of the group. "Can't nothin' bring Eddy back," he said. "No point flangin' the rest of us to the lions."

More nods and murmurs.

"Maybe nothing can bring Eddy back," Carol Ann said, "but I'd like to get justice, even a tiny bit." She carefully gauged the reaction to these words.

Voices rose. The two opposing camps, the small one in favor of action, the larger one in favor of safety, began to subtly move away from each other, separating physically as well as philosophically. A third group, the largest of all, stayed silent, undecided. Carol Ann struggled to word the compromise that might bring them all together.

A soft cough. Doreen Mills shuffled forward. She was a tall, boxy woman with sparse white hair, dark skin and very red lips. She had been a schoolteacher in her youth and Carol Ann had always been terrified of her. One time she had caught Carol Ann looking too long at a pretty bracelet in the goods store in Kintersville and had immediately seen the petty larceny in her heart. Carol Ann had been sure she was a witch, and now that she was older, she looked the part as well. "Perhaps the time has indeed come," she said with her precise diction, "to take a step out of the shadows." She coughed again. "We have been passively waiting for justice for a long time now."

The three groups shuffled. A few people shifted closer to the side promoting action.

"Would you get us all kill't for what might not come up 'till a ways in the future? Ain't gonna be no future if'n we all dead," Mary Mae Thackett said.

The murmuring and muttering started up again, louder than before. Robey Watkins took a breath and opened his mouth to shout over the top of them.

Carol Ann put up her hand. Small steps. Half measures. "Perhaps," she said quietly, "there is a middle road." Everyone turned to face her. "We can take these men to civil court. We can bring them to justice."

"That's what we saying," Robey said angrily, as if she

didn't understand. "We going to tell the sheriff what happened, make him come do right."

"When Torrence an' them hear we don't mean to sit quiet, all hell gonna bust loose," Micah Branch said. His supporters nodded and murmured agreement. "Civil suit, legal suit, neither one don't make no never mind."

Carol Ann tried to concentrate. A delicate touch was needed here to convince this group to compromise. But she'd observed good leaders all her life—Poppa's skill with a crowd, Peter's ability to charm a buyer, even her former friend Helen Voight's dogged determination to stand fast against whoever stood in her way.

"We do this without the sheriff," Carol Ann said. "By ourselves. When a man kills a servant or a factory worker, his kin can take him to civil court for what he did. It's called," she paused, trying to remember those newspaper articles she had only skimmed.

"Loss of companionship and comfort," Doreen Mills contributed.

Everyone looked at her. "What that mean?" Mary Mae asked.

"It means," Carol Ann said, "that Poppa and Rita, they can take those men to court and make them stand up, person to person."

"Wouldn't that be just as bad as a regular court case? Ain't they just gonna say he were defending his woman?" Micah Branch sneered.

"It's a little different," Carol Ann said. "In a civil suit, we bring in our own lawyers. We don't need the sheriff and the county prosecutor to be on our side."

"Y'all be crazy," Micah Branch said. "You think there gonna be a trial, nice and clean, the jury box full of white men from Kintersville and Early Run and Scottsville gonna say one of their own did wrong?"

"We need good lawyers," Robey Watkins said.

"We ain't got no money for no lawyers," Branch said, "good nor otherwise."

"We could get help, I know people who can raise funds," Carol Ann said, speaking slowly but thinking quickly. She remembered the last time she had asked Helen and Marjorie for money. She remembered the day she had first approached Peter's father, the old buzzard. She heard, in her mind, the tones of the helpless, hapless victim she had been. She knew what she would have to do this time, the difference was, this time she knew she could do it. Helen Voigt, after all, prided herself on being the best charity fundraiser in the city. There were organizations in New York who supported this kind of action, who claimed they wanted to see change. Well let them put their money where their mouth was.

"Maybe the NAACP down here would help," Henry LeClerc said. "I could ask my boy Charlie, he know them from school."

"You think them important organizers come all th'way out here to Sculley's Bend? You purely dreaming," Branch scoffed.

"We can get help. Lots of folks think it's time to take steps. Look at what Mr. White's doing now in the NAACP. It's gettin' loads stronger. There even be some of our boys going to Harvard Law School," LeClerc said.

Branch shook his head and made a face of disgust. "You get yourself the best lawyer at Howard or Harvard, white nor black, ain't gonna make a spit o' difference."

The older children had drifted over to listen. Most of them were swiveling in confusion from one set of adults to the other. Custis Baylor scowled, angry and mutinous. It was clear which side he would choose. Carol Ann would have to make sure he didn't rush to do something rash all on his own.

Her thoughts paused there. Since when was she

responsible for his coming up? Had she really taken over the mantle of leadership so quickly, so completely? She had promised Poppa she would take care of the sheriff, and the wild talk, and that's precisely what she'd do, including keeping Custis safe. Yes, she thought, I am responsible for David, and for Martina, and for all these children. They deserve someone willing to fight for a better world. If she didn't have the courage already, well she would certainly get the practice if they took the path of action.

She turned her attention back to the elders, finally judging the time was ripe to speak. She pointed to the children. "When we get old, when they get old, is there gonna be a whole new pack of lions, and a whole new flock of lambs, birthing and coming up and dying like sheep forever and ever?"

Everyone turned to the children.

"Praise the Lord, no," Willy said. "Ain't none of this woulda happened if my old truck had started. Ain't right. No more children should die cause some old fool ain't fixed his truck right." Willy turned and walked away, slapping at the hands that reached out for him.

A short silence descended. The two sides had been stated and argued. Danger now or danger later? Fight and die? Hide and live in fear? What to do? What was there ever to do?

At last Carol Ann knew what to say. The words came easily, and as she spoke, she could feel muscles in her soul flexing and gathering strength.

"Sooner or later somebody has to fight them," she said gently. "It may be dangerous, and we need to step carefully. We may not win, but we need to try. Are we going to spend our whole lives like sheep, hiding?"

A hesitant chorus of "no's" echoed back to her.

"Getting old hiding?"

Another small chorus of "no's."

"Now is the time to take a first step forward into the

light."

Mary Mae Thackett sighed, "If'n only the world was born different," she said.

"A civil suit," Micah Branch said, shaking his head. "I think you is all dreaming like Mary Mae here." At least he wasn't objecting any longer, Carol Ann thought.

"We have time to think about it," she said. "But we need to be careful. No running off and starting any trouble." She pierced Robey Watkins with a glare, then turned the same look on Custis, holding his eye until he nodded.

"A civil suit," Doreen Mills said, "ain't gonna be no jail time for no one."

"Not even if'n we win?" some asked.

"No."

Whispers of disapproval rippled through the group.

"Then what the point? Just money?"

"Not money," Carol Ann disagreed, "we can even file a suit for one dollar. The point would be to show the world what those men did. To take away their hiding place and their good name."

Carol Ann left the group to their wrangling. She had planted the seed, she would have to work hard to nurture it, but right now it needed to germinate. Inside the church, dim shafts of semi-shadow hid Rita as she sat, so still, so defeated. Carol Ann's mood changed in an instant. The excitement of shaking off her passive persona had lulled her into forgetting the true tragedy of this day. In front of Rita, Eddy lay on his makeshift bier, a blanket over him, surrounded by baskets and bunches of late summer flowers. She walked up the aisle and stood next to Eddy for a minute, absorbing the scent of roses and lavender, praying he would find everlasting peace. He deserved it. She touched his cold lips with her fingertips then sat next to Rita. Her throat ached with unspoken apologies.

Martina nestled against Rita, rubbing her pink plastic comb up and down her cheek with one hand and holding Rita's hand with the other.

Her sister was completely colorless, drained of everything that had once been so vibrant. She reminded Carol Ann of Peter in his coma, still alive, but far beyond the reach of emotion and response. Sadness settled in her chest with an actual ache. She reached out to hold both her daughter and her sister.

"You doing okay?" she asked. A pointless question, merely something to say.

"I don't feel nothing," Rita said. "I ought to feel so bad, but I don't feel nothing at all."

Carol Ann stroked Rita's hair. "Whatsoever you're feeling now, that's the right thing for you."

"I should feel bad," Rita said, "I should feel something." Her tone was inquisitive, but oddly flat. "Not like this. Like I a big, gray hole. A person-shaped hunk of fog. When my Sarah died, I didn't feel like this. I raced around making plans for all the things I had to do, because I knew Sarah was up in Heaven with her Daddy and the angels, all of them looking down on me and Eddy. She rubbed Eddy's hand, briskly, as if trying to chafe warmth into him. "Me and Eddy, missing them both together."

"There needs to be justice for Eddy," Carol Ann said.

"Ain't never been no justice for us. Ain't never gonna be none."

"Carol Ann let a moment of silence go by "Maybe there's a way to try."

"I don't believe you."

"Even to try would be something, I think."

"Since when you such a fighter, all a sudden?" Rita turned her flat, slitted eyes on Carol Ann.

"It's pretty new. I'm kinda feeling my way along it."

"Well, you go do whatever you need, Sister. Whatsoever make you right with the Lord."

"Helping fight for Eddy would make me feel right."

"Can't be done." Rita turned away. She leaned forward and adjusted the cuff of Eddy's clean Sunday shirt.

"Folks is getting stirred up," Carol Ann said.

"Well so they should," Rita said, without any emotion behind it. "That Marcus and his nightmare wife, they shot my boy and left him lying in the dirt." A flicker of anger. "They didn't even bring him home." She paused for breath, inhaling with a stutter.

"A civil suit, Rita. Shine a light on what they did. Lies can't grow in the light." Carol Ann put her hand on Rita's arm. "Not for money, not for jail time, but just for love."

"You made up your mind." Rita shut her eyes. "You gonna do this thing, no matter what I think."

Carol Ann shook her head vehemently. "I want to do the right thing for you. The right thing for Poppa. If you don't like my idea, I'll go back outside and tell folks the time ain't right just now."

"I don't know." Rita sighed. "I don't care. Maybe tomorrow I'll care."

Carol Ann sat quietly, waiting.

"You made up your mind," Rita repeated. "You gonna go back to New York City and make this happen." She paused. "Will you leave Martina here with me when you go?"

Carol Ann was stunned. She'd never thought of such an astounding idea. The word "no" leaped to her lips, but she stopped it. She looked at her daughter and her sister, huddled in the pool of their shared warmth, and as much as she wanted to protest, she knew she could not separate them now that they'd found each other, this girl who had lost the father who had lit her day and night, this woman who had lost one child after another and was left with only other people's children to love.

Carol Ann began to cry. Her heart wanted to tear in two. She wanted to protest that this final blow was so unfair, she had lost so much, was it really to be an eye for an eye, a child for a child? But here in this haven Martina would be cherished and safe. "I hadn't thought about it," she said, but another glance at them together and she knew there was nothing to consider. Martina had no more business leaving Sculley's Bend than Carol Ann had staying. She wiped her eyes and drew a breath, as if plunging into deep water. "Yes, she needs you more than she needs me."

Rita nodded. "Thank you," she said, and her arm settled a little more possessively across Martina's shoulders.

Carol Ann started to speak again, but her voice broke, and she sobbed, bending over and dropping her face into her hands.

At her side, Martina began to sing of angels and glory.

Eventually the tears dried. Carol Ann watched the dust dance in the sunlight as she thought about the road ahead, how clear the path. She would go back and fight for Eddy, and for Rita, and Poppa. For Peter. For David and Martina. The right word came to her. *Family.* She would fight for her family. With crystalline clarity she suddenly understood why Poppa always called her "Daughter."

Mary Mae Thackett walked up next to them. "It be time," she said softly.

More footsteps echoed at the back of the church. David and Zebediah entered, dark coats and ties neatly in place, carrying the pine box Poppa had so lovingly created. She caught David's eye, surprised that he returned her gaze, straight on, not ducking down or looking away. What was he thinking? How he must be hurting!

Poppa followed last, relying on Willy Hume's stolid

shoulder for support.

Watching Rita rise from the pew was almost physically painful. Carol Ann ached with every awkward, tearful movement.

The men placed the coffin on the floor next to Eddy's body and removed the lid. Inside, Poppa had placed a clean sheet and a small, white pillow.

Rita sobbed.

"You sure you wants to be here for this part, Miz Rita?" Absalom asked.

Rita clung to Martina, who seemed oblivious to the weight.

The men gently, oh so gently, lifted Eddy off the makeshift bier he rested on and lowered him into the coffin on the floor.

Rita took a breath and knelt down to tuck the pillow under Eddy's head. "Don't that feel better Baby?" she asked him.

"Eddy's sleeping now," Martina intoned. "Eddy's sleeping with Jesus-our-one-lord."

"Yes," Rita mumbled, still on her knees. "He's just sleeping. I know he's just sleeping, that's all."

Carol Ann knelt down next to her sister, readjusted the handkerchief over Eddy's face, and folded his arms across his chest.

Absalom placed the lid of the coffin in position, aligning the corners with precision.

He picked up a hammer and took a handful of nails out of his pockets.

"No!" Poppa lunged forward, grabbed the hammer and threw it behind him. He dropped to his knees and shoved at the lid. "Take me," he screamed. "Take me instead."

Carol Ann and Willy Hume rushed forward to lift Poppa and lead him away. Mary Mae and Portya Baylor surrounded

Rita, who had begun wailing and gasping for every breath. Martina, shrieking high and loud, tumbled into David's arms, her whole body rigid and terrified.

Others came rushing in, children pinned against the walls, faces flat with fear.

Carol Ann tugged and cajoled, eventually propelling Poppa down the aisle and out the door into the blinding sun. Rita and the women staggered behind, with the rest of the fragile community. David led Martina last. She was quiet but stiff, rubbing the pink comb against her cheek so hard she was scraping the side of her face raw.

As everyone milled around not knowing what to do, the muffled explosions of nails driven home assaulted them. With each report, like the gunshot that had taken Eddy, the people of Sculley's Bend shuddered as one being.

Eventually the horrible thumping ceased. Stillness descended. Sculley's Bend drew a breath, then filed reluctantly back into the dark, cool, patient church. Willy Hume led, practically carried, Poppa to the front pew and sat him down next to Rita and Martina, leaving space for Carol Ann and David to join them.

Who would speak for them? Carol Ann caught her breath with realization. Poppa was their Reverend, he led the services. Clearly Poppa was not capable of preaching today. Heads swiveled as they scanned each other, waiting for one among them to step into the breach. That's what it was, Carol Ann thought, a gap in the defenses of their lives.

Willy coughed, and moved forward, but Poppa put out a hand and stopped him. With slow, shuddering movements he stood, pushing his hands against his knees for leverage, bending at the waist like a man out of breath. Step by single step, he dragged himself up to the rough-hewn pulpit and took his place behind it. With deliberation, forcing each movement against the weight of grief bearing down on him, he raised his head and faced the congregation.

He spoke without introduction or preamble. "In the path of righteousness is life, and in its pathway there is no death." He heaved a breath. "Eddy was a strong light in a world of shadows. He held us to a higher standard, he made us better by the simple act of setting a good example in the way he walked through each day with honor and integrity."

Carol Ann was awed as never before by her father's strength as he spoke, carrying the congregation to a place of calm, of humility. Next to her, David bowed his head. A tear made a dark spot on the cloth of his trousers, and she reached out and touched it. He grabbed her hand in a tight clasp and whispered, "Such courage. Like Father. The courage to do the hard work."

The idea nipped at her mind. A little while ago she would have scoffed at the idea that Peter, charming Peter, had this kind of courage, but now she thought perhaps David was right. Perhaps all the men in her life had this fundamentally solid core.

At the pulpit, Poppa raised his voice in determination. "Whatsoever we feel in our hearts, we will not find justice by taking revenge. We will not find justice by seeking more violence. We will find it Eddy's way, by learning to be stronger, to be better, to light the way for others."

Murmurs rose in the congregation as Poppa led them through the service, bringing them, and perhaps himself, to a gentler grief. "Now let us recite," he intoned. "The Lord is my shepherd, I shall not want."

Full voices responded. It was too beautiful a day to bury someone you loved, but that decision was not left to them.

When the service ended, David and several of the men, including Poppa, lifted the coffin and bore it through the golden sunlight to the small cemetery behind the church. Carol Ann held one of Rita's arms and Martina walked beside them.

As they reached the newly dug grave, Rita spoke. "A civil suit, it be just for love?" she asked.

"Yes," Carol Ann said. "Not for money."

Rita nodded. "Eddy would like that."

CHAPTER 33

Dr. R. Hibbeler   Monday, August 24, 1931
Headmaster, The Briarwood Academy
Schuylerdam, New York

Dear Sir,

Last spring when my mother informed you that I would
not be returning to The Briarwood Academy due to the change
in our family finances, you generously offered me the support
of a scholarship. At the time I declined, but recent events have
led me to reconsider. I know that for this year, my place in the
class has been filled and the money no longer available.
However, if you would consider my readmission for next year,
I would be honored to return.

I must tell you before you address this request, I have
recently discovered that I am of mixed heritage. My mother is
not French, as you might have previously believed, but is an
octoroon from Virginia. This discovery, along with other
events that occurred this summer, has forced me to examine
many aspects of my life and reassess the value of pride. Yet as
Socrates once said, "the unexamined life is not worth living." I
have been the cause of wrongs that remain to be righted. I

know not where my road may lead, but wherever it does, I believe I can fight these wrongs most effectively with the best education I can obtain. This would come, of course, from The Briarwood Academy.

If you feel under the circumstances that my return to school would not be possible, I will understand. Please be sure that I will always remember my days there, and your advice, with the highest respect.

Yours Sincerely,

David C. Vandenholm
Sculley's Bend
near Earlysville, Virginia

CHAPTER 34

MARTINA

The other mother one is a fallen sparrow. Just like me. Jesus-our-one-lord watches over us, and together we are right safe to home. Eddy is not here to make the circles come for the other mother one, so I will make the circles come for her. What have I to dread, what have I to fear, leaning on the everlasting arms?

CHAPTER 35

DAVID

David watched the train pulling out of the Charlottesville station feeling a combination of loss, longing and anticipation. The plume of smoke from the engine twisted and danced in the light breeze above the tracks until there was nothing left of it, and the screech of the wheels could no longer be heard. Mother was gone, back to New York. They had said brief goodbyes, planning to rendezvous in a few short days, but somehow it felt as if they were both saying goodbye to their old selves, shedding their white skins and taking on their new forms.

He turned his back on the station and walked to where Aunt Rita waited with Martina, holding her hand. Grandpoppa strode ahead, stiff and silent. David walked deliberately slowly, letting him get even farther ahead. He wished he could make amends but knew he could not. There was, however, one act left undone. He had waited until Mother had gone so he would not be tempted to rely on her help.

Rita studied him from his battered cap to his tattered shoes, then shook her head. "You shouldn't have gone and given your Momma all your money. And ticket, too. You a fool, boy. You don't know how to be black, and you sure don't know how to be poor."

"But I need to find out. Besides, Mother needs all the money she can get to start that legal work for Eddy."

He thought about the courage it had taken Grandpoppa to stand up and speak over Eddy's body. He thought about what Father would want him to do. He drew a deep breath and counted to three. He was nearly nauseous with fear, knowing what he had to do next. He started to shudder, just as he used to do when he'd had to speak in front of the class, but he knew that was no excuse for delaying any longer.

"It was me," he stated. "I slept with Amelia McKinley. It's my fault that Eddy's dead."

"You? It was you?" Rita froze in the middle of the sidewalk.

"Yes, ma'am," David said, staring at a stone embedded in the cement.

"You did that an' then let Eddy pay the price? He was your cousin! He was your kin!" She dropped Martina's arm and clawed her hands into the front of David shirt.

"I tried to stop them," he started to protest, then shut his mouth.

"Not hard enough!"

"No," David agreed miserably. "I was too slow, too late, and too stupid. I'm sorry."

"Sorry?" Rita shrieked. "Sorry?" She was shaking with the force of her fury, and shaking David. "I don't know what—", she stopped. "I don't know—". Without warning she released his shirt and slapped him so hard he fell backward against a lamppost. She surged forward and slapped him again. Then she was flailing at him without any control, striking the lamppost as often as David. He put his arms up to protect his face but did nothing else to deflect the punishment.

Behind them Martina began to shriek and people down the block turned to stare. Rita quit as suddenly as she had started. Her hair stood in wild wisps, her face was shiny with sweat and tears, her eyelids were red. She shushed Martina, gentling her until the girl was calm again, stifling her own rage with nearly physical effort.

She pointed down the road to Poppa in the distance. "You next to kill'd that man. He next to dead right this minute. You think on that as you go through life—you think on the people you done killed here."

David bowed his head. "I'll go tell him what I did," he said. "I'll do that now." Although Granpoppa already knew.

"You gonna do none such thing," Aunt Rita snapped. "You leave him think it were some other hand. Ain't no use to him nor no one if'n that McKinley come after you next."

"Yes ma'am," David demurred. "You know best, I know that now."

"You done killed my Eddy," Rita spat. "Leastwise you learned one thing."

"Eddy is with Jesus-our-lord," Martina said.

"Yes, he is," Rita said, stroking the girl's hand.

David touched Martina's cheek. "I'm going away for a while, sweetie, but I'll be back when I can."

"Play chess," she demanded.

"Yes, and then we'll play chess."

"Long as you live you ain't never gonna be half the man my Eddy already was." Aunt Rita stalked away from him, pulling Martina with her.

The ghosts of his mistakes settled down over him, companions for the rest of his life. He had thought he would be able to stay and make up for what he had done, or at least try to, but in reality that would never have been possible. He could only face forward and do his best. "Half of Eddy's integrity would be a good goal," David whispered to Aunt Rita's retreating back. He squared his shoulders to carry his burden with more dignity. He was heading onward, it was true, but he would always be anchored here in this place, in this time.

David finally reached the wooden bridge and followed the main road out of Charlottesville for almost a mile, past the C&O freight yard. When he sighted the big elm tree, he turned off onto a side road that headed more directly south.

"Head east past tha' big ole shade king, and keep your ears open," Absalom had told him. "Listen for the whistle and follow on along. Don't try to jump a train right in the yard, them bulls won't let you. But outside the gates, nobody don't much care. This time a year, they mostly sleeps and looks the other way." The creases in his skin deepened with his smile. "Weather's too nice, even for the old bulls to be nasty."

"And then what?" David asked.

"Wh'd'ya mean, 'and then what?' Then haul yourself into a boxcar what got an open door and slide it shut so it ain't too obvious you inside. Pick one what be moving slow, so's ya don't kill yourself first time out."

"How do I know where it's going?"

"Ask the other 'bos what freight go through to where."

David tucked his right hand in his pocket and rubbed his thumb over the edge of the envelope tucked deep down there, and the few coins he hadn't given to Mother. He turned left, passed a billboard advertising Lucky Strike Greens, and continued in the direction Absalom and Zeb said would lead to easy access to the rail line.

Sooner than he expected, he rounded a curve in the road and the hobo jungle sprang up before him. It occupied a large, open lot, more than a block across, and was solidly populated with men. Shacks made of tin, cardboard and scraps were scattered in a haphazard array. A few fires spluttered feebly, with desolate figures huddled close by. The wind shifted toward him for a minute; acrid smoke from burning garbage caught him unawares and he choked. The ground was littered with muddy scraps of paper, broken glass, gravel, and the occasional clump of stringy weeds that had escaped being trodden into oblivion.

It was like an anthill, David thought. The longer he watched, the more movement crept into his perception, men drifting from shack to shack, from fire to fire. The fires danced and flickered, smoke twisted and rose. A few women slid in and out of David's field of vision at the edge of the camp, a cluster of children scampered madly, chasing after strips of leather knotted into an uneven ball. He hovered on the boundary, aware of what stepping off into that other world meant.

His feet stayed glued to the pavement.

With a mental shake, he took a breath and stepped. Down, he thought, down off the road, down to reality, down and down.

He edged up to the nearest fire, boots crunching roughly on the rocks and gravel, alert to the danger of violating any unwritten rules. The three men sitting there could have been brothers. They were uniformly gray and uniformly dirty. Their faces held an identical mix of lackluster disinterest and long suffering resignation. The stink of poorly washed clothes and equally poorly washed men, accosted him. With bored eyes they looked at David, saw he had nothing to offer, and turned back to the hypnotic flames.

"I'm trying to get to New York," David said.

The three men ignored him.

"Can you tell me how to get there?"

One of the men shrugged, as if the information would sap the last of his strength. Another looked sideways at David and grinned, exposing a row of crooked, stained teeth. "Ya could take the train," he offered, and they all cackled.

David crouched down with the men, trying to inhale through his mouth to avoid the stench. "I need to get to New

York. How do I find a train that will take me in the right direction?"

The man who'd made the joke leaned away and slid his eyes down. A bony hand rubbed across a stubbled jaw.

Another man finally spoke. "Nought but three choices on this line, friend. Headin' east, headin' west or headin' north. Mostly big trains east and west, going west to Huntington so's it can head north to Detroit, Buffalo or east to the ship yards at Newport News. Trains heading north to DC, they not so big."

The speaker had dirty black hair and a thick beard, deep-set eyes, sunken cheeks. He looked like Abraham Lincoln, except he was about 5'4" and spoke with the heaviest Southern drawl David had ever heard.

Steam appeared over the hill about half mile away, and even from that distance the shriek of the air brakes was loud enough to disrupt conversation. The steady throb of an engine firing up and beginning to move, brought silence and a tense alertness all over the camp. David felt it too. He put his hand up and gripped the strap on his knapsack. But the rhythmic thumping faded as the train picked up speed and headed west, away from them.

From the north, more steam appeared between two rooftops, and another train headed into the freight yard. No one except David paid any attention, but he watched, open-mouthed, as a boxcar door slid open before the train reached the yard's fence and body after body tumbled out. Perhaps a dozen men leaped from the car as it slowed. They bent over and milled around, retrieving packs and hats, then made their way as a ragtag mob to the encampment. There they splintered into individuals and joined the fires already burning. Occasional sounds of renewed acquaintance echoed past.

Steam and engine noise again brought silence to the fires. David sat still, sure this was another false alarm, and was taken by surprise when the Southerner grabbed his arm in a wrenching, strong grip and hauled him to his feet. He barely came up to David's chin, but his pull was strong. "Come along, boy, this one's our'n." He began to run.

David caught his balance and ran with him. His toes itched. Under his cap his scalp tingled. This was it, in a minute he would be on a freight train!

They raced across the pitted ground to the ragged grass alongside the rails. David did what the others did, and when they threw themselves down into the trench below the tracks, he did the same. There, on his stomach in the gravel, he felt the rails humming with the weight of the oncoming train. He raised his head enough to peer down the track, and in the distance, on the far side of the yard, soft puffs of steam appeared, and the black square of the approaching engine. The hairs on the back of his neck stood up and his sweat chilled, as if he were facing a wild animal. As if he were one.

Motionless, he waited with the other men while the train took its time creeping toward them. Then it was on top of them. David felt a rush of air across his face and a rush of air through his lungs, as the men rose together and began running, matching speed with the slowly moving train. The scream of iron wheels made speech impossible, but David was so intensely ready for this train, so tightly keyed up, he could see and understand what the others were mouthing. One man pointed down the line of cars, and the others looked, and moved eagerly toward the same spot. David ran with them, toward the open door of a boxcar approaching them. He raced for the car and flung himself up in a single, terrified burst of speed.

He flew through the air. He had nearly launched himself too far forward of the door but managed to catch hold of the wooden siding and roll inside. He didn't realize the momentum of the train would carry the top of his body forward faster than his legs, which swung behind him and slammed sharply against the edge of the doorframe. Pairs of hands reached out, pulled him away from the opening, and helped him to lean against a stack of crates that, from the smell, contained something packed in vinegar. A jar must have broken open. David wiped his face and tried to swallow.

"You okay there, boy?" It was the Southerner. "You took quite a crack on the shins."

David drew a shaky breath, then nodded. "Thanks," he said to the men around who had helped him in. Someone pulled the door shut, sending shadows into every corner.

The Southerner reached down and ran his hands roughly up and down David's legs, then grabbed each foot and twisted it right and left. David gasped when he pressed on the bruise. "I was a medic in the Big One. Good job nothing's broken," the man said. "You surely came close, leaping in so crooked. First timer, I'm guessing."

"Yes," David answered.

"Well, first time for everything." He smiled, and David smiled back. "But you did well enough, better than I did my first time around."

As the train picked up speed and the excitement of boarding ebbed, talk began, loud enough to be heard over the clatter.

"How far you think we're going?" someone asked.

"4-6-4 on the front. Engine this big, we going all the way to Baltimore," another answered

"Nah, ain't going much yonder of Fricksburg."

"Shit. Nothing there but cows."

The voices rambled on. Although it was still morning, with the boxcar slider shut it was nearly dark inside; David could see only the outlines of the speakers. He tried to figure out if any of them were black. Other than himself, he amended.

The pain in his leg began to subside. David examined his

surroundings and his companions. There were eleven of them, and David wondered if that was a normal number for a train leaving Charlottesville. He leaned against rough crates, mesmerized by the flickering light that stabbed through chinks in the side and top panels of the boxcar. As the car rocked, the shafts of light tripped across the row of men, touching faces here and there. Sparks coming off the rails flashed between the cracks in the floor. The racking, jolting motion of the freight car had nothing in common with the smooth swaying of a passenger carriage.

Below the steady beat of the engine, and the squeal and clack of the wheels along the rails and ties, another noise resonated. It was a low sibilance, barely audible, barely noticeable, and it was of animal origin, not mechanical. David worked to identify it, closing his eyes and straining to hear it better. It seemed important to know what it was.

Breathing. It was the sound of men breathing. Everyone in the car was inhaling and exhaling. It separated them from the train and the crates, David thought. It separated them from being just freight that moved across the land. David struggled to form a concept he had never needed before. "What separates me from animals? What separates these men from a boxcar of cattle going off to be slaughtered in the stockyard?" A few months ago he might have answered, "This is obvious. I go to school, I learn mathematics, it's clear I am a human and not an animal." But there, in the boxcar, massed with a group of anonymous men he'd never met, and could barely see, he could not make the same argument. "We are different from cattle," he thought, "because we choose to be here." But he was dissatisfied with that answer. "We are different from cattle because we strive to be better." Yes, that was closer to the target. He thought of how he had failed, not even tried really, to be a better man this summer, with Eddy, and with Amelia. Then he thought of the consequences. The rest of his life he would remember what could come of sinking into selfishness and pride.

David's thoughts tumbled and rolled. Against the rhythm of the rails, four or five men in another corner of the car were singing together, the occasional old ballad sounding familiar and comforting. The tenor and one of the basses were particularly good, and David hummed along quietly. His tension had evolved into a warm, strong feeling of excitement and new beginnings.

"So you're awake again," the Southerner said. He pulled a deck of playing cards from his pocket and fanned them from hand to hand. "I like these things. I can't play in this light, but they keep my hands busy, so I don't miss cigarettes as much."

"Yes, sir," David said.

"Didn't sleep much before you leaped onto this train."

"No, sir." He hadn't been asleep, but he didn't want to contradict the man who'd been nice enough to help him.

The man chuckled. "It was the same with me. Left a wife and two kids with her mother. I didn't think I'd miss that woman as much as I do."

David's leg throbbed. He leaned forward and rubbed it gingerly.

The man stroked his Abraham Lincoln beard. "So what's a well-brought-up boy like you doing in a boxcar? Your old man take a flier out a window, or something?"

"Auto crash."

"Jeez, I'm sorry. I was kidding. Millie, that's my wife, she's always telling me I should keep my mouth shut. 'You have no sense, whatever thought comes into your head, comes out of your mouth. So for heaven's sake keep it closed,' that's what she says to me. For instance, take the time I said to the neighbor lady, 'Miss Sherry, you look great, you've lost a chunk of weight.' Was that so terrible?"

David opened his mouth to reply, but didn't get the

chance.

"Well, apparently, yes it was so terrible, because she didn't think she had any extra poundage to lose, and she thought everyone was going to tell her she looked delightfully slender. But the truth is, she was downright fat, and probably still is."

The rumble of the train mixed with the stream of words. David struggled to pay attention to the flow of stories, and couldn't. "And that's another reason Millie tells me I should stop being so nosy."

David realized he'd missed at least one entire anecdote.

Time passed slowly, the monotonous beat of their travel sending David into fitful dozing after all. At one point the train slowed, then stopped. "Taking on cars," the Southerner said. As the train ponderously resumed its progress, light flooded through the unexpectedly opened door as four more men leaped in.

"Colored boys sit over there," a voice called out. An arm lifted and pointed.

The new men headed for the far corner. They huddled together, talking only to each other. The rest of the riders glanced at them once or twice, as if to make sure they stayed in place and did nothing they shouldn't have, then ignored them. David looked at them once more and one of them stared back. David turned his head away quickly, but out of the corner of his eye he watched the man lean toward his companions and whisper. All four turned to watch David. Did they think he was going to make trouble, or could they tell he was black, too? David stiffened up, waiting for one of them to say something. Then the boxcar door was pulled to, and the attention of the black men melted into the gloom.

A jolt of the rails made David aware of how full his bladder was. He had noticed the others periodically moving to the narrow space at the sliding door frame. This was yet another new skill he would have to learn on the fly, as it were.

Nervously, he stood.

"Don't get caught by the brakes," a voice called out.

David turned back, and someone laughed. "If the brakes come on while you're hanging your pecker out in the wind, you're going to have one tiny pecker." He laughed again, a loud, deep and merry sound. As if, thought David, his getting maimed would at least liven up a dull trip to nowhere.

He hurried to the door, more nervous than before. At the opening, one hand on his fly and the other on the wooden doorframe, he paused. Hundreds of red and brown cows calmly munched in their field, ignoring the train racing past. It was a sight he had seen many times before, going back and forth to school, but he had never considered these serene beasts with envy before. They didn't know what lay before them; they didn't care whether the farmer or the bank owned the grass on which they grazed. Was it better to be aware of himself here in this box hurtling to a future that might hold out promise of better things? Or to be a sheep on the hillside: well fed, well watered and blissfully unaware of the stockyard looming ahead?

David shook his thoughts loose and unbuttoned his pants. The wind rushing so fast past the train caught him by surprise. He tried to lean forward to keep the wind that cut around the opening from blowing urine back on him, but was only partly successful. He felt the wetness seeping across his thigh, but he refused to look down and admit his mistake, the others could see him so clearly here, outlined against the sunshine. Were the black men watching as well? What were they thinking? Were they studying him for miniscule signs of heritage? Did his skin look darker in the light? Was there something telling about the way he moved, the shape of his hands, or the angle of his head? He stood up straight and tried to appear confident and uninterested in the audience behind him, but he was unable to turn around and meet anyone's eyes.

Was this why Mother's movements had always been so taut? How could she have done this for twenty years?

"Hey kid, you feeling all right?" the southerner called out over the ever-present rumbling. "You're looking mighty strange, standing by the door, staring at nothing. I've seen old timers get like that, but this is your first day out, kid. Don't let it hit you so hard."

David returned to his place against the crates, and was half asleep when the fight broke out. In the dim recess of the boxcar, fists were flailing and bodies were rolling. Eager spectators watched the scuffle without joining in, but three white men and two black men rolled back and forth, throwing punches fast and hard.

"What happened?" David whispered to his companion.

"One of them coloreds started to eat, and one of them country boys called him a thief," he nodded in each direction as he spoke. "Said as how he wanted his vittles back."

David didn't wait. He stood up, strode to the fighting men, grabbed one of the white men by the collar, and shoved him hard toward the far corner of the freight car. Miz Thackett had been right – over the summer he'd grown into his height, and the orchard work had hammered his arms and legs into iron bars.

The man levered himself back to his feet. "What you do that for? Them filthy darkies stole my food." He crouched low, ready to attack.

"It was yours originally, was it?" David's voice dripped disbelief. "At least now it's a fair fight," he said. "Three against three."

"Stay outta this, kid, it ain't your fight," the man said.

"I'm making it my fight," David replied.

A knife flashed in the man's fist. Not a pocketknife to cut string or open cans, but a long, full-throated, hunting blade.

Fear spread through the car like spilled ink. Even those

who could not have seen that brief flicker of steel grew quiet, tense and aware that something malignant had slithered in to join them. The four other men stopped fighting and slid away from David and his opponent.

It would be easy, David thought, to fling himself on that blade and maybe die in the process, but his death would not balance Eddy's. Harder, but better, would be to take on this battle to win. The war for justice would be a long one, and at times the weapons would not be words. David balanced on the balls of his feet and moved easily with the rocking of the train. It was ludicrous, looking back, how seriously he'd taken the sparring and fencing in the Briarwood school gym, but it had prepared him for this moment. He kept his eye on the blade and his peripheral vision on the man's feet. He had no need to pay attention to the head or the shoulders, from those would come only feints and false thrusts.

He watched the knife and waited. He twitched but did not retreat with the first make-believe surge. He did not react at all to the second one, but he was ready when the third pass started as a feint and changed into a clumsy, left footed charge. David danced out of the way, clubbing the man on the ear with his fist as he passed.

The man hauled up and turned, panting, his eyes in shadow. He stamped his foot and charged like a bull. To David it was like watching a filmstrip in slow motion. He grabbed the hand holding the knife as it came toward him, yanked it up and clear, not at all worried as it whisked close to his face. He plowed his fist into the man's jaw, and when the grip on the knife loosened, he banged the man's hand hard against the wall. He hauled his arm back for a second punch and threw his weight forward. As luck would have it, the train rocked with him, and the blow landed with double force. The man slumped to the floor. David snatched up the knife and flung it out the door into the wind rushing past.

Perhaps facing down a weapon was not the kind of courage Grandpoppa had shown, but it had been needful. "I sincerely hope everyone has exhausted the need to argue," he shouted, and his voice roared loud, deep and ferocious, like Grandpoppa at his pulpit. Everyone stared. "Go back to your corners and settle down until we get where we're going. Let's have a little peace and quiet here."

Everyone shifted and shuffled back to their positions against the crates and walls.

David moved to the far end of the car. He inhaled slowly, exhaled slowly. He didn't know what he would have done if his attempt at leadership had failed. He would have tried something else, he supposed. *Father will be proud when I tell him about this.*

He looked around the boxcar and knew what he had to do next. What he wanted to do next. He felt the rightness of it seep completely through him.

"Hey boy, where you going?" the southerner asked.

"Over to sit with my people," he said. "Thanks for all your help this morning."

"Well holy Jesus-mother-and-child," the man said, more surprised than angry.

David took a breath and stepped carefully over to the corner where the four black men sat. They shifted to make a space for him as he slid down to lean against another stack of wooden crates. They didn't say anything, but after a while, one of them leaned forward, bumped David lightly on the shoulder with a gentle fist, and smiled, so hard to see in this low light. David smiled back. Such simple things, he thought, a shared moment in a dim space, such everyday events from which a sense of belonging grows.

CHAPTER 36

CAROL ANN

Carol Ann pointed out the elegant brownstone, standing tall above the wrought iron railings that guarded the entry from the unwashed and unwanted. This property had been in the Vandenholm family for generations, a fact that had been emphasized to Carol Ann by her future father-in-law, the one and only time Peter had brought her here for a visit. It was where Peter had grown up, and what he had rightly been heir to, until she'd stepped into his life and forced a split between him and his father.

"Well here we are. This is where your grandfather lives," she said, then chuckled. "Your other grandfather."

"I know," David said.

She turned to look at him, not disguising her surprise.

"I came here once, just to see what he looked like," David confessed. "I know you and Father weren't talking to him, but I wanted to see him." He shrugged. "He never came out, but I found his picture on the wall at Briarwood."

Carol Ann nodded, understanding. "Between my lies and your father's secrets, we kept you from knowing your heritage, as well as your family." She put her hand on his arm. "I can't make that up to you, but I can help you move forward. However, protecting you from the old buzzard was not a bad thing." She noted David's expression. "You'll see. He is going to have a fit when he hears what we've decided, but it's best that he hears it from us. If he has the embarrassment of hearing it from one of his society friends first, he'll never let us visit your father. At least this way, there's a chance he'll come around to our side in the long run."

A white curtain fluttered at an open window on the third floor. A very young nurse in cap and uniform sat there, reading a book and surreptitiously smoking, holding her hand out of the window between puffs. When she caught sight of them she quickly dropped the cigarette and it fluttered to the ground and out of sight. Aha! Now she knew where Peter's bedroom was. No doubt old man Vandenholm did not at all approve of women smoking, or voting either, for that matter.

Carol Ann led the way firmly up the steps, with David at her side.

The butler let them in as far as the front entry foyer. "I will check to see if Mr. Vandenholm will receive you," he said, pointedly not offering to take the hats and gloves they held out to him.

"I know the way," Carol Ann said, sweeping past him, placing her hat and gloves on a small side table with a delicate shrug. She sensed David's hesitation, but as she moved away, she heard his footsteps following. He'd grown up quite a bit recently. Well, so had she.

At the door to the study she knocked once out of basic courtesy, then opened it without waiting for a reply. She wasn't hanging on this man's whim or timing ever again.

Henry Vandenholm sat barricaded behind his immense walnut desk, glaring at her. Dour ancestors with identical expressions surrounded her, staring down their noses from their ornate gilt frames. The room was filled with shapes and textures designed to intimidate. Dark paneled walls with whirls of wood grain, an immense Persian carpet and deep leather chairs, glass cases with gleaming rows of yachting and fencing awards. One didn't have to squint to see the Briarwood Academy crests, the Yale coat of arms, the elegant burgee of the New York Yacht Club. Maybe this trumpeting of victory was unintentional; maybe this was just what the old man liked – gloom, threats, and tangible evidence of the power he held over any visitors to his lair.

Carol Ann began to suffocate. It felt as though the floor had dropped away, leaving her hanging in mid air, with no support, no safety net, no oxygen. Why had she come, and brought David as well? She pressed her trembling hands against her sides, breathed deeply through her nose, struggled to collect her scattered thoughts.

"I didn't invite you here," the old man snarled.

Carol Ann's momentary fear snapped like a twig. Her trembling stopped, and her breathing returned to normal. No, he hadn't invited them; she'd come on her own. This was her decision, her time to be in charge. She glanced up at the row of dark browed ancestors. Thank goodness Peter hadn't been like them, he clearly took after his mother. She wondered where the old man had hidden her portrait. She wondered if the young wife had hated this room too. Carol Ann could feel the strength of her resolve, full and round in her chest. She sank into one of the chairs across from the desk and waved David into the other.

"This is my son, David. You two have never been formally introduced."

"What is it you want from me, woman?"

Carol Ann took a deep breath. "Before I ask for anything, I want to apologize."

Henry Vandenholm arched one eyebrow.

"I lied to you, and I lied to your son. I lied to my children." She caught his fierce gaze and did not look away. "If some girl off the streets got her hooks into David," she placed a protective hand on his shoulder, "with a lie on her lips and deceit in her heart, I would think the worst of her as well. I do everything I can to protect him from such dangers." She dropped her hand back in her lap. "I behaved badly, I know that, and there is no way I can undo what I've done, but I did not mean to come between you and your son. I did not mean to cause hurt or harm. Misguided as it was, I did it only because I loved Peter so much."

"Pretty words," the old man snorted. "Worthless now."

"I know. But it's all I have. I cannot undo the past."

"Fine. You've apologized. Now let's hear favor you really came to ask for."

Carol Ann nodded. " Very well. David and I would like to start visiting Peter."

"No."

"Whatever you think of me, I loved him and he loved me. He loved his children. Keeping us apart now serves no purpose other than to hurt us. I think it hurts Peter too, and this is a time when he needs all the love he can get."

"No." Vandenholm shook his head. "I won't allow it. He's my son."

"I'm sorry," Carol Ann said. "If you try to prevent me I can make things unpleasant for you. But really," she held out one hand to him, "I don't want to do that."

"Ridiculous," the old man said, "nothing's changed. We've been through this more than once, and I've made my position clear. I will withdraw my support of Peter's medical treatment, and the two of you will die together in a ghetto somewhere in Harlem or Virginia, I don't care which."

Carol Ann could see the poisonous words as if they were painted on the air in front of her, but they just hung there, impotent, unable to touch her. "I don't think you mean that," she said, "He's your son."

Henry Vandenholm spun his chair around, facing away from them.

Carol Ann coughed to catch his attention. "There's one other thing we came to tell you," she said. "I'm going to be telling people my secret. Wiping the slate clean and starting over."

He turned around to face them. "You wouldn't do that," he said, but his voice held the slightest trace of uncertainty.

"I not only would," Carol Ann assured him, "I will. That changes the balance of the scales, I think. It was one thing when you turned your back on Peter so completely, all those years ago, as long as no one knew the reason why. I know they'd think our marriage was an abomination, but they would think poorly of you if you abandon him now, just because he married a black woman. Not when he's dying. Not now." She sat back, trembling, but calm and confident.

"You are seriously mistaken about that, missy," he snarled. The momentary softening in his attitude was gone.

"Only time will tell, I suppose. But believe me, everyone will know, I'll make sure of that. I need to make sure of that, for my own sake." She lifted her chin. "Even at Briarwood," she waved a hand in David's direction. "Your grandson is going back, he'll be a Briarwood boy once again."

Paper crackled as David pulled a well-thumbed telegram out of his pocket. "Headmaster Hibbeler has made a place for me to return this year and has released scholarship money. He said I should be prepared for battles ahead, but he's willing to fight them, if I am."

David offered the telegram across the desk.

The old man didn't move to take it, but his eyes registered shock. "A scholarship student? With the Vandenholm name?" He stopped, fury purpling his face, and his voice rose. "I forbid it!"

"Then work with us, not against us," Carol Ann said mildly, turning her hands palm up as if offering him this obvious truth as a gift.

"I will fight you every inch of the way. I will fight both of you and any other misguided idiot who tries to help you." Spittle frothed at the corner of his mouth. "Briarwood will never see you cross their threshold again, I swear it."

David blinked and sat up straighter. "I'm sorry you feel that way, sir."

Pride filled Carol Ann as David spoke, and she knew it was plain on her face, in her eyes. She looked around the walls at the ancestors whose time was past. She looked at the old man hiding behind the bastion of the wide desk. Surprisingly, she felt pity for him. He was just starting to realize he'd lost everything: the fight, his son, his grandson, and perhaps even his good name. She even felt a touch tender toward him. He was a wounded creature, snarling to keep friend and foe alike at bay.

"I wish you could join us in this celebration," she said. "This is your grandson, your family, and no matter what you think of me, no matter what you think of my race, no matter what you think of your own son for falling in love with me, you cannot help but recognize the courage, the dignity and the strength you see in front of you." She smiled at David. "Briarwood is so impressed by his good qualities that they are willing to fight for him. And he's strong enough to fight for his rights as well. This, truly, is the future of the Vandenholm name. The future of your lineage."

"A Black. A charity student. Never!" He rose and pointed dramatically at the door. "Get out."

Carol Ann could have laughed, but she held herself back. Winning him over was her new battle and it would be a long one, but she had time. She would gain nothing by alienating him, what purpose would that serve? His family was almost gone, his old ways were almost gone, he was almost at the end of his life. Being here with him was like watching a towering cliff crumble into sand and wash impotently into the ocean.

She and David left the room.

Once outside the door, she put her finger to her lips, motioning David to silence. She moved swiftly down the carpeted hallway and mounted the ornate stairs. On the third floor, in a sunlit front room with white lace curtains, Peter lay in his bed, his color as pale as the sheets. The nurse who had been reading by his bedside was surprised by their sudden arrival, but moved out of their way as they approached.

"Hello, my love, I'm here." Carol Ann lifted the skeletal hand and wove her fingers through Peter's. The odors in the room told of how the days passed: borax and rubbing alcohol, lemon oil and bleach. Only a hint of human essence hovered, every indication of bodily function was rigorously scrubbed away as soon as it appeared. He was better off here than he had been in that charity ward. Yes, she had done the best she could back then, but letting go, not holding on, had been the wiser choice.

She reached into her purse, lifted his wedding band out of a folded handkerchief, and slid it onto his ring finger, where it hung loosely. She pulled it off and replaced it on his middle finger. She took it off again, and tried to slide it onto his thumb, where it stuck at the first joint. She dabbed some lipstick from her purse onto his skin, then twisted the ring back and forth until it scooted over the knuckle and settled into place. She folded his fingers tightly around it. "There! Let the old buzzard try to take it off you now. From now on, I'll be right here, and I'll tell you everything I couldn't tell you before." Under her hand, she thought that Peter's fingers twitched ever so slightly. She peered eagerly into his face, then sighed. Nothing. Perhaps one day there would be.

David moved to the other side of the bed and pressed his lips against Peter's smooth cheek, lifted the other limp hand from the blanket, and bowed his head over it. Her whole body hurt with the idea of how far off course her children had been thrown: their life, their family, David's whole golden future, Martina's gentle world, safe from attack.

"I wanted to be the man of the family, but I failed," he whispered. "I made a terrible mistake and I can't go back in time, but I promise you," he gulped, "one day you will be proud of me."

Across Peter's still form Carol Ann caught David's hand. It was not a happy ending, but rather, a new beginning, on meager but honest foundations. She thought of David's strength, of her own, of Martina's. "We both failed, and we both made mistakes, but we learned. He'd be proud of us now."

ACKNOWLEDGMENTS

There are so many people without whom this story would never have seen the light of day. A novel is a complex tapestry of characters and themes, my heartfelt thanks to all the people who patiently supported and guided my work.

My friends and readers, for their unbelievable patience and perception, and for providing quiet writing spaces: Elaine, Nancy, Ruth, Cherri, Judy, Pam, Mary, Joan, Janet, Lisa.

My crack legal team for answering those obscure questions about law and history: Dan, Jenny, Stu.

The educators who helped me try to understand the tough issues, no matter how uncomfortable: Robert Smith at America's Black Holocaust Museum, David Bradley at Breadloaf Writing Conference, Alan Nelson from Union College, and the generous librarians at the University of Virginia and the Schomburg Center for Research in Black Culture.

The men, women and children around the world who bear up under hatred of all kinds and set the standard for what courage really means.

And of course, my family, for never once complaining I spent too much time inside my own head instead of being present with them: Kim, Ian and Graham.

ABOUT THE AUTHOR

Elissa Matthews was born and raised in New Jersey, close enough to visit New York City and watch the turmoil of Civil Rights, Women's Rights, and anti-war demonstrations first hand, then return to the quiet of the country to absorb and understand. She is the author of several short stories, all of them dealing, in one way or another, with our lies, our masks, and the issues we need courage to face. She has visited almost every state in the USA and more than 30 countries around the globe, but still lives 12 miles down the road from where she grew up. *Where the River Bends* is her first novel.

42183170R00163

Made in the USA
Middletown, DE
04 April 2017